UNWRAPPED

Claudia Dain
"Every Square Inch"

"Sizzling sensuality and fabulous storytelling seamlessly blend in this stellar debut by a dazzling new talent. *Tell Me Lies* is a potent, guilty pleasure of a read."

—*Romantic Times* on *Tell Me Lies*

Shirl Henke
"Surprise Package"

"Sensational Shirl Henke is one of the top ten authors of American romance."

—*Affaire de Couer*

Nina Bangs
"Man with a Golden Bow"

"Funny characters, sizzling dialogue and plenty of HEAT! Nina Bangs dishes up the perfect recipe for an incredible read."

—Kimberly Raye, bestselling author of *Something Wild,* on *An Original Sin*

D0964930

Other Christmas anthologies from
Leisure and *Love Spell:*

MISTLETOE & MAGIC
FIVE GOLD RINGS
THE MAGIC OF CHRISTMAS
BLUE CHRISTMAS
SANTA PAWS
CHRISTMAS SPIRIT
A TIME-TRAVEL CHRISTMAS
HOLIDAY INN
A WILDERNESS CHRISTMAS
THE NIGHT BEFORE CHRISTMAS
THEIR FIRST NOEL
A FRONTIER CHRISTMAS
AN OLD-FASHIONED SOUTHERN
  CHRISTMAS

Unwrapped

Nina Bangs,
Claudia Dain,
Shirl Henke

LOVE SPELL BOOKS NEW YORK CITY

A LOVE SPELL BOOK®

October 2000

Published by

Dorchester Publishing Co., Inc.
276 Fifth Avenue
New York, NY 10001

ISBN 0-505-52403-1

Every Square Inch

Claudia Dain

With special thanks to Grace,
who led me through the maze of Navy letters and protocols.

Prologue

It was one of the few days she got home from work early, only 6:30 and still enough light to see the lock and fit the key without fumbling. The air was crisp and clean and filled with the smells of October. Her summer flowers, impatiens and Mexican heather and geraniums, were exploding with lush color and dark greenery; still, it was nearly time to pull them up and put down some pansies for winter. The south knew how to manage winter. Raleigh was a place where it was always warm enough for something to be blooming.

She'd get to it, had to get to it before Halloween. It was almost against the law not to have the mums out for Halloween. She wouldn't be the kind of neighbor who didn't manage her yard with care, knowing one weedy, ill-kept lawn could ruin the look of a whole street. She'd get to it, even if she'd never get to look at it.

How often was she ever home before dark?

Not often enough to bother to keep track.

Mary Scott, possessed of a fine southern double first name, opened the door and stepped in, stepping all over her mail. At least it hadn't been raining. Putting her purse on the antique chest in the foyer, she bent down and picked up the mail. It was mostly junk. Her mother had convinced her that a slot in her door was much more convenient than a mailbox—no going out in the rain, and the mail safely inside the house while she was gone all day. But since she had to get on her hands and knees to retrieve it every day, it wasn't such a convenience, after all. And now she had a rectangular hole in her door.

The doorbell rang while she was straightening the fringe on the Persian carpet in the foyer. She stood up, straightening both her skirt and her hair, and opened the door. Without looking first to see who it was. Raleigh was that kind of city.

He was in uniform, a naval uniform, and her heart jumped into her throat before she could blink. And then she did blink. It wasn't him. It wasn't anyone who could make her heart do anything but what it was supposed to do, which was beat placidly inside her chest, where it belonged.

Standing before her was a man in a navy uniform, his hat tucked under his arm, his expression solemn. Next to him stood an older man in a black suit.

"Mrs. Adams?" the officer asked.

Yes, he would call her that. Anyone connected with the Navy would think of her that way. It was nothing to be alarmed about.

A boy rode by on his bike, one of those off-road types that all the kids rode today. It looked heavy. His dog, a black Lab, loped next to the bike, his leash looped around the boy's wrist. If the dog decided to bolt, the boy could get dragged down the street. It would be bad if that happened.

Something bad was going to happen.

"Mrs. David Adams?" he repeated, clearing his throat.

He was handsome, with soft brown eyes.

The little boy on the bike was out of sight, down the road with his dog, playing in the last light of an October night.

"Yes?" she said, not looking at his eyes.

The light was slanting through the oak trees that lined the street, huge, ancient trees with trunks the size of small cars. The leaves were still on, brown and gold and red, fluttering and clapping, blocking out the evening sky with their motion. They could block out everything,

everything, even the man in uniform standing on her porch.

But they didn't.

"Yes, I'm Mrs. Adams," she said evenly.

"I'm sorry to have to inform you, Mrs. Adams, but your husband was killed in action . . ."

He kept talking, but she didn't hear any of it.

Another boy, smaller than the first, churned down the street on roller blades, leaning forward, arms pumping, struggling to catch up. But he couldn't catch up. The boy on the bike was gone.

Gone.

The leaves were still on the oaks. They wouldn't fall until Thanksgiving, and then the streets would be choked with dead leaves, curled and brown, crushed to ash with every step. The lawns would be buried, and people all over town would rush out with their leaf blowers to roar the debris off their bright green grass, desperate to save it. Desperate to keep their grass alive.

"I'm sorry, Mrs. Adams. I'm sorry. Are you all right?"

"All right?" she said slowly, taking her eyes off the leaves that still fluttered as if absolutely nothing had happened. "Yes, I'm all right. Thank you. Thank you for telling me."

She closed the door then, not quite sure she hadn't closed the door in his face.

The mail was still in her hand. She walked to the antique chest she'd bought only last month and put down the envelopes. It seemed a very complicated act. She felt that she'd managed it quite well. Her purse was still there; it hadn't moved in the last ten minutes, though it might have. Everything in her life had shifted in the last ten minutes. It seemed she needed something from her purse, she couldn't think what, but she rummaged around, hoping whatever it was would leap into her hand. It did, eventually.

Her purse-size organizer; yes, she'd need that now.

The phone was . . . in the kitchen.

Mary Scott walked through the house to the kitchen in the back. Yes, the phone was still hanging from the wall, just where it had been that morning. How strange.

Finding the number and dialing wasn't so hard; she could do that, had done it all her life. But her voice, once she managed to make it come out, sounded hollow and thin, like a recording from the 1920s.

He wasn't home. He was probably working late, the way she should have been. She shouldn't have come home so early. . . .

". . . leave your message, and I'll return your call as soon as I can. 'Bye."

The beep that signaled commencement sounded in her ear, and then that strange 1920s voice that was supposed to be her own said, "Robin, it's Mary Scott Burke. I just received news that my husband is dead. You can drop the divorce proceedings."

Chapter One

Mary Scott moved thorough the darkness of her yard to the front door. Dead geranium blossoms, translucent red, lay on the walk like confetti. The impatiens had long ago succumbed to the cold, their stalks lying dark and wet like seaweed stranded by the tide. The Mexican heather had simply withered and disappeared.

Mary Scott sighed. She just didn't have the energy for pansies.

There weren't many places left that were still selling pansies. Christmas wreaths and garlands and trees were crowding the nurseries now, dressed with bows of red or shimmering gold, with not a purple pansy in sight. She'd missed the season. Her neighbors must think her a terrible laggard; the least she could do was clean up the leaves that covered her lawn and her planting beds. That, or get a landscaping service to do it for her.

She'd do it; once Christmas was over, she'd do it. The office was quiet then because of the holidays; she'd have time to either get out in her yard with a rake or make a quick phone call and hire someone else's rake. One more thing to do.

She'd get it done. She always got it done.

She'd installed a timer on her porch light so that now she didn't have to fumble in the dark with her key. She never got home before dark, so that had seemed a practical necessity. And it was a welcoming feeling, coming home to a house that was lit, even partially.

On the way home from work every night, these winter nights that began so early and stayed so late, she drove slowly, looking into the windows of the neighboring strangers who surrounded her. She saw living rooms painted salmon or coral and glowing with welcoming light from a pair of lamps set in a pair of windows facing the front, the color dramatic even from the street and looking as warm and inviting as a fire. Sometimes it was taupe walls set off by white trim and lit by brass lamps topped by black shades that beckoned her, ball fringe hanging from valances, as she drove past, trying not to look like a voyeur. But she was.

She was looking into homes, into lives, that

looked warmer and happier than hers.

Because, even with the timer, even with the porch light on, she knew the house would be empty when she opened the door.

Mary Scott opened the door to her house, her beautiful sixty-year-old house on a seventy-year-old tree-lined street, and flicked on the lights to both the living room and foyer, flooding the space with a gentle glow. She walked to the chest in the foyer and set down her purse and went back to kneel down and pick up the mail strewn on the floor. Even from that angle, her living room was a lovely sight to any drive-by voyeurs. She knew. She'd checked.

Her foyer wore a white-on-white damask design wallpaper, the floor white marble with black squares. They didn't make floors like that anymore; it was one of the pleasures of owning an old home. The rug that protected the marble was an antique Persian from her great-grandmother, and the colors had faded to soft red and bleached blue on an ivory ground the color of summer linen. The antique chest, so recent an addition as to still catch her eye and make her smile every time she saw it, was a curved piece of walnut almost a hundred and fifty years old, and with the original hardware. Even her mother had said she'd done well on that piece in her infant antique collection.

A wide opening led to the living room, painted soft blue-gray with white trim. Floor-length curtains of heavy white cotton with white fringe almost always stood open. The curtains were for show, not for privacy. What would she ever do in the living room that would require privacy? Besides, she wanted her home to look beautiful and serene and compelling to passersby. Though when the leaves were down and the days cold, the room could look the slightest bit chilly. Especially since the upholstery was all in a somewhat darker shade of that pale blue-gray.

Her mother had thought she was insane, choosing one upholstery fabric for the whole room, and one without a print, besides, but she liked the serenity of it. Her mother had come over one Saturday afternoon with an antique chair in the Tudor revival style, the seat covered in an aged needlepoint. She'd loved it. It now sat in baronial splendor next to the fireplace. For her birthday, her mother had had a pillow made for her out of an antique scrap of Oriental carpet. It, too, looked just right. Mary Scott had a feeling that she'd be getting more tapestry or needlepoint for Christmas, since her mother clearly felt that the room needed more color and texture.

The debate now was whether to paint the dining room deep coral, her mother's preference—and, it seemed, everyone else's in Raleigh—or iced yellow. She'd paint the room yellow and then watch while her mother added dashes of coral by way of accessories. These decorating battles were old ground between them, and Mary Scott got more amusement out of it than irritation.

Next on her list of planned purchases was a better rug for the living room. She wanted something beautiful, intricate, a future heirloom to pass down to ... someone. What she had at the moment was a square of pile carpet in off white. It would have to do for a while longer.

Mary Scott got up off her knees, mail firmly in hand, and walked into the kitchen. It was painted eggshell white and was going to stay that way. It was an old kitchen with new appliances and shining granite countertops and a big scrubbed-pine table pushed up against the large window overlooking the tiny backyard. It was where she lived.

She was starving. It was after eight, and she hadn't had anything to eat since one. And she was exhausted. It was Friday night, and it had been a long week, and she wasn't going to tempt fate by going upstairs to change, only to find herself facedown on her bed tomorrow morning, her stomach an empty hole that reached to her knees. That had happened more than once since she'd started at the brokerage firm. She was just getting started, and that meant long hours and few rewards. But she was doing well. She already had an office with a window.

Dropping the mail on the table, she walked to the refrigerator and opened the door. A lot of empty white space greeted her. A wedge of cheese, half a head of lettuce, bottled water, two apples, four eggs, half a bag of English muffins, and two inches of V8. No milk. She'd meant to go to the grocery store on Wednesday, but on Wednesday she'd worked until after midnight, and on Thursday she'd been too tired to think beyond the comforts of a nice, firm mattress. And now it was Friday, and she didn't have much in the way of solid food. Lasagna would taste good. Too bad no one had made any.

Tomorrow was Saturday. She'd do it tomorrow. Now, perhaps, if she could find some nuts in the cupboard, she could toss together a reasonable Waldorf salad. If only chopping the lettuce weren't such an effort.

The empty gnawing of her stomach urged her on, and she got out a knife, suddenly motivated to start chopping food into bite-sized particles. It would be a Waldorf without the nuts; she didn't want to take the time to search for nuts.

The doorbell rang just as she'd laid the lettuce on the cutting board.

She'd ignore it. She was too tired to be sociable and too hungry to fend off a salesman.

It rang again. It was probably a neighbor, coming to complain about her lack of civic pride, her lack of pansies, her lack of even a wreath for her door. She'd get a wreath tomorrow. She'd do it all tomorrow. She had to eat *now*.

But if it was a neighbor, she couldn't hide in the kitchen. While she loved her old home, it didn't have the one thing that every house built in the last forty years had: a garage. Her car was parked in her driveway, announcing to the world that she was most definitely home.

She was already in enough trouble about the pansies; she shouldn't compound it by not answering the door. She shouldn't add being unfriendly to her list of heinous landscaping crimes.

Putting down the knife, Mary Scott walked back through the house to the front door, glad that she hadn't changed into her dressing gown before starting dinner. If she was going to face an irritated neighbor, she wanted to do it well-dressed. In her tailored suit and pumps she looked very respectable, even if her yard was windblown and her grass patchy.

Prepared to smile, Mary Scott opened the door.

She didn't get a chance to smile.

He stood under the porch light, the stark illumination leaving only planes and valleys of shadow.

And then he reached for her, grabbing her to him as he lifted her over the threshold and carried her inside the house, slamming the door shut with one foot.

He was beautiful in a dark and masculine way; there was nothing pretty about him, not in his blunt nose or in the thin scar that sliced down through his upper lip or in the startling blue of his eyes against skin tanned brown. His hair was short and dark, dark brown, his jawbone prominent, his legs long, his shoulders wide.

Mary Scott closed her eyes as he set her on her feet and pressed her against him, lifting her face to his kiss. She didn't need to look at him; she knew exactly what he looked like, down to the small chicken pox scar he had next to his right ear. She remembered every inch of him.

His kiss was hard and hungry. She could only stand numb before such an onslaught. Then the spark of desire that she had banked into a slug of cold charcoal roared to life, mocking her.

Holding his head down to her, she assaulted his mouth, kissing him deeply with her tongue and nibbling on his lower lip. He rubbed against her, holding her hips to his, his hands pressing, insistent. She could feel the length of him like a club against her, and she ground her hips against him, pulling at his shirt, wanting to feel his skin against hers. Wanting the hot, hard length of him to possess her.

He wanted the same. In this, they were always united.

He tugged at her jacket, pushing it off her shoulders and down to her elbows, his hands caressing her, struggling with the inconvenience of her bra. She pulled at her sleeves, yanking her arms out, caught, panting her frustration at being trapped in her clothes. He kicked off his shoes and reached for the button at the top of his shirt with one hand; with the other he mangled her bra, leaving her half exposed, one nipple freed of restriction and tight with need.

Finally free of her jacket, she let it drop to the floor, forgotten. She reached for his shirt, pulling him to her by his collar, fumbling with the buttons as she kissed him, pouring her heart into the kiss, letting passion sweep away thought so that only feeling remained. She was clumsy with desire, the buttons wouldn't give, and so she yanked the shirt from his body, sending buttons flying.

It didn't matter. Nothing mattered. He was free of the shirt, and now she could press her skin against the solid heat of his chest.

Dizzy with need, she leaned against him, working at the small hook on her skirt, only to give up and pull at the button of his slacks. She throbbed with need, the ache reaching up to her heart and into her throat, where she sobbed with want and frustration.

Grabbing her to him, he fell into a damask-covered chair and pulled her into his lap, forcing her to straddle him, her wool skirt hiked up to her waist. Throbbing heat, shaking need, were all she felt, all she heeded in the tumult he fired in her with the first touch. Panty hose ripped, shoes falling with twin thuds to the floor, hands in his hair, his mouth on her breast, and then he was inside her. Filling her. Stretching her with glorious brutality. She was ready for him. Ready for this thing that was between them that she had never thought to feel again.

Her throbbing response was instant, explosive, more powerful for having been denied these last months. She had been starving for him. She gorged herself now, giving in totally to the waves of intense pleasure that brought her to the edge of pain and panic.

She lost herself in him as he was drawn into her.

And when it ended, when the last tremor whispered out of her like a ghost, it still didn't end.

She pulled his head up by his warrior hair and kissed him, hard, pouring all the pain and all the longing she felt into it, reveling in the knowledge that he was alive. He was so gloriously alive.

He stood, still planted deep inside her, and laid her down on the floor. He slid from her for just an instant and then rushed back in with the force of the tide. She sighed her satisfaction, need met, ache assuaged.

There was nothing left of thought in her; all

was emotion and sensation and the driving, impossible need to be filled by him to the last cell of her being, to be possessed by him. To be one.

Her second orgasm came hard, harder than the first, and she grunted against the force of it as it came shattering out of her, escaping the momentary oneness of their union. It left her shaking and bumping against the edge of unconsciousness.

He slipped out of her then, and she could hear herself groan her distress. Oneness lost.

Dimly, lethargically, she felt him take off her skirt and pull off her tattered hose and torn panties. She couldn't find the strength to lift her head or open her eyes. She heard the soft thud of pants hit the floor, and then he was lifting her, his body deliciously naked against hers. Heat against heat, muscle against skin; she buried her face against his neck and suckled him, wanting to mark him, wanting the taste of him in her mouth.

She felt him rise up and poke her in the buttocks. She smiled and sucked harder.

Another kick, and a door was opened. He laid her on a bed, so soft against her back, and then he was touching her everywhere, torturing her with his caress while he withheld his possession. It was torture, and he knew it. She watched him with sex-drugged eyes and knew it. And she was too weak with spent passion to do anything about it. Except endure it.

23

He was handsome, even in the dark. His body rose up, breaking the full weight of the darkness, his back broad and his shoulders stooped to his task. His task of arousing her.

He seemed to glory in her shape, running his fingertips over her breasts and down her sides, over the tops of her thighs and down still farther to her calves, ankles, feet. He massaged each foot in turn, instep, arch, sole, toes, loving her with his hands. Ministering to her like a body slave of Roman times, yet she was the slave, enslaved to his touch, to the very scent of him.

And then his mouth replaced his hands, and he was kissing her toes, the high arch of her foot, the indentation below her ankle. She sighed and stretched, her restlessness growing as the need for him grew. Again.

It was never enough; no matter how many times she took him into her, she never could get enough of him. There was always an ache, the ache of desire unleashed, the ache of passion fulfilled, the ache of longing for something he seemed unable to give her, no matter the mastery of his hands and mouth.

"David," she murmured, watching him as he bent over her, his kisses both teasing and promising, his hands running lightly over her skin in what should have been a tickle. But she was too bone-deep relaxed within his embrace for the skittishness of a tickle. His touch brought only deeper desire and greater languor. Her limbs were heavy with passion spent and passion renewed.

He was not done with her yet.

"David," she breathed.

He looked up, and she caressed his face, her hands flat along the planes of his cheeks. The curtains were closed, but the cold light of the street lamp slid in anyway, to illuminate his face in stark lines of gray and black. His eyes were shadowed, but she could see them sparkle as they gazed intently down upon her.

He entered her slowly, deliberately, and she arched to catch all of him, bringing her legs up to wrap around his waist, holding him to her.

In silence, they joined, their eyes locked as well as their bodies. Slowly, methodically, he pumped himself into her, the heat and friction of him a glorious thing. This oneness that he brought to her, this weight of two souls mingling, twining, was his gift.

He was alive.

Mary Scott ran her fingers over the sharp angle of one eyebrow and down the cheek to the ridge of jaw. She knew every line of him, every texture, every color, every scent. She knew the mole that rode high on his back. She knew the scar that sliced his lip and how he'd gotten it. She knew the way his hair would spike from a cowlick on the right side of his forehead after a tossed sleep. She knew the way water would bead on his skin after a shower and which way the drops would run down the muscles of his chest to the line of hair below his navel. She knew . . . he was alive.

His tempo increased, and she stayed with him, needing him, needing everything he could give her and all that he would not.

"Come with me, Scottie, just a bit more," he whispered, palming her breasts.

She shot through the last barrier of restraint, her orgasm taking her suddenly without the warning of a tremor. Heat, heavy and low, pulsed within her, and she would not close her eyes against it. No, she wanted to take him in with her eyes, too, to take him in any way she could, for as long as she could.

He was alive.

Tears fell softly from the corners of her eyes; she knew she was crying, and she didn't care. She didn't have the strength to care. David lay on top of her, and she kissed his shoulder, tasting smooth heat and the sweat on his skin. She held him to her, finding comfort in his weight on her body.

He ran a hand over her hair and kissed her temple, tasting her salt, the salt of tears.

They said nothing.

David slid out of her with a twitch of his hips and rolled onto his side, taking her with him. In a tangle of arms and legs, they fell asleep in the same instant, entwined.

Chapter Two

It was the sound of the back door slamming that woke her, every muscle jerking as she sat straight up in bed. The bed in the guest room. With David lazily stretching by her side.

What had been a romantic dream last night looked embarrassing by the light of day. Of course, if she knew David, and she did, he wouldn't think so. He would think it all hilariously funny and, if he could manage it, would do something to make the whole horrible situation worse.

She just wouldn't give him a chance to manage it, that's all. It was her house, her bed, and her maid coming in to clean, and she would have her say about all of it, and David would just have to cooperate.

How often had she tried to get David to co-operate? And how often had she succeeded?

"Miz Burke?" Ruthie called from downstairs. "You want me to start on those upstairs baths like we talked about? There's a mess down here in the living room, clothes piled and thrown every way but up. . . ." She trailed off, mumbling.

Oh, God, do a quick and simple miracle and make those clothes disappear . . . and make David disappear with them. At least until she could make Ruthie disappear. Or get some clothes on. Or both.

Mary Scott didn't have any clothes in the guest room. David didn't have any clothes that weren't lying on the floor of the living room. And Ruthie was coming up the stairs.

Mary Scott looked down at David; he was lying on his back with his hands behind his head, grinning up at her. David was at his most troublesome when he was grinning.

"If she's going to change the sheets, we'd better get up and give her some room to maneuver." He flipped back the blanket and lay there, naked. And aroused. Grinning.

She flipped the sheet back over him and grabbed for the comforter. "You . . . stay where you are!" she snapped, pushing her hair off her face and trying to get the blanket wrapped around her in any way she could. "Ruthie!" she called, fumbling with the blanket, swatting David's hand away when he made a grab for the back of it and pulled it off her shoulders.

"Yes, ma'am?" Ruthie called, her voice much closer now. She had to be halfway up the stairs.

"Just a minute, just wait a minute," Mary Scott said in a rush, scooting off the bed.

Why did things like this always happen to her? But that wasn't right; they only happened to her when David was around. Without David her life was calm and orderly and free of embarrassment.

"It won't take more than a minute." David laughed and threw back the sheet, showing her how hard and ready he was to do his minute's worth of work.

"Stop it!" she hissed, escaping the bed when he lunged for her. Scooting to the door, the bulky comforter draped around her like a mutant pillow, Mary Scott hurried into the hall. She bumped into Ruthie on the second-floor landing.

Ruthie looked up at Mary Scott from her petite five-foot, one-inch height, noted the blanket, and said, "Did you want me to change the linens today, Miz Burke? Because I thought we agreed that I was to do the bathrooms and the baseboards before Christmas and then before New Year's do the floors and the linens and then after the holidays go back to my regular routine.

Because I thought that you wanted me to do the dusting and the kitchen every other Saturday and then the windows once a month. Because I thought we talked about not keeping to a regular schedule with the holidays coming since I have family in town and you said I didn't have to work a full day again until they left town and they're not leaving until January third. Because my husband's—"

"No," Mary Scott interrupted. Ruthie always talked this way. It was actually a relief when she ran the vacuum, but even then Mary Scott could see her mouth moving as she talked to herself. "No, you're right, and I don't want you to change the linens today. You go ahead and do what we talked about, but start in the downstairs bath, since I overslept and still need to shower. . . ."

Mary Scott trailed off, since Ruthie wasn't looking at her and wasn't listening to her; she was looking into the guest bedroom with her mouth hanging open and, for once, unmoving. Mary Scott took a deep breath and made herself look and see what Ruthie was looking at and seeing.

It could have been worse, but only by a little. David was sitting up in bed, the sheet pooled around his hips, grinning and waving to the women in the doorway, as if he was issuing an invitation. Or half an invitation.

David didn't give them a chance to say a

word; he just jumped right in and said the worst possible thing, like he always did.

"Morning, Ruthie." He grinned, completely and disgustingly at ease with his own nudity and blissfully expecting everyone else to feel the same way about it. "I'm Scottie's husband, David. Just give us a minute"—and he winked at Mary Scott as he said *that*—"and we'll be out of your way."

Ruthie stood there with her mouth open for a moment longer. Mary Scott clenched her blanket around her. David sat comfortably, leaning against the mahogany headboard, a pillow shoved into the gap behind the small of his back. He actually looked as if he was perfectly at ease. He actually looked as if he owned the place. Mary Scott actually had a very potent visual image of herself shaking him until he turned red.

It was then that Ruthie turned to her and said, loudly, "I thought you were divorced."

Mary Scott felt the blood in her face drain down into her knees. She stared at David, waiting for his reaction. He was amused, perhaps puzzled. She didn't wait any longer than that.

"Ruthie, you go on and do the downstairs bath," she said calmly.

"Do you want me to do anything about them clothes in—"

"No, I'll take care of that," Mary Scott interrupted, fighting her embarrassment. "You go ahead and do what we agreed you'd do today."

"Yes, ma'am," Ruthie mumbled, turning to go back downstairs with a final curious look at David. David returned the look with a cheerful wave.

"Divorced?" he said.

Mary Scott didn't look at him; she just clutched her blanket and walked into the master bedroom across the hall. It was the only bedroom that had its own bath, and she desperately needed the privacy of her own bath right now. David could use the bathroom down the hall.

"The bathroom's down there," she pointed, not looking back. "Second door on the right. The towels are clean."

"Divorced?" he said again, now up and following her. "Why would your maid think you were divorced? Widowed, I'd expect, but divorced—"

"She'll be back up soon to do the baths," Mary Scott interrupted, "so you'd better get washed while you can." She turned the shower tap on and pulled the balloon valance down. David was standing in the doorway. He'd left the sheet behind on the bed. He was still ready for his one-minute duty.

"Your bath is down the hall. Second door—"

"On the right." He smiled. "But this shower looks big enough for two."

"It isn't," she said, running a hand under the

water. It was an old house; the water took a while to run hot.

"Let's check it out." He came in, closing the bathroom door behind him.

"Ruthie'll be up here soon!"

"Not in the next minute or so." He grinned, coming toward her.

Same old David. Same blue eyes that made her melt and feel squishy inside; same grin that had her smiling in return even when she didn't know the joke; same preoccupation, wanting to spend every waking hour in her arms and in her bed. When had that started rubbing her wrong?

Mary Scott jumped into the shower, dragging half the blanket with her, soaking it. The water wasn't warm yet, and she couldn't help the yelp that rushed out of her.

"No need for a cold shower, Scottie. I'm right here to take care of you," David said from his side of the shower curtain.

"Down the hall," she said over the noise of the shower. At least the water was finally getting hot.

"Okay," he said. "I won't crowd you."

That was almost funny, coming from David. Not crowd her? He always crowded her, sexually. In every other way, he left her dizzingly alone.

"So why did Ruthie think you were divorced?" he said softly.

Mary Scott soaped herself thoroughly and

scraped a razor over her legs and under her arms. She wasn't doing it for David; she shaved every morning, for herself.

"She knew I was alone," Mary Scott said tersely. "Divorce is more common than widowhood, I guess." Standing under the scalding heat of the shower, she said softly, "I did think . . . they told me you were dead. What happened?"

"They were wrong," he said, the timbre of his voice closing the subject. Same old David. Closing her out, wanting nothing from her except open arms and open legs. And giving her nothing in return.

"Can't hear you," she said, the pain in her voice awful to hear. She buried her head under the stream of hot water and grabbed for the shampoo.

"I'll join you, and then you'll hear me just fine," he said, peeking around the shower curtain.

"I'd rather bathe alone," she said stiffly as she rubbed the shampoo into her hair. She knew the sight of her, her arms up over her head, the shampoo bubbles sliding down over her breasts and belly, would arouse him. She didn't care. As far as that went, it didn't take much to arouse him.

"Same old Scottie." He smirked, the shower mist leaving beads all over his face and hair. He looked as mischievous as a water sprite. "Once the sex is over, you pull back into your tank and swing your guns into position."

She didn't say a word to that. There was nothing to say. They'd been over this ground too many times already. Nothing had changed, even though he'd come back from the dead. Last night had been . . . a dream, maybe even a gift, but last night was gone, and now reality was back.

Only a fool lived in dreams.

She turned off the shower and wrung the water from her hair. David had ducked his head back outside the curtain. She was grateful for that.

"Would you hand me a towel, please?" she asked.

"Sure," he said easily. She was instantly suspicious. And for good reason. Through the gap in the shower curtain, he passed her a hand towel the size of an oven mitt.

"David! Never mind, I'll get it myself."

"Can't. I moved them all."

"I'll never get dry with this."

"Come on out, and I'll get you dry."

"Never mind," she grumbled, "I'll manage."

"You always do."

"If you're trying to insult me, you missed."

"I'm not trying to insult you," he said softly. "Come on out."

"I'm embarrassed," she breathed, her head tucked down.

"Why? I've seen it all before."

"You're making it worse," she said, pulling at the hand towel, stretching it. She gained maybe an eighth of an inch.

"What are you going to cover, your top or your bottom?"

She could hear the smile in his voice. He loved embarrassing her. He could make a living at it if only someone would pay him for it.

"My face," she said.

"Works for me." He laughed.

"Does it matter that it doesn't work for me?" Did everything have to go his way?

"Sure it does," he said solemnly. And he handed in another hand towel.

There was no getting away from it; she'd have to leave the shower with only two minuscule hand towels to cover her. The only up side was that the bedroom was just a few feet away and her robe was hanging in the front of her closet. And he had seen it all before.

With all the dignity of the Queen Mother, Mary Scott held the two towels to her breasts and walked out of the shower. David only smiled. He could be very gracious in victory.

"Now tell me why Ruthie thinks you're divorced," he said, his victory grin still in place.

She didn't want to tell him. She didn't want the fight that would follow. She didn't want to have to explain to him what he never could understand, and she didn't want to defend herself to a man who made a living by shredding an enemy's defenses. And she would be the enemy, if he ever found out that she'd been more than halfway to divorcing him. What she was going to do about that now, she didn't know. He'd shown up last night, after she'd thrown away all thoughts of ever seeing him again. All she'd done was feel. Gratitude that he was alive, passion to be in his arms again, tenderness and awe at the oneness that being sexually possessed by him caused to rise up in her. But it didn't last. It never lasted.

Mary Scott grabbed for her ivory silk robe and wrapped it around her, tying the belt tightly. She toweled the remaining wetness from her hair with the two little hand towels and then faced him. David stood in the doorway to the bath, his arms crossed over his bare chest, his erection gone. His minute must have been up. What was it about David that he could stand in front of her as naked as a baby and feel just as unashamed?

"Maybe because you weren't around," she said sharply. He was never around, and when he was, he was usually naked. Like now.

"You didn't tell her about me?"

"My maid?" she snorted. "We talk about rust deposits in the sinks."

"I tell everybody about you."

"I'm not flattered."

"You should be." He grinned. Couldn't he find a towel for himself?

She walked back past him, tossing him a soggy towel, and went into the bathroom to comb her hair. If she didn't get it styled while it was still damp, she'd look like a cyclone survivor for the rest of the day. Though why she should care what she looked like for David, who liked her best flat on her back—

"You cut your hair," he said, interrupting her angry thoughts.

"It's easier. I didn't have time—"

"It looks good. You look good."

It was cut to just below her chin—not so very short. She knew he liked long hair. It had been past her shoulders when she saw him last, just a few months ago. He had lost weight since then, but he still looked good. The muscles of his arms and chest were more sharply defined and his jaw more pronounced, but he was just as handsome, just as devastating to her equilibrium as he'd always been. From the very first look.

"So do you," she whispered, looking at him in the mirror's reflection. "They told me you were dead." Her voice cracked as she said it, the pain in it telling him too much when she wanted so much to hide.

"They exaggerated," he said to her, facing her image in the mirror.

"The Navy doesn't usually do that."

"I'm a special case," he said lightly.

He wasn't going to tell her what had happened to him. He wasn't going to let her in. He never did.

"Are you all right?" she asked, her voice low and hesitant.

"Don't I look it?" He smiled arrogantly.

He was gorgeous, in a purely masculine way, and he knew it. She wasn't going to feed that ego willingly. And not with him standing naked in her bathroom.

"You finished in there, Miz Burke?" Ruthie called from the doorway to the bedroom.

Mary Scott dropped her brush on the counter and turned with a jerk toward Ruthie's voice. David just kept looking at her in the bathroom mirror, his blue eyes searching hers, but she wouldn't look at him. Ruthie had broken the tension between them, and she was nothing but thankful.

"Just about, but give me a couple more minutes."

"You can start on the bathroom down the hall, Ruthie," David said. "Second door on the right. I'll be using this bathroom."

"Then get to it," Mary Scott hissed to her husband. "I pay her by the hour." And she walked out of the bathroom and closed the door behind her, shutting a still naked David in.

He walked right out, a bath towel now

wrapped around his waist. Where had he hidden it? She wasn't going to stay and ask him. He wouldn't tell her anyway.

Mary Scott walked out of the bedroom and into the hall. She was going downstairs to make herself some chamomile tea and try to get a little peace and serenity back in her Saturday morning.

David, wrapped in a white towel with embroidered edging, followed her down the hall and down the stairs and into the kitchen.

"What's for breakfast?" he said cheerily, as if he actually lived with her.

"Hot water," she said, putting a single mug of water in the microwave to heat. David hated herbal tea, and she didn't have any coffee. "And I'd appreciate it if you'd get some clothes on."

David looked down at his towel, his abdominal muscles crunching at the motion. Her heart fluttered, and she felt ripples of emotion under her ribs.

He had done that on purpose.

"Too informal for Saturday breakfast?"

"A towel? You know it is. Go get dressed," she snapped.

The microwave beeped its readiness to provide her with boiling water for her tea, and she whirled to face the machine, turning her back willingly on David and his abdominals.

"Really? You didn't seem to mind that time we ate berries for breakfast in that little apartment in Newport News. I was dressed in less than this. And so were you."

And she remembered what he had done with those berries, too. Mary Scott flinched in shameful recollection and sloshed boiling water over the backs of her fingers.

"Ouch!"

He was by her side instantly, grabbing her hand and shoving it under the faucet, turning on the cold water in the same moment. Mary Scott enjoyed the cool relief and moved her fingers under the rushing water. It wasn't much of a burn, wouldn't even leave a blister. But David's hand, so brown and large, holding hers, seared her brain with memory and longing and pain. And she couldn't stop looking at their hands clasped under the stream of cold water.

David had held her hand when he had asked her to marry him. They'd been standing in a parking lot in the middle of the afternoon, just last May. A thunderstorm had been rolling in off the ocean. He'd asked her then, when she was in a rush to be off and with nothing even remotely romantic about the moment. But once he'd said it, once he'd asked her to marry him, she'd had to say yes. Because one look into his impossibly blue eyes and it had become the most romantic moment of her life. A candle-light dinner and flowers with another man would have been trite after David's proposal in the sweltering parking lot of the church, the

41

rain starting to fall in noisy plops to the ground.

David had held her hand in his when they first made love, hanging on to her when she felt she was going to fly off and hit the ceiling with the force of her climax. He had held her hand, holding her to him, giving her his strength and his presence, promising without words that he would protect her and cherish her.

David had held her hand in the car, just before she'd gone in to request a private office. He had held her hand gently, rubbing his thumb over her fingers one by one, while he told her that she was going to get that office, and if she had any feelings that the interview was going badly, she should pull a Sharon Stone and cinch the deal. And then he'd asked if she'd worn her black thong. She'd laughed so hard in the car that she'd gone into the interview as loose as a sleeping cat, grinning every time she recrossed her legs. She'd gotten the private office.

David had held her hand when he'd said good-bye. David had held her hand hard and said little, and that's how she knew it was going to be bad. And it had been bad. He'd been reported killed in action. She'd never thought to see his hand holding hers again.

But she was. He was.

"You okay?" he said, studying her hand, his dark head bent down.

"Don't I look okay?" she breathed.

He looked up at her then, his face so close to

hers, his eyes so intense and so blue. She saw the flare of intimacy, of desire, spark in his eyes, and she felt the answer in her heart.

"You look better than okay."

She wasn't going to do this again. She wasn't going to forget all the hurt and fall into his arms. She could forget everything in his arms, but she couldn't live there, and when real life sliced into the haze of passion he built around them, she was left hurt and angry and alone. She didn't want to do that again. She didn't want to lose herself in him and find that she was all alone in the losing.

"So do you," she mouthed. She didn't even give breath to the words; they had no volume, only shape. But he heard her.

He pulled her to him by that hand he had saved from a burn and kissed her gently, his mouth moving over hers like a tentative explorer, thorough, cautious, eager. She didn't want the pain he always brought with him, but she wanted this. She always wanted this.

Passion, always simmering in her when he was near, exploded at the touch of his lips on hers, and she pressed herself against him, the throbbing between her legs instantaneous and intense. It was always like this. Just like this.

He wore only the towel, and her robe was thin; it would be so easy to spread her legs and invite him in. It would be so glorious to have him inside her again, filling her, possessing her.

David lifted her so that she sat on the kitchen counter. He pushed her knees apart, and her robe opened. His hands traced the delicate skin of her inner thighs, and she shivered, holding him to her, her hands gripping his hair. It was always like this.

An upstairs toilet flushed. Ruthie. Reality.

She broke the kiss and laid her forehead on his shoulder, breathing deeply and brokenly. David rubbed her back, even his comfort sensuous in her aroused state.

"Get dressed," she whispered, her voice ragged. "Please."

"Yes, ma'am," he said softly, kissing her hair.

He backed up, leaving her sitting on the counter next to her mug of warm water, and adjusted his towel. With a wink and a grin, he left the kitchen and went into the living room.

Ruthie had piled their clothes in the needlepoint chair Mary Scott's mother had bought her, getting them up off the floor, at least. She had noticed that when she came down. Once Ruthie left, she'd put her clothes away, though they'd most likely need to go to the dry cleaner after spending a night on the floor in a wrinkled heap. Save for his shirt buttons, David's clothes would be fine, she was sure. She'd been wearing a wool business suit, while he'd been wearing . . . what had he been wearing? She couldn't remember anything beyond her initial recognition of him and then the feel of his body next to hers. Oh, well, men's clothes stood up to rougher handling than—

"I can't wear these," David said from the living room.

"What?" she said in instant alarm, leaving the kitchen to walk down the short hall into the living room.

David stood in the living room in his towel and held up his pants and shirt. Khakis. He'd been wearing khakis and a blue broadcloth shirt.

"Wrinkled."

Mary Scott could hear Ruthie talking to herself; she must be about finished by now, and she would come down the stairs and see David standing in her living room in nothing but a towel.

"I'm sure they'll be fine once you get them on," she said. "You can work the wrinkles out by wearing them."

"No," David said decisively. "I can't wear these." How had she forgotten how fussy he was about his clothes? He was worse than any woman. "I'll go out to the car and get my suitcase."

He was already turning toward the foyer and the front door. It was almost 10:00 AM on a Saturday; everybody in the world would be home, watching David in his scrap of a towel.

"Like that?" she squealed.

"It'll just take me a minute."

"Wait! Put on your pants! Put on *something!*" The door opened. He was outside. In his towel. In her neighborhood.

She liked this house; she didn't want to move.

Mary Scott stood in the living room, feeling helpless and furious at once. And then she felt humiliated. Because she didn't have to move a step to see David striding down her walk in his towel, didn't have to even move her head to see him reach into the back of his bright red truck and pull out his bag; she could see it all, right from where she stood in her elegant living room. And last night, the whole world and her neighbors and any cars passing by could have seen them ripping their clothes off and attacking each other like teenagers in the first flush of hormones. Her beautiful living room, with windows to the floor and drapes that weren't meant to be closed, had been a well-lit stage last night.

She and David had been the players.

She really was going to have to move.

Mary Scott watched in numb horror as David, his white towel a beacon of indecency, walked through her front yard.

A woman with her infant in a stroller was jogging; she swiveled her head and picked up her pace to a dead run.

Her neighbor two doors down and across the street was edging his lawn; he cut through a small shrub before letting the edger sputter to a stop.

A teenage girl with a blond ponytail was walking her dog; she stood and stared at David, her mouth agape, until her dog pulled her off balance and she reluctantly continued down the street, walking backward so she could keep David in her line of sight.

Her next-door neighbor, Fran, was out plumping the bow on her Christmas wreaths; she took one look at David, scurried back inside, and slammed the door so hard that the wreath fell to the ground.

David, to make it all worse, smiled at everyone and waved as if he were the star attraction of the Christmas parade.

She still hadn't moved when David came back into the house. She couldn't. She was in shock with the growing realization that she would have to sell and move out of the zip code; a block or two away wouldn't be enough. No, this level of shame would follow for miles.

David had the nerve to be smiling.

"Nice neighborhood," he said, plopping his bag down on her antique chest. There was a zipper on his bag; he'd probably scratched the wood. "People seem real friendly."

"Get some clothes on," she managed to say, her voice a thread of suppressed anger.

David didn't bother to look up at her; he didn't care that he'd just ruined her chances of making any friends at all in this neighborhood.

"That's the idea," he said as he pulled out a

pair of jeans and tugged them on. He didn't bother with underwear. He dumped his towel on one of her damask chairs. He did all this in front of the living room window.

A car passed and hit the brakes hard—the first mooning of a car from a house. It was a dark green minivan; she hoped she didn't know its occupants. Probably parents with a car full of kids going to church for choir practice. She'd probably be arrested for contributing to the delinquency of minors. The parents would probably sue her for traumatizing their children. She'd have to sell the house to pay for her legal fees. Well, she'd have to sell the house anyway.

And David kept smiling, his cheer impenetrable. It had occurred to her more than once in the time she'd known him, and it occurred to her now: he must be doing it on purpose. No one could humiliate a person so relentlessly by accident. He thought it was funny to stomp all over her life, making things difficult for her. He thought all he'd ever have to do was smile that devastating smile of his and throw her to the floor for the wildest sex ever achieved by man and she'd be powerless to stop his easy humiliation of her.

He didn't know that everything had changed.

"Could you take your bag off the chest?" she snapped. "You're scratching it."

"Sure. Sorry." He went to the chest, his jeans

still unzipped, and pulled the bag off. Her mail went flying. "Sorry. I'll get it," he said, bending down, the muscles in his back twisting and bunching.

It didn't matter what his back muscles did; she wasn't going to let it get to her. Things had changed. Things had to have changed.

David picked up the mail. He began reading the envelopes. And then he stood and looked at her. He wasn't smiling.

"Since when did your last name stop being the same as mine?"

Mary Scott met his look, but she couldn't hold out against the raw confusion she saw in his eyes. She turned and walked back into the kitchen. David followed, the mail clutched in his hand.

"Scottie?" he said, his voice throaty.

She faced the refrigerator, keeping him at her back. She knew what she would see in his face, and she didn't want to see it. She'd wanted their divorce to be distant, unemotional, painless. There was nothing painless about the sound of his voice. She didn't want a confrontation that would leave her feeling guilty and upset. She didn't want a confrontation with David at all, ever; he was so good at it, and she was so inept.

"When?" he asked.

"I thought you were dead," she said to the white face of the refrigerator.

"My Aunt Sylvia's been a widow for ten years, and she hasn't changed her name."

"I'm different."

"And quick," he shot back. "When did you get the notice?"

He was pinning her down, or trying to, and she didn't want to give him that. He didn't need to know any of this.

"I don't see any point in such a painful conversation," she said, opening the refrigerator and looking in, pretending she was seeing food, planning a menu. All she was looking for was an escape.

David pressed the refrigerator closed with one hand and then stood in front of it, forcing her back. He looked wildly male, angry and charged with energy, his jeans gaping open and his body hard and hairy. He was the most incredible-looking man she'd ever seen, and he made her feel things that no one had told her about, but she couldn't stay married to him. He was stepping all over her, and he didn't even see it. She was dying in this relationship. Every time he made love to her, she died a little more. And she didn't know how to make him understand.

"Painful to you or to me?" he asked, knowing the answer, or thinking he did.

Leaning against the refrigerator door, David asked the one question he'd been asking all morning. And she was finally ready to answer it.

"You were divorcing me, weren't you?" he asked, his voice raw with emotion.

Mary Scott looked at him and met his blue eyes without flinching. "Yes."

Chapter Three

She stood there, her gray-blue eyes unblinking, and told him that she'd planned to throw him out of her life. Cool as glass. She stood there in her white robe looking as if nothing could touch her, as if marriage to him hadn't touched her, as if divorcing him wouldn't even raise a sweat. His SEAL team had called her "the popsicle," and he'd laughed, knowing how hot she was with him, glad that no one else could see the white fire in her. But he didn't see any fire now, just ice.

She'd been acting weird since . . . well, not last night, that had been great, but since this morning, and he hadn't been able to place why. Now he knew.

But he wasn't going to let it happen. He loved her. He'd married her, and a man didn't do that lightly. She'd gotten some bee in her bonnet about him, probably kept alive by her mother, and she'd decided to cut him loose. But she couldn't do that without some kind of agreement from him, could she? No-fault divorce was one thing, but didn't he at least have to sign something? He hadn't signed anything, and he never would.

"How could you divorce me? I didn't agree to it," he said, studying her face.

Scottie licked her lips and flipped back the pale blond sheet of her straight hair; she was nervous. Maybe she was only as cool as cracked glass.

"I was proceeding with the divorce—"

"*Our* divorce," he said. He wasn't going to let her get away with putting any distance between it and her.

Scottie glared at him and continued, "—when I got notification of your death."

"So . . . ?"

"So, I told my lawyer he didn't have to continue with it."

"So, we're not divorced."

"Not legally," she said stiffly.

"What other way is there besides legally?" he said, coming off the refrigerator.

She backed up until she was pressed against the opposite counter. The morning sun was coming in the back window and lit her like a white candle; white robe, pale skin, pale hair, and pale gray eyes like an exotic cat's. But he wasn't going to let himself get sidetracked by how gorgeous she was. He was going to nail this divorce thing down.

"I thought you were dead!" she said, playing with the ends of her belt.

"And that was better news to you? You were trying to divorce me—long-distance, no less— and then I turned up conveniently dead. That must have been the best news you had all year! Congratulations, Mrs. Adams, your husband is dead, and you can save yourself the cost and aggravation of a divorce!"

"It wasn't like that at all!" she snapped.

"It had to be that way!" he snapped back, pacing the kitchen and staying as far away from her as he could. If he got anywhere near her, he'd shake her until her ears rang. "You wanted to be free of me. My death accomplished that. Better than a divorce. If you really want to escape a man, how much better does it get than to have him dead?"

"I wasn't happy to find out . . . to think you were . . . and that's not the point anyway!" she scrambled, going on the offensive. "Your feelings are hurt, fine, but we didn't have much of a marriage. You can't be surprised."

"We have a great marriage. I'm damned surprised."

Something clicked behind her eyes then, something he'd seen before in her but couldn't name. The angry sound of a metal gate slamming closed, the heavy sliding of a bolt; those were the sounds he put to the look in her eyes.

"And that's the problem," she said with a rasp of emotion. "You *shouldn't* be surprised."

"Why? Why shouldn't I be surprised?" he asked, stopping in front of the kitchen table. "I love you. You love me. We love being together."

"Right," she said sarcastically, "we have such great conversations, such soul-stirring talks where we share our thoughts and dreams."

What? What was she talking about? Did she want mutual analysis, talking psychobabble to each other?

"We talk," he said.

"Really?" she said with false brightness. "Tell me again how you came to be reported dead, just the parts that aren't classified."

Anger flared, and he closed the distance between them. "Tell me again how you don't love being with me, especially after that demonstration last night."

Scottie's cheeks turned pink, but she didn't drop her eyes. "That is exactly what I'm talking about."

"Well, so am I, so keep talking."

"We never talk. You don't even know if it's another man. You haven't even asked."

David leaned over her, close enough to be almost touching. Scottie's eyes dilated, and her breath got short, just like it always did when he got close. He knew the effect he had on her—the same as she had on him. He knew her, better than she thought he did.

"I don't need to ask," he said. "You're not the kind of woman who'd sleep with me if there was someone else. There's no one else, not for you."

God, let it be the truth.

The doorbell rang, breaking the angry tension only slightly. Scottie turned abruptly and walked to the front door. She moved like a dancer, every step graceful and accentuated by the thin silk robe she wore. She'd lost weight in the few months he'd been gone, and she was thin enough to start with; she needed to eat more.

David followed a few steps behind, zipping up his pants as he did. He could hear a man's voice, and he closed the distance fast; Scottie was only wearing that little bit of silk.

"She swears she saw a naked man in your yard and wanted me to check, make sure things were all right over here," he said.

"Thank you so much," Scottie gushed. He could hear her smile from six feet behind her back. "I'm just fine, Cyrus, and you tell Fran I appreciate her watching out for me."

"So . . . you know the man?"

"Well, yes, he's a gue—"

David pushed forward, opening the door

wider, and held out his hand. No way was he going to be described as a guest of his wife.

"Good morning! I'm Scottie's husband, David."

"Uh, good morning," Cyrus said, shaking David's hand. "I didn't know Mary Scott was married."

"I've been away a while." David smiled, wrapping an arm around Scottie's waist and pulling her in tight. "It's good to be home. And it's good to know we've got neighbors who'll watch out for her when I'm not here—Cyrus, did I hear your name was?"

"Yes, Cyrus Holbrook, and my wife's Fran."

"Excuse me, I should have introduced you," Scottie murmured politely, trying to step away from David. He just smiled and held on.

"And where do you live?" David asked.

Cyrus gestured with a flick of his hand. "Right next door."

"Lived here long?"

"About twenty-five years. We moved in a few years after we got married; it's home."

"Twenty-five years." David grinned, stepping out onto the porch. "That explains why your lawn is so perfect. Not a blade of grass out of place. What's your secret, or does it just take years of effort? Please, tell me I have a chance."

Cyrus smiled and shook his head. "I'm not looking for any more competition in the grass department. I'm just holding my own with Sam

Rule three houses down; he's the man to beat."

"Really? Which house? The Cape Cod?"

"You named it." Cyrus laughed. "It looks great even from this distance; that's how good he is."

"And how long has he been here?" David asked, moving out into the yard. Scottie wouldn't have any cause to complain; he was wearing pants.

"Maybe seven years."

"Ah, so it can be done in less than twenty-five years. I do have a chance." David grinned.

"Got me." Cyrus laughed in return. "But if you really want to know my secret, it's in having a sharp blade on the mower every time I cut the lawn. No torn stems, no ragged tips."

"Really? It's not in the mower itself? What do you use?"

"I was using a self-propelled until a few years back, then switched back to what I'd used as a boy doing my daddy's yard."

"A push mower," David said.

"Not just a push mower." Cyrus smiled. "A rotary."

"You did give in to nostalgia. I'll bet it's a good way to stay in shape. And easier to sharpen."

"Yeah, but hard to find. I had to try a few yard sales before this one—"

"If you'll excuse me," Mary Scott interrupted, "I need to get dressed. Thanks for coming by, Cyrus."

"Oh, my pleasure, Mary Scott," he said, already turning his back on her and heading off down the walk with David, talking lawn mowers and weed 'n' feed.

Mary Scott closed the door, closing out the sound of David chatting it up with a neighbor she'd done little more than wave to in the four months she'd been in the house. She resisted the urge to lock the door only because she didn't want David walking around all day in her neighborhood without a shirt on.

And when she faced him next, she was going to have on more than her robe—though she'd been fully dressed last night, and it hadn't made a bit of difference. She'd been surprised, she reasoned, caught completely off guard; today would be different. There'd be no giving in to heady, self-destructive impulses today. She'd wear wool—nice, thick wool—and good, sturdy shoes; that would help. The silk robe had been a bad idea. And Cyrus Holbrooke had seen her in it, too, at past ten on a Saturday. No pansies, and hanging around in her robe; she'd have a fine reputation as a sloth. They'd probably get up a petition to run her out of the neighborhood.

Shaking off the negative cycle of her thoughts, Mary Scott went upstairs. Ruthie was just finishing.

"If you'll just dust and vacuum downstairs, that'll be all, Ruthie."

"You don't want me to do the kitchen? It's been three weeks since I did that oven."

"It's fine," Mary Scott said from the doorway to her bedroom, already closing the door. She'd never been less than fully dressed when Ruthie came on Saturday morning to clean, and here she was, still in her robe. Well, it was better than the blanket she'd been wearing when Ruthie first showed up.

"But with Christmas just a few days off—"

"I won't be doing much in that kitchen between now and New Year's. It's fine."

"Not even with your husband come home? He'll be wanting a—"

"There's no need for you to do the kitchen, Ruthie. Just dust. And vacuum."

Mary Scott closed the door on Ruthie's grumbles and leaned back against it. She took a deep breath and then walked over to her closet. It was huge. The previous owner had annexed a small bedroom on the shared wall, so the master bedroom now stretched the length of one side of the house, and a third of that was closet. And it was all hers.

She had to get control of herself with Ruthie. Ruthie was the best maid in this part of town, and it had taken her mother weeks of scrambling to get the woman to agree to come and do her house. At that, she'd had to come on Saturdays, since all her weekdays were booked. Over time, Mary Scott would work herself into a prime weekday slot, and then she wouldn't have to share her house with her maid on one of her few days off.

Mary Scott hung up her robe and considered her choices. Definitely wool, and some color David didn't like. She realized her problem immediately; she didn't have any idea what colors David liked or didn't like. He'd never said a word about it one way or the other. All right then, layers, lots of tedious layers that would make it impossible for him to get his hands on her skin. Just the thought of it, of David reaching under her clothes to unsnap her bra or slide a hand down her pants made her nipples tighten in readiness.

Flushed and flustered, she hurriedly put on her underwear and grabbed a pair of charcoal wool pants and pulled them on. It wasn't very cold out, but she wanted those layers, so she picked a white Egyptian cotton shirt and threw a black boiled wool vest with pale gray embroidered ivy leaves on over it. That looked somber enough. Hardly anything to inspire lust. She slipped on a pair of black shoes with black socks, very mannish. A pair of pearl earrings that her mother had brought back from a trip to Japan and her watch completed her toilette. Mary Scott looked in the full-length mirror in her closet; she looked severe and plain and decidedly unfeminine. Perfect.

Now, she had to get out of this bedroom before David came back in. She didn't look like a femme fatal, but there was no point in taking foolish chances. It didn't take much to set David off; she'd learned that time and again.

The more painful lesson was that it didn't take much to set her off, either. Last night was a perfect illustration of that. She'd taken one look at him, and every rational thought, every instinct for self-preservation, had deserted her, to be replaced by blind need and hungry passion.

In four months, months of stern lectures to herself, months of strict self-denial, she'd accomplished nothing. Last night had proved that. Nothing had changed between them. This morning had proved that.

She wasn't going to feel guilty, no matter what David said. The divorce had been a good idea and was still a good idea. They'd talk, and he'd see that, he'd understand.

But that was the problem: he'd never understand. That's why she needed to get the divorce. And she wasn't going to feel guilty about it.

David came back in as Ruthie was dusting the chest in the foyer. He took a quick look; there didn't seem to be a scratch in the finish. One less thing for Scottie to be mad about. She seemed to be mad about everything lately, even before he'd left on his mission. Thinking about it that way, her idea of getting a divorce didn't seem quite as far-fetched. Not that he was going to give her one. Divorce just wasn't an option, not for them.

"Ruthie," he said in greeting, and then went over to his bag to dig around for a shirt. It wasn't exactly cold out, but it was December and not the time of year to be running around outside without a shirt on. He dug around some more and pulled out a pair of socks.

"Mr. Burke," she answered, eyeing him as he buttoned his navy flannel shirt.

"Burke's my wife's maiden name, Ruthie. My name is Adams."

"Sorry," she said.

"No problem." He sat down in an old-style chair in the living room and pulled on his socks. "I guess she didn't mention me?"

Ruthie kept dusting. "Not that I remember, but we don't talk much except business. I clean for her mother, too."

"Oh." David smiled and leaned back in his chair. "So you know Mary Nell. How's she doing?"

"She's off on one of her cruises again."

"Where to this time?"

"One of them old-timey tours of Greece," Ruthie said, warming up. "She went with Miz Winn and Miz Cunningham and Miz Finch; they all play bridge together. This is one of them tours where they have bridge tournaments every day. I clean for them, too."

"Gone for Christmas?" he asked. That wasn't right, leaving Scottie all alone and a new widow. Or so they'd thought.

"Gone till just after New Year's," Ruthie humphed, evidently thinking the same thing.

"What do you have planned for Christmas? Is your family in town?"

"Oh, we all get together at my house for Christmas Eve and then my sister's for Christmas Day. We're a big family, lots of food to get cooked. I do the potatoes and sweets for her on Christmas Day. She brings the same to me on Christmas Eve. It works out."

"Lots of kids in the clan?" he asked, sitting back in his chair while Ruthie dusted the picture frames.

"Yes, sir, sixteen of 'em, and my brother's wife is expecting twins in February. She won't do no cooking this year—has to stay off her feet, according to the doctor. Needs to keep her feet up. They're swelled like two muskmelons right now. My brother'll just bring some drinks to help out."

"Sixteen kids," David said. "And how many are yours?"

"Five are mine, with only one grandchild so far, but I'm hoping for more by summer."

"Grandchild? You don't look old enough for that."

Ruthie humphed and laughed soundlessly. "How old you got to be? I had my first at eighteen, and my oldest had his at eighteen. Be young with your kids, that's what I say." Ruthie had finished with the dusting in the living room, giving a final swipe to the baseboard abutting the fireplace. She was standing right next to David. "You two ought to have kids; it'd keep you together."

David looked at her and smiled. "You think so?"

"Yes, sir, I do," she answered emphatically. "When you got kids, you're too busy to be unhappy; they don't give you any time at all to notice it."

"It may be too late for that." He shrugged.

"Lawd, the way Miz Burke looked this morning?" She laughed. "It ain't too late. Could be you already took care of it."

David just grinned and winked at her. Ruthie laughed again and walked into the foyer. Before she went down the hall to the kitchen, she turned and said, "My sister, Pamie, she had some trouble in her marriage last year. The pastor fixed them up good, and now they're expecting their fourth. You go see somebody, get this thing worked out. Divorce ain't right."

David stood up and followed Ruthie into the kitchen. Seemed that no matter what Scottie had to say about what was to be cleaned in her house, Ruthie wasn't going to leave the kitchen alone. She was wiping out the oven when David rounded the corner.

"You think Scottie would listen to a pastor?" he asked. This could work; he couldn't imagine a pastor advocating divorce.

"She goes to church, doesn't she?" Ruthie asked rhetorically, her head in the oven.

"Do you know where?"

" 'Course I know. She goes to Pinewood Baptist."

Ruthie finished with the oven and went to inspect the interior of the microwave. David left her to it. Tomorrow was Sunday. They'd go to church together, and he'd make a point of meeting the pastor, and he'd lay the whole thing out; he'd even sit through some counseling sessions if he had to. He'd go that far to get her to drop this divorce madness.

Mary-Scott waited upstairs until she couldn't hear David's voice anymore. She knew he must be talking to Ruthie and decided to wait him out. She was dressed in layers and wearing gray wool, looking as puritanical as possible, but she didn't see the need to act recklessly. Being anywhere near David and a flat surface was a reckless act.

Ruthie was in the kitchen when she came down, giving the floors a quick damp mop. Mary Scott didn't say a word about it; it was the reason Ruthie was so much in demand. She was thorough and came to look upon the houses she cleaned as her own, and the people in them, too.

Mary Scott reheated her water and steeped her herbal tea in silence while Ruthie mumbled about rising divorce rates and the emptiness of a marriage without children. She sipped her tea and bit into an apple when Ruthie started talking about what a nice man Mr. Adams seemed to be. She tossed the core into the compost pile when Ruthie advised her to have a good, long talk with her pastor. And then she waved Ruthie good-bye and wished her a Merry Christmas, still holding her tongue.

Ruthie might have said half those things on her own, but she knew David well enough to know he was responsible for the other half.

She was still going through with the divorce, no matter how many people he recruited to his side.

David came in through the back door, which led into the kitchen, as she was rinsing out her cup. His shoes were covered with bits of grass, the toes stained light green.

"You should take better care of the lawn, Scottie," he said, walking across the floor and leaving bits of grass in his wake. "You've got some patches of moss out there bordering Cyrus's yard, and that stuff likes to spread."

"That was you out mowing?" she asked in amazement. She'd heard a mower but had never figured it would be hers. What was he doing mowing her lawn?

"Yeah," he answered, coming to stand next to her at the sink.

She edged away. He looked wonderful in his blue flannel; she wanted to bury her face in his chest and wrap her arms around his neck. And when that urge had been satisfied, she wanted to kill him for clumping through her life and leaving bits of grass behind on her fresh-mopped kitchen floor.

David took down a glass and got some water from the tap; she had filtered water in the refrigerator and almost offered it but forced herself to keep still. Tap water was just fine for David.

"You've got to get some lime down, too. I was talking to Cyrus about it. It's not too late in the year, what with it being so warm." He looked at her wool vest, and she closed the edges over her breasts. It didn't matter how warm it was, she was wearing layers.

"Seems you and Cyrus hit it off just fine," she said stiffly. She'd lived here for months and was barely on speaking terms with her neighbors; David showed up, in a towel, and was instantly on the receiving end of gardening tips. That was one of the most irritating things about David: Everyone warmed up to him so fast. Everybody liked him, no matter what he did or how he behaved. "What else did you talk about?"

"Nothing much," he said between swallows. She tried to keep her eyes off the strong line of his throat . . . and the bruise she had left. "Just yard stuff. We need to go out and get that lime today, and maybe some flowers for the beds; Cyrus had some nice ones in front of his house, yellow and all kinds of purple. Those beds are a mess, Scottie; it looks like they haven't been touched since summer. And we need to get a wreath for the door and a tree. We'd better run out now and get them before they're all gone. Christmas is just a couple of days away."

Mary Scott could feel her anger pulsing through her like a charge of electricity. This was *exactly* why she was going through with the divorce.

"I know when Christmas is. I know my planting beds are a mess. Those little yellow and purple flowers at the Holbrooks' are pansies, and I haven't had time to get a wreath! And I don't need you to tell me what to do with my own house!"

David just smiled and leaned a hip against the kitchen counter. "Did you know about the moss, too?"

Naturally, he'd turn it into a joke. He pushed into her life and took it over, and it was a joke. It didn't matter what she felt, it didn't matter what she wanted, as long as he was having a good time and got what he wanted. Well, not this time, no matter how good he looked in blue flannel.

"I'm going to the market," she said coldly.

"Wait. Give me a chance to shower, and I'll go with you."

"I'm ready, and I'm going now," she said, daring him to stop her. Mary Scott walked out of the kitchen and got her purse from the foyer chest and opened the front door, David walking behind her all the way. If he touched her, she'd hit him with her purse; that would leave him staggering. She almost hoped he'd try.

She opened the door and walked out onto the stoop. A red pickup truck was parked behind her silver Lexus in the driveway. She was blocked in. She turned to face him, her face as stiff as ice.

"Move your truck."

"After I shower."

It was a standoff.

"Where are your keys?" she gritted out.

"On me." He grinned and opened up his arms, silently encouraging her to frisk him.

She was tempted, if only for the excuse to slap him down, but she wouldn't. No more reckless acts.

"I'm leaving in five minutes, even if I have to walk."

"I'll be ready," he said, charging up the stairs with his bag.

He was back in four, wearing clean shoes, a black T-shirt, and a gray flannel button-down with his jeans.

"Why'd you change your shirt?"

David shrugged as he tucked in the tails. "Layers and gray seemed to be the order of the day."

Mary Scott flushed and turned to walk out the door, wanting to leave him and his observations behind. He was right behind her.

"Let's take my truck."

"Absolutely not." She was not going to be seen riding around in a bright red truck with a handsome man, as if she was a mindless teenager looking for thrills.

"Why not? It's more convenient."

"There won't be anyplace secure to put the groceries and . . . trucks are too hard to park."

David looked at her with a skeptical smile, but she held her ground.

"I'll move the truck, but you have to promise not to take off in your Lexus while I'm doing it."

"I'm not a child!"

"Is that a yes?"

"I'm not going to promise anything!"

"We can stand here all day, giving Cyrus and Fran a show. You know I don't care," he said, waving to Cyrus and Fran Holbrook as they stood looking from their lawn.

Mary Scott smiled at her neighbors and gritted through her teeth, "Move your stupid truck. I'll wait for you in the car."

"Is *that* a promise?"

"It's closer to a threat."

"Okay, Scottie." He chuckled. "I know you keep all your threats."

He parked on the street, under the big oak, while she swallowed oaths in the car. David got into the passenger side cheerfully and waved to the Holbrooks as they backed out.

"You're almost obscenely happy," she said as they started down the street.

"I'm with you, aren't I?"

"Don't waste your charm on me," she said, accelerating.

"Who should I waste it on?"

"The Holbrooks."

"They seem nice enough."

"You'd know," she muttered.

David didn't say anything to that and looked out the window as they drove through the neighborhood.

"Nice neighborhood."

"I like it," she said, thinking of how she'd probably have to move.

"Old. Has a stable feel to it, as if lots of families have raised families here over the years."

He'd been talking to Ruthie, all right. Mary Scott kept her eyes on the road and her mouth closed.

"When did you leave Newport News?"

They'd met in Newport News, on the coast of Virginia near Norfolk, married in Raleigh, and lived in Newport News, while he'd commuted to the base in Norfolk at Little Creek. But they hadn't built a life in any of those towns; she'd come to Raleigh to do that.

"August," she said after a few moments' silence. He'd gone off to training in August.

"Still with the same firm?" he asked softly.

"Yes, that wasn't a problem; they have branches everywhere."

"But you bought a house here," he said. She wouldn't be going back to Virginia.

He sounded so forlorn in that moment, she wanted to comfort him. She fought the urge, certain it would weaken her position; still, she had to offer something by way of explanation.

"Mother is here, just a few blocks over. I wanted to be closer to her. She wanted me here."

"Did you know before I shipped out?" he said, not looking at her.

She couldn't answer that. She wouldn't. She wanted to divorce him; she didn't want to hurt him. Her refusal to answer told him everything.

They drove in silence until she pulled into the parking lot of the Piggly Wiggly. The lot was crowded. It was the Saturday before Christmas.

"You must be doing well up here if you could buy a Lexus," he said. She'd driven a Honda in Newport News.

"It's used," she said, pulling into a space and putting the car in park.

David laughed and looked over at her, the

shadows in the car disintegrating at the sound. "That sounds like my Scottie."

"Why buy new? A car's a depreciating asset."

"I knew you'd say that." He chuckled.

"Well . . . it's true."

"I know," he said softly, his eyes sparkling with humor. He leaned over and kissed her lightly on the lips before she had the wit to pull herself away.

She stared at him, at the humor in his eyes, at the hurt that lay beneath, and reveled, just for a moment, in the sight of him. He turned her heart over without so much as blinking. He was so very dangerous to her.

David reached over and turned off the ignition. "Let's go shopping."

The spell broken, Mary Scott and David walked into Piggly Wiggly. It was a small grocery store by modern standards, but Mary Scott liked it for just that reason. It had the same sense of age and comfort as the neighborhoods that surrounded it.

Mary Scott nodded to the girl at the checkout and pulled a cart free. David strolled behind her, his hands in his pockets and a satisfied expression on his face. He had no reason to look so pleased with himself, and yet she knew exactly why he did; grocery shopping together was entirely too intimate an act for a couple on the brink of divorce. They had slept in each other's arms, they had awakened in the same bed, he had mowed the lawn, and now they were buying food together; it was the routine of a happily married couple. But they were not happily married. At least she was not happily married. If only she could convince David of that.

She pushed her cart with fierce energy, eager to make her choices and get out. Lettuce, tomatoes, apples, oranges, new potatoes, sweet potatoes, green onions. David tossed in a bunch of bananas. She never bought bananas; she couldn't eat them fast enough, and they always spoiled. She left the produce department with a shrill squeak of cart wheels. T-bone steaks, a rib roast, lamb chops, stew meat, hamburger. David threw in a few packages of swordfish and shrimp. She didn't like fish, and she especially didn't like the way cooking it made the house smell.

"Maybe you should get your own cart," she said.

"Why, do you think we're going to fill this one up?" he said.

Before she could answer, David stopped and grabbed her by the arm. He pointed down into the butcher's case, an expression of shock on his face.

"What *is* that?"

Mary Scott looked into the case and grinned. "Pickled pig's feet."

"What do people *do* with them?"

"Eat 'em," she said, trying for a straight face. "A little farther down, there's pickled tongue. You ought to like that."

"Tell me you've never served this to me," he said, turning away from the case and gulping, grabbing his chest.

"What's in it for me?" she chuckled.

"I won't throw up all over your feet."

"You just motivated me. You've never eaten pickled pig's feet, not at my table."

"What about these—barbecued pig's feet?"

"Is this a new deal, or are we operating under the old one?"

"I can feel it coming up." He gagged.

"You've never had it!" She laughed. "No pig's feet of any kind!"

"Thank God."

"I thought soldiers could eat anything," she said, heading for the dairy aisle.

"I'm in the Navy—better food than the Army gets."

"That's why you joined up? The food?"

"Well, I considered it," he said in mock affront. "A man has to consider his appetites." He leered cheerfully.

"Dairy aisle," Mary Scott announced, pushing the cart away from him. "Lots of cold air down there. Just what you need."

"Is that where they keep the popsicles?" he asked, tagging along behind her.

"Yes, but who wants popsicles in winter?"

"I do. I want popsicles all the time."

There was something in the way he said it, something that had the scent of a joke, and since she couldn't figure it out, that meant that she was the butt of the joke. She wasn't going to play.

"Help yourself," she said when she turned into the dairy aisle.

"Thank you," he said, looking down at her. The look in his eyes was so suddenly fierce and sexual that she felt heat instantly flare in the pit of her stomach. "I love to lick them and watch them slowly melt."

Oh, no, she knew that look, and she felt the swelling of her own arousal answer him. His blue eyes were eating her up, and she wanted nothing more in that instant than to throw him on the floor and climb on top of him, capturing him inside her. And he knew it. It was seeing that certainty in his eyes that saved her. This was what he always did, and he wasn't going to get away with it anymore.

"I need eggs," she said bluntly and turned away from him.

"I'll get the popsicles," he said easily. "Any preference?"

"They'll be all for you, so get what you want."

"All for me," he murmured, and a chill went up her spine. It was cold in the dairy aisle, even with layers and wool.

She got the eggs and the milk and the cheese

while David dropped three boxes of various popsicles into the cart.

"That's a lot of popsicles for one person," she said as they entered the bakery aisle.

"I can handle it." He winked.

The wink convinced her; she wasn't going to talk to him about popsicles again.

She picked out wheat bread; he loaded in rye. She needed some more English muffins. He wanted bagels. And then he ran back to the dairy aisle for cream cheese. He came back with cream cheese and whipped cream.

She didn't ask.

The cart was piled fairly high by the time she wheeled into the checkout line. Michele was on duty, a twenty-year-old with over-sprayed hair and too much blush and a great body. Michele was the daughter of a church friend of her mother's, so there was a slight social connection between them. She was chewing gum, but discreetly. The management at Piggly Wiggly didn't allow its employees to chew gum. Mary Scott had had Michele check her out most Saturdays, and she had never seen her without the gum. She had also never really seen her eyes, since Michele was busy pushing products across the scanner and checking the readout. But today she was all eyes, and they were directed at David.

It wouldn't have been fair to describe David as all eyes, but he was certainly all smiles.

"Hey, Michele," Mary Scott said. "You ready for Christmas?"

"Hey," she said, answering Mary Scott but looking at David.

"Hey back." He grinned. When he said it, it didn't sound like the casual greeting it was. It sounded like an invitation.

"So," Mary Scott tried again, "all your Christmas shopping done?"

David broke visual contact and started unloading the cart. Michele managed to look at Mary Scott then.

"I guess so. Maybe."

"I haven't even started," David offered, handing Michele the rib roast. Michele popped her gum and slid the roast over the scanner. "Doesn't look like I'll get the chance, what with the weekend I'm going to have."

Both Michele and Mary Scott looked at him.

"Got a hot weekend planned with this gorgeous woman. 'Course, I hardly know her. She just picked me up in that silver Lexus out there, but I figure, I'm game for a good time. And she's buying the food."

Michele looked at Mary Scott, and her mouth dropped open. Mary Scott could see her gum. It was green.

"He's my husband!" Mary Scott barked out. They knew her in this store, knew her mother. What was he trying to do? Humiliate her, naturally.

79

"You have a husband?" the bagger said. He was sixteen and had pimples on his chin and was wearing pants two sizes too big.

"Yes! This is my husband," Mary Scott announced.

"I didn't know you were married," a woman in the next line said. Mary Scott looked behind her; it was the wife of one of the other brokers in the office. She remembered her from the office Christmas party three weeks ago. Naturally, she couldn't remember her name at the moment. The moment when her very private life was becoming screechingly public.

"Oh, hello," she said awkwardly. "Yes, I'm married."

"But not for long," David chimed in, lifting out the milk to set it on the conveyor belt. "She wants to get a divorce. Would *you* divorce me, Michele?" he asked, all smiles and innuendo.

Michele's gum fell out of her mouth to the floor.

The rest of the store fell silent.

"Of course, I really don't blame Scottie. My popsicle habit alone would break a lesser woman."

Michele looked down blankly at the popsicle boxes he'd piled up and slowly slid them over the scanner.

"Popsicles?" the woman behind Mary Scott asked of no one in particular, as if she really wasn't sure what she had just heard.

Mary Scott felt exactly the same way.

Somehow, they made it out of the store. She'd have to go to a new store from now on. Well, that would work out, since she'd already concluded she had to leave the neighborhood.

"That was fun," David said when they were back in the car.

Mary Scott looked over at him as she backed out of the space. How many years would she serve for vehicular manslaughter?

"And your having fun is what it's all about, right?" she snapped as she sharply accelerated.

"I like to have fun," he said innocently.

"I suppose you had fun humiliating me back there! I know those people!"

"Then it's even more fun," he said. "They know it's a joke."

She didn't know them *that* well, but she wasn't going to admit that. David made friends easily, effortlessly, and constantly. She didn't. It took her longer, and she was more cautious, but she never had a chance to take relationships at her own speed when David flew into the middle of things, churning everything up with his "jokes."

"I'll tell you what the joke is," she said. "It's you thinking you're going to have a 'hot' weekend. The only way that's going to happen is if you have it with Michele."

"You think she's available?" he said. He said it so seriously that she knew he was joking. But she looked over at him just to make sure.

He was laughing at her, silently laughing, his eyes misted with humor.

"More available than I am," she said, fighting the urge to smile.

David could charm the rattle from a snake. It was grossly unfair.

"I'll stick with you," he said. "You have the popsicles."

She didn't say anything to that; she was going to avoid any conversation about popsicles.

They unloaded the groceries when they got home, David carrying the bags into the kitchen while she emptied them and put everything away. It was so much easier when there were two people to share the labor. They performed their duties companionably, domestically. Naturally, it was very irritating.

It didn't matter that she enjoyed his company. It didn't matter that he wanted to stay married. It didn't matter that when she looked at him, she wanted to bury herself in his arms and breathe in the scent of him. She wouldn't let any of it matter. She was going to get a divorce.

It was troubling that she had to keep reminding herself of that.

Proximity, that was the problem. Too much proximity. Standing in the kitchen together, putting the groceries away, saying little bits of nothing, like, "Where do you want the potatoes?" and "I'll put the wine over here," was wearing on her. She was remembering the good times they'd shared, the easy times when he was acting like the man she remembered marrying. But those times were too rare. A marriage couldn't stand on such tiny bits of ground.

Being with David was confusion, isolation, and passion. She had to remember that. She had to get away from him so that she could remember that.

"I need to go to Mother's," she said when the groceries had been put up.

"I'll go with you."

"No," she said, moving toward the front door. "I just need to get her mail and check her plants. She's on a cruise."

"I heard, and I'm coming," he said, holding the door for her.

He was in the car before she could stop him. She really didn't know what she'd do in any case; she couldn't wrestle him to the ground. Or if she did, she knew what would happen next. The ground was a very large flat surface.

Her mother's house was less than two miles from hers and on a nicer street with bigger homes and larger lots. It wasn't quite the truth that she'd grown up in the house, but her mother and father had moved there when she was thirteen, so she had lived there as a child. She loved the place. It was a big white colonial with black shutters and a snaky vine that arched over the front door.

David was silent as they pulled into the driveway. Mary Scott let the silence settle between them. She got out and checked the mailbox and then went up the walk to the front door. David followed just behind her.

"Why doesn't Mary Nell just stop her mail while she's on vacation?"

"She doesn't want anyone to know she's out of town. A house down the street was burglarized a couple of years ago, and that's what they'd done."

"So you come over here six days a week to pick up her mail."

"You saw how close I am," she said, defending herself instinctively.

"And you have a key to her house, right on your own ring. That's handy, since you use it so much."

"Yes. It is," she said. Why did he make her feel guilty for having the key to her mother's house on her key ring?

They walked in, the house silent with the special silence of emptiness. Mary Scott walked into the kitchen and sorted through her mother's mail, throwing out the junk, and then put the rest on the pile that was already three inches tall. Her mother liked to go through the mail chronologically, so Mary Scott was very careful how she stacked it. David had stayed be-

hind and was in the living room when she came
back through to check the plants; the Christmas
lily needed water.

David was being very quiet, and she was surprised at how nervous that made her. He was a
man who liked to talk and laugh, and his silence
left her feeling stranded. He picked up a framed
photograph and studied it. It was a picture of
her mother with some of her friends in Rio. The
mantel was clogged with photographs in silver
frames of her mother in exotic locations; her
mother loved to travel and did so at every opportunity.

"You moved to Raleigh to be close to your
mom," David said, putting the picture back.
"Why? Seems like she's gone more than she's
here."

"It may seem like that, but—"

David cut her off. "Is this your dad?"

Mary Scott looked at the picture, but she
didn't need to look. There was only one photograph of her daddy, and it was huge.

"Yes, that's Daddy."

"I know you told me, but tell me again; how
old were you when he died?"

"Fourteen. We'd been in the house less than
a year."

"Must have been hard on your mom. And
you," he said softly, studying her.

She flushed under the scrutiny, intensely uncomfortable with it. "It was, but Mother and I had each other."

David just stared at her, saying nothing.

"What?" she asked, staring back.

David shrugged and then suddenly grinned. "So where's your old room? I'd like to see it."

"What for?"

Again he shrugged. "Just because."

"Just because what?"

"Just because I was wondering how big a bed you had. How big was it? A double? A single? We could have some fun on a single."

"I should have known," she snapped, forcing away the image of David making love to her on her old single bed. She pulled at her vest, which seemed to be pressing against the sudden tenderness of her breasts.

"Yeah, you should have." He grinned.

"The tour is over," she said, standing by the front door and opening it.

He pressed her back against the open door, his knee between her thighs, and kissed her hard on the mouth. She responded instantly, opening her mouth to him and rubbing the ache between her legs against his thigh, humiliating herself even further. She knew every neighbor on this street. And they knew her.

"Meet you back in the tour bus," he whispered, laughing.

She pushed her hair off her face with a flick of her hand and then pushed him out of her mother's house with her hand to his chest. "Get in the car or you're walking back."

"I'm going." He smiled, walking to the car like a very satisfied man. But he wasn't going to be satisfied, not with her.

When they were on their way back to her house, David was quiet, but he was looking at her and smiling. Still looking very satisfied.

She was slowing to turn into her drive when he said, "Park on the street so we can get the truck out."

"You're leaving? Great." But she felt her heart trying to squeeze through her ribs, flattened and pressed down. She hadn't thought he'd leave her so soon, even though she did want to divorce him.

David looked at her and then reached out and brushed back the hair next to her face. "No, I'm not leaving, Scottie. I need to do some shopping, and I want to take the truck. And you."

The relief she felt at his words embarrassed her. She shouldn't feel so needy, not with him. She was divorcing him. As soon as the holidays were over, she'd call her lawyer and get things started again. Her mother would be back then, too; it would be easier to proceed with her mother around to give her emotional support.

"What do you need?"

"You know," he said, getting out of the car. "Lime, pansies, maybe some mulch for those planting beds, a wreath, a tree for Christmas. Why don't you have your tree yet?"

Mary Scott got out of her car and locked it. She followed David to his truck and hesitated about getting in. He didn't need her with him to go buy lime. But it wasn't his lawn; it was hers. He didn't need to be thinking about lime at all. And she didn't want to talk about her lack of decorations for Christmas.

"You and Cyrus really bonded, didn't you? And all over a bag of lime."

"We didn't have any beer handy," David said, opening the passenger door for her and waiting. "What kind of tree do you want?"

"It's too late; all the lots will be empty."

"What kind of tree do you want?" he repeated, waiting for her to get in.

Her house was in front of her, empty and quiet. David and his red truck beckoned. What would she do if she went inside alone? Watch TV, maybe rent a movie, change the sheets, fill the bird feeder, and stare at the clock, watching time pass.

Mary Scott got into the truck.

"I want blue spruce, but I'll settle for Douglas fir."

"Blue spruce it is," he said, closing the door behind her.

"And I don't want to talk about the divorce," she said as he got in and put the key in the ignition.

"Neither do I. No divorce talk. I'm all for that."

She knew he meant it differently, but she didn't want to talk about it, not today, not anymore. They didn't have to talk about it, not when she was so set on doing it.

Southern States was fairly empty, since no one but David was interested in yard work right before Christmas. There was only one flat of pansies left, mixed colors, and David scooped that up right away. He got two bags of lime and arranged for six bales of pine straw to be loaded into the back of his truck. He debated the fullness of the handful of wreaths that were left for sale, finally deciding to buy two, one for the front door and one for the back.

"But no one will see the one in the back," she argued.

"We'll see it," he said cheerfully, closing the subject.

There was one blue spruce left, small and squat and perfect. David grinned when he saw it and indicated with a flick of his finger that it should be loaded up with the rest of his purchases. His purchases for her house. She couldn't let him buy for her; it was so . . . intimate.

"Our first Christmas tree," he said, sliding an arm around her waist, under the protective wool of her vest. She could feel the heat of his hand against the soft cotton of her shirt. Too much intimacy, of all the wrong kind. He was so good at this.

She moved away from him. "Is that everything?"

"No." He let her put physical distance between them. The emotional distance was far greater. "Cyrus was telling me about this great pair of pruning shears. Do you have pruning shears?"

"No, but why would you need—"

"In case you want to prune something, like shaping the Christmas tree or those bushes in your front yard; they were looking a little thin."

"Those are azaleas, and if you prune them now you'll take off the flower buds!"

"I'm going to look for the shears anyway. He got his here. You can always use a good tool."

"So says every man in America," she muttered.

David just smiled and started cruising the aisles. For a man on the hunt for pruning shears, he was very easily distracted. He had to stop and examine the aerators, then the post hole diggers, then the latest in lawn edgers. "Do you have one of these?" he asked longingly.

"No, and I don't need one."

"You're sure? Because it looks like it would do great and wonderful things to the edge of the lawn."

"I'm sure. I'm going to get a service to do the yard."

"That takes all the fun out of it," he grumbled.

She tried very hard not to laugh at the woe-begone look on his face as he passed up the edger.

It was when they were in the hand tool aisle that David made a friend.

He was crouched down, studying the labels on the pruning shears, when he struck up a conversation with a man who was standing next to him, comparing two pairs of leather work gloves. Mary Scott was at the end of the aisle, trying to find something to lean against that wouldn't leave smudges on her wool pants. She wasn't having any luck.

She stayed at her end of the aisle, watching the two men talk. David talked to everyone, charmed them into instant warmth and good-will. It was amazing. He'd done the same with her when they'd first met, and she hadn't had any defenses against the firepower of his smile. She only had one now: a strong instinct for self-preservation. It was just barely enough.

He'd come into the firm, looking for a broker to give him investment advice. She'd been just starting out and was slated as broker of the day, taking every walk-in client that Monday. David Adams had walked in, sat down at her cramped desk in the bull pen, and treated her with respect. That had gone a long way toward warming her. He'd asked intelligent questions, listened to her advice, and stayed for two hours.

He'd left her with a check for five thousand dollars, a lot of money for a walk-in, and called her twice a week to talk investments.

After a month, he'd asked her to lunch. She'd gone, writing it off as a business lunch with a client. After six lunches, he'd asked her to dinner. She'd written that off, too.

By the third dinner, she'd known it wasn't business anymore.

Not only had he treated her as if she was the most irresistible woman he'd ever met, he had listened to her and continued to take her financial advice. It was a heady combination. She'd had no defense against it.

She'd never met anyone who had.

But she knew now what she hadn't known before; there was something missing in his charm and his warmth, something she hadn't seen until they'd been married a few months. Something he didn't see and couldn't fix. And it was something she couldn't live without.

"Scottie! Come over and meet Kevin Kennedy; he knows Cyrus, too!"

Mary Scott walked down the aisle, a pleasant smile pasted on her face. It always happened; David couldn't go anywhere without attaching a few people to himself.

"Hello," she said and held out her hand.

"Hey," Kevin said, "I hear we're neighbors. I live over on Colonial Drive. David says you live next door to Cyrus? He's a great guy."

"He told Kevin about the pruning shears, too," David offered, a true testament to the greatness of the man. "Kevin went to VMI."

"VMI?" she said, not quite sure what that was.

"Virginia Military Institute," Kevin supplied.

Naturally, it would be something military. That alone would cement them as instant friends.

"Listen," David said, every gesture singing with enthusiasm, "Kevin has some yard work he needs to do, and we thought that we'd help each other out; he'd come to our place, and I'd go to his."

"I called my wife," Kevin added, "and she says she'd love to have you over for dinner."

"Oh, I couldn't do that," Mary Scott said in mild panic. Eat dinner with total strangers? And be forced to play the happy housewife in front of an audience? "It's such short notice, and so close to Christmas, I'm sure she—"

"He's already called her on his cell phone," David said. "She's thawing the meat right now. We're expected."

He could hardly have said anything to tie her down more; she felt positively trapped.

"I hear your mother is Mary Nell Burke," Kevin said into her wide-eyed silence. "I met her at church a few weeks back; she's a greeter, isn't she? Real nice lady."

"You know my mother?" she said softly.

"Not only that," David said with a grin, "he

and his wife go to your church. Just joined."

David had said just the thing that would tie her down more. And he knew it. She could read it in his grin. She couldn't back out of a date, no matter how impromptu, with new members of her church.

"Dinner would be lovely. I'll bring a salad and wine, okay? I'm not coming empty-handed."

"That would be great." Kevin grinned. "I'll call and tell my wife."

David didn't say a word; he just grinned and stuck his hands in his pockets. She didn't say a word either, but she wasn't grinning. A whole evening to play the role of happily married newlyweds; David would be having a fine old time, while she would know it for the joke it was. They weren't happy, and they were just barely still married, but she wouldn't betray any of that to the Kennedys. That would be unspeakably rude. She'd have to save it all up for David later, when they were alone.

But it was hours before they were alone again.

Kevin came to her house first, and between the two men, they made short work of clearing, planting, and mulching the beds and tossing out lime by the handfuls. David was kicking himself for not buying a spreader—so much more fun than using his bare hands to spread granules around in the dirt. The wreaths she hung using brass hangers her mother had given her, and the tree they put on the porch, to set up later. She made a quick salad and chose a nice bottle of merlot to bring to the impromptu dinner. She also changed out of her mannish black shoes into a pair of metallic pewter flats.

Twilight was fast approaching when they headed for Kevin's house. Mary Scott was introduced to Kevin's wife, Donna, and the two women set the table and laid out the food while David and Kevin took turns manhandling a heavy aerator over the lawn. Any awkwardness Mary Scott felt had to do with David, so she and Donna got along well, talking about church and work and the decorating plans they had for their houses. Donna was wearing a cute pair of shoes, and, being a normal American woman, when Mary Scott complimented her on them, it prompted a twenty-minute discussion about the best shoe stores in town. For them, it was the equivalent of bonding over an edger and a pair of leather work gloves, only much more logical. It was shoes, after all. They were still talking shoes when the men came back in, looking sweaty and supremely satisfied.

Dinner was comfortable, the food good, the conversation easy. It was all extremely alarming.

She didn't want to make "couple" friends with David now, not when she was on the verge of being single again. She didn't want to see him laughing and talking with people, drawing them into the warmth of his smile, coaxing them into social intimacy. She didn't want to pretend to these lovely people, who went to her church and knew her mother, that she was a happily married woman and that the act she and David were playing out before them would continue to other nights and other shared meals and other laughing conversations. David would leave; he would go back to the coast, leaving her behind to answer the questions they would ask.

Most of all, she didn't like seeing David play the part he always played, the part he'd played in the beginning. This was the David she had fallen in love with, this attentive man who leaned into his conversation with you and made you feel that the rest of the world had faded away to mere shadows. This David was engaging and sweet, and he convinced you that he was giving all of himself to you and only wanted you to give all of yourself back to him. And she had, as the Kennedys were now, believing that he cared and that he truly wanted to touch minds and hearts and lives. But he didn't. It was an illusion.

The evening ended at ten, early because of church the next morning. She couldn't have been happier; the charade of marital bliss was wearing heavily on her. On the way to the front door, David offered to drive Kevin in his truck to pick up pine straw and help him spread it out after Christmas. Donna coaxed her into a joint shopping trip to a great shoe store in Burlington sometime after New Year's. The basis for friendship had been laid, but it had been laid on sand; the friendship that the Kennedys were reaching for with the Adamses had no foundation. Very soon there would be no David and Scottie Adams. There would be just Mary Scott Burke.

She felt so guilty, she thought she'd choke.

And it was all David's fault.

"So, you're going to church tomorrow? You sounded very eager about it," she said as they drove off, waving to the Kennedys, who were standing and waving from their front door, arms around each other. She felt sick.

David looked over at her briefly and kept driving. "A left at the stop sign?"

"Yes, and answer the question. Are you planning to go to church tomorrow?"

"Of course."

He turned left. The streets of Raleigh were quiet and still, gilded by Christmas lights and the high glow of streetlamps. It was Saturday night, and the whole town would be up early for church. It was on Sunday morning, not Saturday night, that the streets were clogged with cars.

"Go through the light and then make a quick right," she said, her arms crossed over her breasts, her eyes narrowed in irritation.

"Right," he said in acknowledgment. "You

know, I've been meaning to tell you all day how good you look. That vest . . . it's the sexiest thing I've ever seen you wear."

He couldn't be serious. She looked at him, a streetlamp casting him in slanted light. He was grinning—leering, actually—and then he winked.

"Keep your eyes on the road," she snapped.

"Hard to, when you're in the car next to me," he said, looking slowly back at the road in front of him. "A lot of things are hard right now."

She should have known; this was David, and they were alone, after he'd surrounded them with people all day. After he'd invaded her life and humiliated her countless times and taken care of her yard work. After he'd made them feel married.

"*Nothing's* going to happen. I don't care how *hard* it is for you."

"Very funny." He chuckled.

"And nothing's changed," she said as they pulled up in front of her house.

David didn't press it; he could see how angry and scared she was, and for all that, he knew that if he touched the back of her neck or kissed the edge of her jaw, she'd melt and pour fire all over him. She was a popsicle, melting at the first wave of heat. But he wasn't going to press it, not tonight. They'd had a long day full of the things married people did together; he'd shown her what she was giving up, what he could offer.

Tomorrow, he'd get the pastor of Pinewood Baptist on his team, and then she'd have nowhere to run. She'd have to stay married to him. She'd have to, because he wasn't giving her up.

David slept in the guest room. It was a long, hard night.

Chapter Four

They caused a minor riot when they walked into the sanctuary Sunday morning. Everyone knew Mary Scott, knew her mother, knew her family, but nobody knew the good-looking man walking at her side. They made a handsome pair. Mary Scott with her pale, slender elegance, and her escort, dark-haired, thick with muscle, and with a look about him that said he could handle anything that ran at him.

Mary Scott faced the furor they were causing with a cool smile and stiff carriage as the usher led them to a pew. The man with her smiled and nodded at every pair of eyes trained on him, easy with the scrutiny. And why shouldn't he be? It didn't take long for word to spread that this was the man who'd made Mary Scott a widow.

David Adams didn't look a bit dead.

So why didn't Mary Scott look happier?

If there was one thing she hated, it was being the center of attention, especially this kind of attention. David didn't mind in the least. He spotted Kevin and Donna Kennedy and waved across the church to them. Cyrus passed the plate for the offering, and David nodded his greeting, smiling broadly.

The quiet hubbub settled down somewhat when Mr. Bradley, the music minister, stepped up to the podium and led the singing. David sang out in his rich baritone, while Mary Scott kept her second soprano in modest check. The singing finished, Pastor Swain took his place at the podium and began his sermon. Mary Scott hardly heard it. The only thing she was aware of was David's thigh alongside hers. David's chest breathing slowly in and out. David's after shave wafting to her with every rotation of the ceiling fan. It was obvious to her that David should have stayed at home.

It became very obvious to her when the service was finished why he had not.

While the rest of the congregation was heading for the doors, David had her by the hand and was pushing against the throng to stand before Pastor Swain. Pastor Swain smiled. David smiled. Mary Scott gulped. She knew David well enough to be apprehensive.

She was so right.

"Pastor Swain," David said, holding out his free hand. He wasn't letting go of Mary Scott. "Great sermon. I'm David Adams, Scottie's husband."

"Thank you. It's nice to meet you," Tim Swain answered, smiling, "but I thought Mary Scott was a widow."

"You mean she didn't tell you she was divorced?"

Mary Scott closed her eyes and with all her heart prayed that every last person was out of the sanctuary and out of earshot; she didn't want any of this bandied about at Sunday lunch all over town.

Pastor Swain looked at Mary Scott with a quizzical smile. She didn't smile back.

"No, she told me she was a widow."

"She thought she was," David said. "But she wants to be divorced. From me. I think we need some counseling."

That made her eyes snap open. He was using her own pastor, enlisting him in his plan to keep her married to him. No wonder David had been so eager to come to church; he must have been planning this since yesterday. No doubt Ruthie had been his inspiration. Ruthie talked incessantly; Mary Scott knew about her sister, Pamie. Every woman who had her house cleaned by Ruthie knew about Pamie.

But it wasn't going to work. She was sick of David manipulating her and every situation, working it to his own ends. This time, she'd fight back. And he wouldn't even see it coming.

"Counseling is often a good idea," Pastor Swain said. "Mary Scott?"

"I have nothing against counseling," she said.

David looked at her, his blue eyes both hopeful and suspicious. She tamped down the itch of guilt and kept her face serene. She was going to win this skirmish.

"Then how about I meet with you later this afternoon? Say, around four o'clock?"

"Today? On Sunday?" David said. This was faster than he'd hoped.

"Sunday is a working day for me," Tom Swain said. "Is four convenient?"

"Four is fine," Mary Scott said.

"Four is perfect," David added, his voice overwhelming hers.

"Then I'll see you at four, my office."

And that was that. Mary Scott and David walked down the aisle in the nearly empty church, saying nothing to each other, the silence between them awkward and heavy.

In the parking lot, they ran into the Kennedys, who invited them to join the Holbrooks and another couple at K&W Cafeteria for lunch. David accepted before Mary Scott could take a breath. Mary Scott went along with it, adding this latest bit of high-handedness to his growing list of offenses, though she hardly needed to. The list against David was long enough to strangle an elephant.

K&W was full of churchgoers, making it difficult to find a table for eight. Eventually, they pushed two tables together and sat down in the smoking section. The smoking section of the restaurant was always nearly empty at Sunday lunch. It was the one quiet spot in the restaurant.

Mary Scott kept a polite conversation going with Donna Kennedy and Fran and Cyrus Holbrook, who were sitting at her end of the table, but most of her attention was on David. He was in his element. He'd just been introduced to two new people he could charm, drawing them into conversation, making sure everyone was included, leading the talk away from himself when it strayed onto his military career.

He'd never talk about that. He might live with his SEAL team for six months, but he wouldn't share a minute of it with her. He kept a very closed mouth about himself, while enticing the most intimate confessions from a stranger. Kevin Kennedy was just now admitting that he'd been jilted at the altar before falling in love with Donna. Why would a man share something like that at the K&W with someone he'd met the day before?

"You must be so happy to have your husband back. It must have been awful when you thought he was dead," Fran Holbrook said.

"It was pretty bad," Mary Scott said, not letting herself think about it. It had been devastating.

"He seems untouched by whatever happened," Fran said.

"Yes, he does," Mary Scott said. He did. He always did. She had come to hate that about him.

"My father was in the second World War, in the Navy, and he would tell us great stories about some of the things that happened on his ship. He could get us really laughing," Fran said.

David wouldn't ever tell stories about what he did in the Navy, serving his country, and if he did, she was fairly certain that they wouldn't make her laugh.

Mary Scott glanced over at Donna. She was picking at her salad, not saying anything about the subject and not looking as if she intended to. Donna was a very wise woman and had the makings of a dear friend.

"He told one story, about someone firing off his sidearm . . ."

Mary Scott let Fran's voice slide out of her mental focus. She didn't want to hear about Fran's father; she wanted to hear what David

had to say. But David never said anything remotely self-revealing.

They got to the pastor's office at five minutes to
four, which was something of a minor miracle,
since they hadn't spoken all afternoon.

After lunch, David had tried to charm her into
talking about her job. She wasn't interested in
a one-way conversation and had told him so.
She'd changed her clothes behind a closed door
and gone for a long walk in the neighborhood.
David had changed his clothes behind an open
door and grabbed up the new pruning shears,
slamming out of the house. The last thing she'd
said to him was that if he trimmed any of her
azaleas, she'd use those pruning shears to snip
off something he dearly loved.

He'd left the azaleas alone.

She'd come home at three-thirty, walked into
the house, snatched her purse off the foyer
chest, and walked back out to the car. He'd been
waiting in the passenger seat by the time she
got home. They'd driven to the church in stony
silence, each busily checking their ammunition.
It was going to be a bloodbath in Pastor Swain's
office.

The pastor seemed to sense that as he invited
them to each take a chair. The cozy couch along
the wall didn't seem a likely option for them at
the moment.

"Good afternoon," Tim Swain said, sitting behind his desk, facing them. "How can I help you?"

David jumped right in, doing most of the talking. Just as she'd expected.

"Thanks for seeing us on such short notice, Tim," David began. "We could really use your help. The way it stands is that I love Scottie—loved her when I married her last summer and love her just as much now, but she wants to divorce me. I don't want a divorce. I want our marriage to last for seventy-five years or more. I don't want to lose her or the life we could have together. I don't know why she wants to divorce me; she doesn't believe in divorce any more than I do. We talked about all that before we got married. We both believe marriage is for life. Now, this."

Tim looked at Mary Scott sitting so quietly in her chair, her face impassive and calm. It was taking a lot of effort for her to keep herself that way. She was planning exactly what she was going to say, had been planning it on her long walk all afternoon. All anyone had to do was ask. . . .

"Have you asked Mary Scott why she wants a divorce?" Tim said.

It was a reasonable question. David didn't have a reasonable answer, since he never had asked her that.

"Well, not really," David said, "but that's only because I was trying to talk her out of it."

"Hard to do when you don't know what you're talking about," Tim said, then smiled. "I mean that in the nicest possible way, of course."

"Of course," David mumbled.

David looked miserable. This wasn't going the way he had planned it at all. She wanted to laugh out loud, but she didn't. She was waiting for her chance. It wouldn't be long now.

"Mary Scott?" Tim asked. "Do you want a divorce?"

"Yes, I do."

David made some frustrated noises and shuffled his feet around on the carpet; she made herself ignore him. She'd been making frustrated noises for awhile, and he hadn't paid her any attention.

"Why?"

She was so ready for that question, her answer came pouring out of her like liquid mercury.

"Ever since I married David, ever since he showed up at my door two nights ago, he's surrounded us with people, with allies to his cause."

"Wait a minute—" David interrupted.

"Let her have her say," Tim insisted.

Mary Scott continued. "Whatever he wants, he gets by consensus. He charms and manipulates, building up a force to back his plan. He leaves me out while he's trying to pull me in."

"That doesn't even make sense," David said, his expression dark and angry.

"It makes sense to me," she said, facing him briefly and then turning back to Tim Swain. "There's only one time David wants me to himself, and there's only one reason."

There was no need to be more explicit; they all knew what she was talking about. Tim had enough years of experience at this sort of thing not to be uncomfortable with the turn in the conversation. It usually boiled down to sex one way or another anyway.

"May I speak now?" David asked, his voice hot and hard with rigid anger. Tim nodded. "What she's saying, that's not the way it is. Not at all."

"But that's how it is to Mary Scott," Tim pointed out.

"She's wrong."

"How convenient for you," she said into the air over her head.

"Tell me, David," Tim interjected before the session fell apart completely, "what do you do when you and Mary Scott are alone?"

"We talk."

"About sex," she said.

"And?" Tim prompted.

"We make love," David said in some defiance.

"Whenever he's awake," Mary Scott mumbled, her chin quivering with shame and rage.

"The sex is great!" David said.

"The talking isn't!" she shot back.

"So," Tim said, "you talk about having sexual relations, and you have sexual relations. Anything else? Any shared hobbies? Anything in particular you like to talk about? Politics? Spiritual things? World events? Sports? No?" he said as they each shook their heads. "Well, the problem seems clear enough. You have only one bond, and it's sexual. Marriage is more than that, and you're finding that out. At least Mary Scott is," Tim said mildly. "I would suggest that you both work on your emotional bond to each other, and to do so, that you forego your sexual relationship for a set period of time. You need to learn to be intimate on a different level. Sex, at this time in your marriage, is only getting in your way."

Tim looked at them both, studying their faces. It wasn't going to be easy for them; their passion for each other ran quite hot, and it was blatantly obvious, even on a Sunday afternoon. Still, he didn't see any other course for them; it was tragic that they hadn't reached a higher level of intimacy during their courtship.

"Any questions?" he asked them.

"Yeah," David said, standing up and pulling out Mary Scott's chair. "Can we talk to someone else?"

It was dark when they got back into the car; they'd stayed for the evening service, both of them needing time to cool off from their first marriage-counseling session. It hadn't gone at all as he'd expected. What was worse, Scottie seemed to have enjoyed it. He hadn't. And he didn't seem any closer to getting her to drop the idea of divorce; in fact, it seemed more likely than ever now that sex had been wiped from the equation.

Scottie liked sex.

David laughed and tried to swallow it, looking out the passenger window. Liked sex? She was ready and eager anytime, anywhere, craving him as much as he craved her. It was great, what they had going together in bed. She wouldn't want to give that up any more than he did.

He couldn't give it up, because without it, what did they have? It was the one thing they had together that no one else could share. No, he wasn't going to give up sex with his wife. There just couldn't be anything biblical about that. They'd find another pastor who could give them the right answers, and they'd have great sex in the meantime. No way was he giving up sex.

"Your pastor's got a strange sense of humor, laughing that way about an honest question," David said as Scottie drove them out of the church parking lot.

"You only think that because you didn't see your face when he told you to keep your distance," she said. He could hear the smile in her voice.

It hadn't been funny.

"It was only a suggestion," he said, inching his way to getting her to toss the whole idea.

Scottie stopped at a light and looked over at him, her face more serious than he wanted it to be.

"If you want there to be any chance for us, you'll do it."

"You mean I won't 'do it,' " he said.

She just shrugged. Scottie always did that when what she wanted to say was more than she could make herself say. She was a woman who couldn't take the least bit of flak, who hated conflict in any form. He understood that about her; he tried to protect her from getting upset over things. It was why he spent so much time giving her what she needed: hot sex and lots of laughs. She was strung too tight, and he didn't want to see her snap, that's all. And now he was the bad guy, just for wanting to protect his wife and keep her happy.

Scottie said she didn't want sex. Scottie said she wanted to talk, to find common ground. Scottie wanted him to prove there was more to them than around-the-clock sex.

He wanted Scottie, and he'd do whatever it took to keep her.

"Keep driving," he said, when he saw that they were back in her neighborhood. "Just keep driving, and we'll talk all you want."

She looked over at him in surprise. "Where?"

"There's a lake north of here, right? Drive to the lake."

"I'm not taking us parking!"

"Drive to the lake and turn around. Don't even put the car in park. Let's just talk."

He was convincing, he knew he was, and it was because he meant every word. He wanted her to keep driving, because if they went back home, she'd find herself flat on her back with her legs spread. He was trying to give her what she wanted. And he was a man who knew his own limitations, especially with her.

Scottie turned out of the neighborhood and headed north.

The clustered houses and lit streets of town slowly gave way to strip malls and pillared subdivisions as they made their way north on Old Wake Forest Road. Eventually, even the strip malls disappeared behind them, and the dark black of woods broken by widely spaced subdivisions was all that was left for them to notice. They hadn't said a word.

"You come out here much?" he asked.

"No," she said, "but there's a shoe store just behind us a ways that I like to check out every month or so."

"The saga of the hunt for the perfect pair of shoes," he said.

"Don't laugh. It's not easy to find a great pair of shoes."

"So you go there once a month?" he said. "How often do you come home with a pair of shoes?"

Scottie grinned and said, "Once a month. Last month, three pairs. I got lucky."

"You can't call it luck when you work so hard. Don't sell yourself short."

"You're still laughing."

"Maybe if I saw the shoes . . ."

"No, I don't think it would help. You're a man with four pairs of shoes. You wouldn't understand."

"And you have how many pairs?"

"I stopped counting."

"You stopped counting when you hit . . ."

Scottie smiled and mumbled, "Forty pairs."

David smiled. "Bwana is a mighty hunter."

"Back off, or I'll start buying you shoes, too."

"Would these shoes be in the way of a love token? I'm not as up on sexual fetishes as I used to be."

It was the wrong thing to say. He could feel the change in her; he could see her stiffen, even in the darkness of the car. They continued in silence, the road becoming more hilly and more winding. Scottie pulled off on a wide spot in the road and pointed. A flume of water, white in the darkness, came pouring out of the hillside to fall in a noisy froth and then tumble wildly over boulders and under the bridge just ahead of them, to be lost in the sweep of river to his right.

"Where are we?" he asked.

"The tailrace, where the lake explodes back into the river it used to be. Good fishing, they say. You can't find a place to park on the weekends."

"You like to fish?"

"No. Do you?"

"No," he said. They hadn't known that about each other. He didn't know what she liked to do when she wasn't working.

Scottie had kept the car running, and now she eased back onto the road, continuing north.

"Where now?"

"Wake Forest is just up ahead. Let's keep going," she said.

He wanted to read so much more than a car ride into her words. "Okay," he said.

"I talked to your mom," she said as she drove, the darkness of the road even heavier after the tailrace, "after we heard the news. How is she doing now? She must want you for Christmas, this year especially."

"I want to spend Christmas with my wife. My mom understands that," David said.

"So is the whole family gathering? All your brothers?"

"Yeah," he said. He missed them, more so because things weren't going the way he'd planned with Scottie. He'd never thought she'd want a divorce. "Mark is bringing somebody, so Mom is all excited. She missed our not having a big wedding."

"My mother swears she'll never get over it," Scottie said.

"What about you? You sorry we did it small and simple?"

"Are you kidding? Do you know how much those big weddings cost?"

David laughed and held up his hands in surrender. "Sorry, I forgot for a minute who I was talking to."

"So how did you tell them that you were alive? Have you been up to see them?"

He didn't want to talk about that. It wasn't important. "I called. I'll see them," he said dismissively.

"When?"

"Before I report back for duty."

"And when is that?" she asked quietly.

He didn't want to go there; this conversation wasn't taking him anywhere near where he wanted to be with Scottie.

"All those layers didn't work, you know," he said, reaching over to stroke her hair. It looked silver in the dim light of the car's interior. "You looked pretty hot yesterday with that little vest. You look pretty hot now. You looked hot in gray, but I'd have to say that blue is your color. You look like you're lit up inside." He ran a finger down her cheek to her neck; she arched like a cat. The car slowed.

She was wearing a blue sweater, tight at the neck. He'd go in from the bottom. With his other hand, he rubbed her breast through the soft wool and could feel the catch in her breath.

"Stop it," she said. Her voice was so soft, it sounded like an invitation.

"Okay," he said and took his hand off her breast to slip his fingers underneath her sweater. She shivered.

"I'll drive into a ditch," she gasped.

"Head south. We'll find an empty parking lot."

She jerked away from his touch and slapped his hand off her midriff. "Stop it! You're treating me like a sex toy!"

"I think that's a compliment. You can treat me like a sex toy all you want."

"That's the trouble," she snapped. "What about marriage counseling? What about what Pastor Swain said? You made it, what, forty-five minutes? I can see how much you want to work at our marriage!"

David sat back in his own seat and heaved a heavy sigh of defeat. "I think it's a stupid idea, but if it proves to you how much I want you, then I'll leave you alone. For 'a set period of time.' That's what he said. You want to talk about something, why don't we talk about how long this is going to last?"

Scottie turned around in a gravel driveway

and headed south; he didn't think she was going to be looking for a deserted parking lot.

"Until we can talk about things that are important. Until we *connect*."

"That long, huh?" he grumbled. He wasn't good at touchy-feely stuff.

"At least tell me how long you have before you have to report. That's not a secret, is it?"

She was mad. He shouldn't have suggested they stop in a parking lot for a quick tumble in the backseat, not after just having met with her pastor. His timing had been way off on that.

"I have until New Year's," he said, not wanting to think that far in advance. He was with Scottie now. Now was the only place he wanted to be.

"Maybe we can find something to talk about by then," she said stiffly.

The car headed south, back into town. They didn't find anything to talk about.

Chapter Five

"Hi, Mom! Merry Christmas!" he said into the phone, opening cupboards in the kitchen, trying to find a coffeepot.

"Merry Christmas!" she said to him, and then in an aside, "It's David calling from Raleigh. Go get on the extension."

"How's Dad doing? You guys all ready for everyone to descend on you today?"

"I've been ready for a week," Carol Adams said, "but your father still isn't ready. He wants to clean out the garage."

"That sounds like Dad." David chuckled.

"What are you doing? I hear noises."

"I'm trying to find a coffeepot, with no luck."

"If Scottie didn't leave it out, I'm sure she knows where she put it."

"Scottie's at work. She was out of here by six-thirty this morning."

"On Christmas Eve day? That girl works too hard."

"Well, when the stock market's open, she has to be there."

"Of course she does," Dennis Adams said from one of the many extensions in their large Connecticut house. "She's responsible and industrious—good traits and getting harder to find nowadays."

"Well, they ought to close the stock market on Christmas Eve. People shouldn't have to make money every day of the year," his mom muttered.

"It's closed Christmas Day, Mom. She'll have all day tomorrow."

"And how are you two going to spend Christmas? Any chance you could drive up here tonight? We've room, and we'd all love to see you."

"It's a twelve-hour drive, Mom."

"And I'm sure he doesn't want to spend twenty-four hours in a car on Christmas. That's no way to enjoy the holiday," Dad said.

"So, what are you two doing?" she asked.

David had given up his search for a coffeepot and settled for making himself some hot chocolate he'd found. At least it had caffeine.

"I'm not sure," he said, filling a mug with water from the tap and putting it in the microwave.

There was silence on the other end for a few seconds. Then his mom said, "Things not going well?"

"No, everything's fine," he said quickly.

Too quickly.

"You know," his mom said, "we spoke to Scottie when we got word you'd been killed. She was as lovely as she could be."

"I'll bet she was," he said. Scottie was always lovely and polite and correct in everything she did. It didn't mean anything except that she'd been raised right.

"So what's the problem?" his dad said.

"There's no problem. I just called to talk to you and wish you a Merry Christmas."

"David, you haven't 'just called' us since the day you left for Annapolis," his mom said sternly. "What's wrong between you and Scottie?"

David pulled his mug from the microwave and poured in the chocolate mix. It floated on the top of the water like a brown island. He stirred it. It looked like brown water. He added some milk. It looked like dirty milk. He drank a sip. It wasn't bad.

"This is what's wrong," his dad said to him mom over the extension.

"What?" David said, sloshing his hot chocolate over the rim and down the sides of his cup.

"You're not letting her into your life, and she's getting tired of being penned out of it," his mom said. "You've been like this since you started shaving."

"I never could figure it out," his dad said.

"You couldn't?" his mom snorted. "Your dad was the same way, and your mom used to talk to me about it every Thanksgiving while we basted the turkey."

"Well, she should have talked to my dad about it," Dennis Adams said. "I don't see what she expected *you* to do."

"Maybe just listen," Carol Adams said.

"Did Scottie talk to you about how she feels?" his dad asked, bringing him back into the conversation. David was happier out of it. He didn't want to talk about his marital problems with his parents. He didn't want to talk about his marital problems with his wife.

"We talk," he said, a little defensively, remembering last night.

"You know, son, women need . . . things. They're not like men."

"Dennis, I swear, you don't know what you're talking about half the time!" his mom snapped. "David, women and men need the same things, the same connection, the same level of openness. It's just that women are smart enough to know it."

It sounded exactly like what Scottie had said

122

to him. Did all women speak the same, secret language?

"You've been watching too much Oprah," his dad said to his mom.

"Are you saying that you *don't* think there needs to be complete openness between a couple?"

"I didn't say that," Dennis said. "I only said women and men are different."

"Not in this," Carol said.

"Look, Mom, Dad," David interrupted, "I didn't call to get you into a fight—"

"No, you called because you and your wife are in some kind of trouble," his mom said.

"And we're not fighting," his dad said.

It was a good imitation, David thought. His mother seemed to hear him over the phone lines.

"This isn't fighting, David," she said. "This is just . . . tangling in each other's thoughts and lives. That's what marriage is. You tangle, and you're not afraid of a few bruises. You can't be afraid and be married. You have to trust. A man can't hold a woman at arm's length and expect her to be happy. Are you doing that with Scottie?"

"Holding her at arm's length?" David said. "Not by choice."

David heard the bark of his dad's sudden laughter, and he joined him. He enjoyed the laugh; he needed one.

"I think I hear a car in the drive," his mom said. "Dennis, you keep talking to David, and I'll get the door." There was the sound of a toilet flushing. "Dennis?" his mom asked. "Which extension are you on?"

"The one in the bathroom," he said innocently.

"I swear, I don't know if I'll ever get you civilized enough for mixed company. David, you take everything your father says with a grain of salt, and you might be okay. Merry Christmas. I'll call tomorrow. Say hello to Scottie for me."

"Okay. 'Bye, Mom."

He heard a click, and then there was just his father.

"So, what's going on down there?"

"Nothing good," David said, glad for the chance to talk to another man.

"What's Scottie say?"

"About what Mom said."

"So, what are you doing, cutting her out? Keeping a woman like the one you've got in the kitchen with her apron strings tied over her mouth?"

"It's not like that, Dad. I'm not like that."

"What is it like?"

"I'm just trying to protect her," David said softly. That had to be right; he couldn't be wrong doing that.

"From whom, David? From you?" his dad said.

124

It sounded stupid when his dad said it. Maybe it *was* stupid.

He showed up at her office building at noon; he was going to take his wife to lunch, and they were going to find something to talk about. He was going to give her what she wanted, or he was going to go down trying.

David knew enough about the pecking order in a brokerage house to understand the significance of Scottie's windowed office. Not only did she have a huge window that comprised one whole wall, but she overlooked the landscaped entrance. It was a great office. She must have put in lots of hours and done tens of thousands of dollars in production to rate this outer office. She was on the phone when he got there; her eyes showed surprise when she looked up and saw him, but she kept talking and keying in on her computer. She was busy.

And successful. He knew firsthand how good with investments Scottie was, and he also knew how hard she pushed herself. Clearly it was working. For such a new broker, she was obviously on the fast track in a tough business. Stockbrokers rarely lasted five years, and those five years were full of struggle. Scottie had an outer office and had bought a house and a Lexus; even used, they weren't cheap. Maybe she was tougher than he gave her credit for.

Maybe he didn't have to protect her. Maybe his dad was right.

She hung up and looked at him as he stood in the doorway of her office. He was wearing gray dress slacks, a white shirt, a navy sweater slung over his shoulders, and he still looked rugged and a little dangerous. And wonderful. This forced abstinence was wearing very thin, but she was determined to have more from David than sex, and withholding sex seemed the only way to get it. At least according to Pastor Swain.

"I'm here to take you to lunch," he said, leaning against the doorjamb. "You available?" He grinned.

He was adorable; he really was. She remembered in a sudden sweep of feeling just how she had fallen in love with him. He was so sure of himself that he could let her be sure of herself, too. Her success pleased him because he was pleased for her. He was a man who didn't know how to be patronizing. Even if he did treat her like a sex toy whenever they were alone.

She knew he had meant what he said last night in the car; he would have been flattered if she'd told him he was her sex toy. Maybe any man would have been. She just didn't know. She had little experience with men, and her father was just a black-and-white photographed memory, cherished but mostly forgotten.

"Sure," she said, hitting the log-off button on her computer.

"I'll have you back in an hour."

"In an hour the markets will be closed. They're closing at one for Christmas Eve. I've done enough for today; it's been slow."

"Oh, I didn't know."

"I didn't expect you to," she said easily, meaning it. How could he know? They didn't talk.

He escorted her from the office, and he nodded to the bank of secretaries as he held her by the hand. They all turned their heads and stared as he passed. He was a man to stare at.

They went to Cameron Village, a collection of shops that covered a city block, where her mother often shopped, and had a light lunch. Slowly, gently, they began to talk.

She spoke about a client who had called from Hilton Head to wish her a Merry Christmas, about an investment she was intrigued by, about her mother's cruise, about her decision to buy a house, and eventually, almost imperceptibly, David started to talk about himself. He told her about telling his parents he was alive. He told her that his youngest brother, Steve, had decided not to apply to Annapolis. He told her that he was thinking of leaving the Navy.

Her response was instantaneous; guilt and remorse twisted inside her, twins of equal strength. Was he doing this for her? Did he think this would help their marriage? She would never ask it of him, would never have thought to ask it of him, no matter what her mother said to the contrary.

"Is it because of me?" she whispered, twisting her paper napkin into shreds, avoiding his eyes.

"No," he said softly.

"But your whole family is Navy."

"Not Steve," he joked quietly.

"But you, you've always wanted to make the Navy your permanent career."

"Maybe I want something different now," he said gently. "Besides, I'm just talking, just thinking out loud."

"You can think out loud with me anytime you want, about anything," she said, looking deeply into his twinkling blue eyes. "I like it when you 'just talk.' "

"Good," he whispered. "I'm trying."

"I know," she whispered back, feeling tears prick at the back of her eyes.

The connection she felt with David at that moment was almost sexual in its intimacy and its intensity. Could he feel it?

David stood abruptly and said, "I need to go Christmas shopping. How about you? Any good stores in here?"

She stood with him, pushing back any feeling of tears. "They're all good in my opinion, though according to my mother it's been going downhill since 1986."

"I'm sure I'll like it then," he said. "Meet you

back at the car at four, and no peeking."

"Don't spend too much."

"I can manage my own gift-purchasing financial package, Scottie. You can dictate to your heart's content on the rest of my mega-millions."

"Give me twenty-five years, and that won't be a joke."

"I'll give you the next one hundred," he said, suddenly serious.

She stared up at him, wanting him so desperately in that instant that she ached, the pain of emptiness sharp and insistent. But she was going to follow Pastor Swain's advice, though it felt as if it was killing her.

"Four o'clock," he repeated and turned away from her. Her heart dropped to her hips at the sudden physical loss of him. "And make sure you get your stuff wrapped; I like to peek."

They made dinner together, ate together at her pine table with a bottle of white wine between them, and cleaned up the kitchen together. She felt very married.

And when David brushed against her as she leaned against the kitchen counter or laid a light kiss on the top of her head as he reached over her to open the tall cupboard over the refrigerator, she felt very courted. Because nothing was going to happen. Her breath would catch, and she'd feel the heavy heat of desire pool in her belly, and there it would sit, with no hope of release. Denial only made the desire more intense.

She only hoped David was in as much sweet misery as she was.

They played Christmas carols on the CD while they decorated the tree in the foyer. He wanted to listen to Manheim Steamroller, and she wanted Bing Crosby. He didn't understand why anyone would set up their tree in the foyer and kept moving the stand toward the living room. She explained that in the foyer it would look prettier from the street and turned up the volume on Bing. She didn't have much in the way of decorations—a few strings of tiny white lights and four boxes of glass ornaments—but the tree was so pretty and full, it didn't need much. The smell alone shouted Christmas.

When they were finished, when the tree was up and the few presents arranged underneath, Mary Scott turned off most of the lamps so that they could admire their handiwork. David turned on the gas logs in the fireplace and brought their wine from the kitchen. He also removed Bing and substituted Mannheim Steamroller, turning the volume down low. The setting was romantic and dim, lit by the fire and the tiny white lights. She didn't walk out. She didn't turn on the lamps. She didn't look away.

"Talk to me," she said, taking the wine from his hand and sitting on the couch.

"Talk to you?" he said, sitting next to her.

"Please," she said softly. "I want to hear your voice. I want to hear about your day."

"I was with you for most of it."

"Please talk to me," she said. "What did you do this morning before you came to get me for lunch? Do I need to check the azaleas?"

David chuckled and leaned back against the couch, setting his wine on the coffee table. "They're safe, for the moment. But don't leave me alone with them too often or I won't take responsibility for my actions."

"That doesn't sound like you," she said, studying the firelight gleaming on his hair.

"You don't know how they call to me. Every man has his breaking point."

"I know," she said. She knew he was not talking about the azaleas, and she smiled at the gift of his restraint; he was trying so diligently to give her what she needed. Underneath it all, he was an honorable man.

"I called my folks this morning, as a matter of fact. Wished them a Merry Christmas, listened to them bicker, got yelled at—it was a great call. My mom wanted us to drive up to spend the day with them in Connecticut, which shows you how much she travels."

"I'll bet they wanted you to come desperately."

"They wanted us both desperately."

"I'll bet it's going to be a white Christmas up

there," she said a bit wistfully. A big family all gathered together, lots of noise and confusion and kids.

"No, they had a white Thanksgiving; it's nothing but frozen slush now."

"How do you know?"

"Weather Channel."

Mary Scott looked over at her husband. "You thought about going, didn't you? You can go. If you leave now, you'll get there by morning. Christmas morning with your family."

"You're my family," he said huskily, his blue eyes full of emotion.

How could she never look into his eyes again? Never hear his voice? Never feel his body next to hers?

Never feel the emptiness of emotional abandonment.

David, charming and playful, never quite let her in. She might not even have known what she was missing, beyond the empty ache in her heart, if she hadn't seen him with some of the men from his SEAL team. With them, the subtle barrier that he kept in place with her disappeared. There was an easiness, a trust, a bone-deep level of openness that she'd never known David was capable of. And once she had known it, and known that he didn't have that with her—worse, that he didn't seem to want that with her—the pain in her heart had quietly exploded.

A marriage couldn't survive that kind of hollow pain.

"More wine?" he said.

Her glass was still half full. "No, thank you. So what else did you talk about with your parents?"

"You still want to talk, huh?" he said, his hand moving along the back of the couch. She grabbed his hand and set it on the couch between them, holding her own fingers over his. Keeping him still.

"Yes, I do. Surprised?"

"Unfortunately, no." He grimaced comically. "We talked about you, Scottie. My mother told me that women were smarter than men—"

"I always liked your mother."

"—and my dad told me that you were tougher than I was giving you credit for."

"What do you mean?" she asked, swatting at his hand as he traced his finger on the inside of her wrist.

"Just that I don't need to work so hard at protecting you."

"*You're* protecting *me!* Is that how you see it?"

She was furious, suddenly and completely— the firelight, the tree, the soft music all instant irritants to her rising anger. Once again, he was the innocent, only trying to do what was best, blaming her for any glitch in his plan. She wanted a divorce. She wanted more than sex in her marriage. She wanted a husband who shared his life, his heart, with her. All problems he had to surmount with a wife who was difficult and demanding and needed protection. He had held back his heart to protect her? He'd love to believe that. The most infuriating thing was that she was sure he did; he believed it completely. She was being unreasonable, and he was being accommodating; that was the world through David's eyes.

She jerked to her feet and faced him, facing off, adversary against adversary. "So you've been protecting me? From what? I've got news for you, David. You're not protecting me. You're protecting yourself!"

David rose from the couch, his six-feet, two-inches towering over her in equal aggression. She wasn't the least bit intimidated. David couldn't scare her; he could only seduce her. But since he hadn't been seducing her lately, he was feeling more aggressive. Well, so was she.

"That from a woman who cares more about her mother than her husband!"

"That's not true, and even if it was, she needs me!"

"I need you!" he shouted.

"For sex!" she shouted back. "You need me for sex. I'm more than that. There's more to me than that." She could feel tears pressing and blinked them back; she wasn't going to win or lose this battle because of a few emotional tears. She was going to win by exchanging one verbal punch with another. She'd been avoiding this argument for too long, because it shamed her so. Her husband liked sex with her but didn't like to *be* with her.

"And you give it all to your mother."

He was wrong. Yes, she was close to her mother. It was just the two of them, after all, and her mother had always relied on her. Mary Scott stopped and listened to herself and grew very still inside. It wasn't just the two of them. There was David. Had she shut David out the way he had shut her out, using someone else to fill the place reserved for a spouse?

"I have to give it to someone," she said, cursing the tightness of her throat. "You don't want it."

"You're wrong," he said, stalking away from her.

"Prove it," she said, taking a breath to face the next assault. She was on safe ground; he'd never be able to prove that he'd ever shown any interest in wanting any of her heart.

"Prove it?" He swung around. "You want me to lay out my life so you can study it, talk about it with your mother, and then walk out and leave me?"

"You're the one who asked me to marry you. If not to share your life, then for what? You're the one who talked to your mother and father about me. You're the one—"

"I'm not the one who left!" he shouted, cutting her off. "You're the one who left. I'm the one who gets left behind."

It was then that she saw David in a way she'd never seen him before, and it shook her to her soles. David was afraid, and anger was the mask he wore to hide it. She'd never seen him so close to losing control.

"You got left behind," she repeated, understanding only that those were the words that had changed the mood of the fight.

David turned away from her, facing the darkness of the hall that led to the kitchen, facing away from the warm, cheerful light of the fire and the Christmas tree.

"You want to know what I'm thinking? What I'm feeling? You want to know about my last mission? You've been asking often enough. You want me to talk about that? You got it."

She was too tense to speak. He didn't seem to need her to speak. For once, David was going to open up and talk.

And now Mary Scott was afraid.

"You knew I was in Colombia." He didn't wait for her to acknowledge that, he just kept speaking, his back to her, his face in darkness. "It got . . . complicated . . . some foul-up. I was in a building when a bomb went off, and it exploded to hell and back, blew out my transmitter. Everything malfunctioned. By the time some native kid and his dog dug me out, my team was gone."

That was impossible, she knew. No one was ever left behind, dead or alive. No one was left behind. SEALs *never* left anyone behind.

"Gone?"

"Yeah, gone, as in 'left,'" he snarled. "My team, the guys I trusted with my life, beyond my life, gone. I trusted them," he said hoarsely. "Trusted them, knew them, like no one else."

"I know," she said softly. This was why he was thinking of leaving the Navy, not because of her. She was glad; she didn't want to be the reason David gave up his dream.

"How badly were you hurt?" she asked softly, closing the distance between them, joining him in the dark.

"Not bad enough to kill me," he said, cracking his knuckles. "I went native, lived on the edge of the jungle mostly, trying to get some strength back and find someone I could hook up with. It took me two months, but I found an American 'adviser' in Buenaventura, which is funny when you think about it. They flew me home that night."

She didn't know what to say. She didn't know what he needed her to say. "I don't think it's funny."

He turned to face her. "That's because you don't know what Buenaventura means. It means good—"

"I know what it means," she interrupted. His face reflected his anger, but she didn't think he was angry with her. He was angry because he'd been abandoned, betrayed by that sense of comradeship and unquestioned loyalty he'd trusted in but that had, in an explosive instant, been called completely into question. "I still don't think it's funny."

"Well, I do," he said, walking past her, back into the living room. "It was even funnier when I got back to base and no one knew where my wife was. I had to go to your old office to find out you'd moved. You'd left."

"I told you why—"

"Sure you did. Your mother needed you," he snapped. She flinched at the abrupt pain in his voice. "Well, guess what, Scottie? So did I." He turned away from her again and stared at the tree, the little white lights shining happily. "I needed you, Scottie. Walking through that jungle, feeling more alone than I ever had in my life, feeling so afraid it made me ashamed, I thought of you. My SEAL team walked out on me, I said, but not Scottie. She's my wife, and she'll never leave me."

"I didn't know. How could I know?" she said, her own voice rising.

"And when I did find you, when I was finally feeling whole for the first time in months, I find out that you were divorcing me—that is, until you found out I was dead. I guess the day the CACO came to your door was the happiest day of your life."

Tears rolled down her cheeks as she looked at him. He was staring out the window, not looking at her, not touching her, but she could feel his pain and his rage and his hurt.

"It's not true," she said, choking on her tears. "I wasn't happy. I'm *not* happy." Didn't he understand about the dead geraniums standing gaunt in her planting beds? Didn't he understand why she'd never planted winter pansies?

He turned to face her then, and she could see tears shimmering over his strong blue eyes. "You've got a great house near your mom and a great job where you're on the fast track to the top. You look like you're doing just fine."

She started laughing then, the kind of hysterical laughter that only women seemed able to emit and that she'd always despised.

"I'm on the fast track because I'm always there. I came to Raleigh to be close to my mom because I had to feel close to *somebody*. But she's never even here. She's got a life. I don't. I work fifteen hours a day because I can't stand being home alone. I don't want to be alone. I wanted to . . . I need to . . . give myself to somebody. But nobody was ever around."

"I'm around," he said, his voice as broken as hers. "I want you."

"All of me, David?" It had to be all, or it would be nothing. She couldn't live on the edge of his heart anymore. She was selfish; she wanted all of him.

"Every square inch," he said, looking at her, the lights of the tree behind him.

"Don't joke," she said brokenly. "Not now. Not when my heart is broken and bleeding—"

"So's mine, Scottie," he said. "And not just my heart—every square inch. Can't you see that I'm giving you all I've got? Can't you see that there's nothing left for me to unwrap?"

He stood before her, and she did see. David had given her everything she'd asked for. She'd wanted him to give her his heart, and he had, even though it was in pieces.

"Yes, I can see," she said. "But there's still something to unwrap."

"What?" he said.

Scottie Adams smiled and unbuttoned the cuffs of her fine silk blouse.

"Me."

"Wait," he said, holding up his hands to fend her off. When had David ever done that? "If I stay in the Navy, it won't be in Raleigh. You'd have to move, away from your mom and your new house. Can you do it? Can you leave all this to come with me?"

Leave the house, the neighborhood, the mother she rarely saw? Leave everything she knew to be with David, all of David, every square inch of David?

Scottie smiled and said, "I've been thinking about moving anyway."

Surprise Package

Shirl Henke

For two good sports,
Kathryn Falk and Carol Stacy

Chapter One

"Someday my prince *will* come," Gilly Newsom muttered fiercely. "If nothing else, he can rescue me from the five-twenty rat race."

Her companion, also elbowing her way through the rush-hour crowds thronging the subway platform, grinned good-naturedly. "Romance is still alive in your cynic's heart, then?" Charis Lawrence asked.

"Not really. Look around you, girlfriend. Most people are toting bags of holiday goodies, while I'm lugging twenty pounds of manuscript—three of the mere two dozen I'm currently assigned."

"Stop whining. Look at it this way—no need to go to the gym," Charis said, patting her briefcase full of marketing reports. "Besides, it's called paying our dues in New York publishing."

"Easy for you to say when you're going home to Bill, not a cold, empty flat in Yonkers. I don't even have a dog, for Pete's sake. You have William Channing Lawrence, Esquire."

A dreamy look came over Charis's pert, pretty face. "True, Bill is very special, but someday there'll be a guy just as great waiting for you. Well, maybe not quite as great—nobody could be."

"You wouldn't be just the least bit prejudiced in the matter, would you?" Gilly teased. Charis had always been able to lighten her mood, ever since they met back at Oberlin College nearly nine years earlier. They'd quickly become best friends as well as roommates in spite of the fact that they came from such diverse backgrounds. Charis's family was upstate New York old money, while Gilly's folks were rust-belt Ohio blue collar.

The subway car—already packed, as usual—pulled into the station, and both women shoved inside with the negligent ease of seasoned New Yorkers. "At least it's semi-warm in here, with all the bodies doing the 'subway sandwich.' The temp may be twenty-two degrees, but the wind chill makes it every bit as cold as northeast Ohio," Gilly groused. "Too crowded to hope for a seat. I could use this time to edit."

"Oh, yeah. I know you're just dying to get back to Gwendolyn Gleeson's Spanish-American War opus," Charis said, rolling her eyes as she held fast to a subway strap when the car started up with a lurch.

"God save me from first book authors like her. That manuscript is filled with almost as many historical errors as it is with purple—no, fuchsia—prose," Gilly replied, shuddering.

"Just because she had the hero going to Washington to consult with the Defense Department and the Pentagon in 1898? Picky, picky."

"That one was easy. I just substituted War Department and let it go. But when I came to her description of the heroine's breasts as 'a milky sea of white velvet topped with wild rosebuds,' I wanted to write in the margin, 'It sounds as if you're confusing a window display at Bloomingdale's with an ad for the Dairy Council.' "

Charis whooped with laughter. "Almost had you ripping *your* bodice with frustration, huh?"

Now it was Gilly's turn to roll her eyes. "I suggested that the phrase was a mixed metaphor, that she'd be better off with something a bit less flowery, like 'ivory with pale pink nipples.' "

"You're following sound editorial dictum—leave as much rewrite as possible to the author's discretion."

"Frustrated writers make lousy editors, that's

for sure," Gilly agreed. "If only I could enjoy my job as much as you do yours."

"You're the one who wanted to be an English major," Charis reminded her.

"I still love to read, and I'm a darn good editor. . . ."

"Just underemployed." Charis had heard this lament before. While she loved her job as assistant director of marketing at a small paperback romance publisher, Gilly was frustrated with hers as an assistant editor. She ached to be in the big leagues, to work for a prestige hardcover house editing literary fiction. "I know it's hard for a Phi Beta Kappa who graduated summa cum laude from Oberlin to edit historical romances, but this is just a stepping-stone for you."

"More like I'm the stone. Honestly, Charis, I've had nearly five years of hearts and flowers. I want a real job."

"What you want is a real hero. A man to bring some romance into your life, so you can believe in it again."

"If I ever did." Gilly had seen enough of men like her father, Whalen Newsom, even before her one time love Frank Blane delivered the final blow to her girlish dreams.

"Next month is Christmas, and you're thinking of Frank again, aren't you?"

"Frank was a loser. I'm much better off without him." She repeated the mantra.

"You've got that right. Imagine having *both* a wife over in Jersey and a kid with his girlfriend here in Midtown. You were lucky to find out when you did."

"Yeah. Almost as lucky as I was when Brian Schwin dumped me to marry that cheerleader our senior year at Oberlin. Let's face it, Charis, I'm just not cut out for happily ever after, which is probably why I dislike editing romance so much. Forget the heroes; I'll settle for a brilliant career in publishing."

"Now all we have to do is figure a way to get Farrar, Straus & Giroux to hire you," Charis replied, tapping one well-manicured nail against her cheek.

"Wouldn't that be sweet?" Gilly said, swaying as the subway began to slow. Then a staticky voice announced, "Forty-second Street," and she gasped, "What was I thinking? This is my stop!"

Charis gave a puzzled look. "You live all the way up in Yonkers."

Already working her way toward the opening doors, Gilly called over her shoulder, "The library won't have late hours again until next Monday, and I have to check that reference book on the Spanish-American War they're holding for me or it'll vanish into the abyss again! See ya tomorrow."

Desperation lent strength to her slender five-foot, three-inch frame when she caught the door just as it started to close on her. Escaping its jaws unscathed, she scooted quickly through the crowd, slinging her heavy tote bag over her shoulder. She began climbing the steep stairway to the cold, windy corner of Fifth Avenue and Forty-second Street, near where two giant stone lions guarded the entrance to the New York Public Library.

Winter had come to the Big Apple early in November this year. The icy slush of midday had once again solidified into diamond-hard shards. Here and there the city snowplows had scraped paths as smooth as greased tinfoil, but lacking ice skates, Gilly opted to walk on the refrozen slush. Like most New Yorkers, she wore sensible shoes while commuting—in this case sturdy Eddie Bauer lace-up boots with rubber grip soles—and left her heels at the office, safely tucked in the bottom drawer of her desk.

A sudden gust of wind almost knocked her off her feet as she neared the daunting series of steps up to the library. Clutching her tote like a talisman, Gilly put her head down and walked into the gale, feeling the crunch of ice beneath her boots. Lord, it was cold! Her breath came out in burning white puffs, her lungs seared from the frigid air being forced into them. She would go back to working out at the gym—she would . . . just as soon as the holiday crush was over and Gwendolyn Gleeson's interminable manuscript went to copyediting!

Jeff Brandt did not see the small figure laboring up the steps directly in his path until it was too late. Like her, he'd had his head lowered against the wind, watching the treacherous steps beneath his feet. Then a small booted foot somehow just appeared in the exact space where his big, sturdy Adidas was coming down. At the precise same instant that he was trying to rearrange his feet, a small woolen bundle smelling faintly of vanilla careened into his belly.

"Oomph!" was all he could manage before they went down together. Somehow the fact that the unguided missile in his path was female and much smaller than his six-foot, two-inch frame must have registered. He turned them in midair so that she fell on top of him rather than the other way around, the only chivalrous thing to do.

When they landed, he was no longer so certain chivalry had been the hot tip. She—or something attached to her person—landed on his gut like a Chuck Norris kick. Then Jeff became a human bobsled, he and his "rider" rocketing down the steps, his head clunking on every stair.

By the time they reached the sidewalk, he couldn't even manage a strangled "umph," just a low, feeble groan as he stared dumbly at the canvas tote gouging his ribs. Its contents were partially spilled, pages of something or other fluttering against the rubber bands holding them together. Above him, he could hear her voice, soft and breathless, concerned. A nice voice, he decided. Then his eyes focused on her face, pale in the artificial lighting from the street. Wind-kissed pink cheekbones set high over softly plump lips, a small button nose, and wide eyes of some light color he could not discern—blue or green. Slim, delicately shaped eyebrows arched with chagrin.

"Oh, I'm so sorry! I ran right into you, practically knocked you down. This stuff is so heavy. I hope I didn't break your ribs or anything," she babbled breathlessly as she crawled about, frantically scooping chunks of paper back into the tote.

To Jeff, this looked about as easy as stuffing cooked spaghetti into a long-neck bottle, but somehow she accomplished it, all the while talking in fast little spurts. His skull pounding, he raised himself up on his elbows, observing her until he had recovered enough wind and presence of mind to say something himself, like *What the hell have you got in that bag, lady, an anvil?* But he refrained. She was obviously flustered enough, and he had been raised to be a gentleman . . . sort of.

Gilly tried to conceal her embarrassment. She could tell the tall stranger had deliberately

twisted her around so that he took the full force
of their fall—a fall she had caused by not watching where she was going. He was nice looking,
too, drat the luck. Why did she always mess up
at times like this? He had a square jaw and dark,
serious eyes, magnified by wire-rimmed
glasses, which were now perched catiwampus
on the end of his straight nose. His features
were angular, striking in a scholarly way, offset
by shoulder-length black hair that gave him a
hippie sort of look. No, make that a university
student sort of look. Double drat. He was probably younger than she.

"The collision was as much my fault as
yours," he replied. "In this wind, everyone is
looking down, trying to breathe without frost-
ing their lungs. Besides"—he grinned—"I'm a
lot bigger. A little thing like you couldn't hurt
me—although the stairs may have flattened the
back of my skull."

He admired the view for another instant, trying to decide if her body was as shapely as he
hoped beneath all the layers of winter clothing,
then sat up and reached for her hand, helping
her to her feet.

He was right about their size difference, Gilly
saw. She wore flat-heeled boots, and he towered
over her. She would definitely need "power"
heels to measure up to this guy. Then her bemused train of thought came to an end when
she realized that she stood with her gloved hand

still held firmly in his grasp, staring up into his face as he reached with his free hand to straighten his glasses.

I must be gawking like a banked carp! She closed her mouth and broke contact, then stooped to pick up her tote—just as he scooped it up to hand it to her. Quickly catching herself, Gilly straightened up—just in time for her head to connect with his jaw. The heavy woolen cap she wore softened the blow, but she could hear his teeth click together. He touched his tongue experimentally against the bleeding edge of his lip.

Great! Maybe I could render him unconscious and drag him back to my apartment to have my way with him! "I'm so sorry. Does it hurt? What am I saying—of course it hurts. You're bleeding. Here, let me . . ." She began to root frantically in her tote, searching for a handkerchief. All she managed to come up with were a couple of dog-eared grocery coupons and a lipstick-smeared tissue.

Jeff dug a handkerchief out of his back pocket and daubed his lip, grinning once again at her flustered agitation. "You know, we might be able to form a really funny circus act, except no one would insure us." Before she could begin apologizing again, he said, "I'm Jeff Brandt. We may have, er, gotten off on the wrong foot, but that's no reason we can't start over."

"I'm Gilly—Gillian Newsom. My friends call

me Gilly." *Idiot*. She was babbling again.

"Then I hope I can call you Gilly. The least I can do is buy you something hot to warm you up after that tumble on the ice. There's a little coffee shop down the next block. I'll even carry your tote. It looks pretty heavy."

"That's very sweet, but I have to do some library research for a book I'm editing." The minute the words tumbled out, Gilly could've kicked herself. How often did she get an opportunity like this dropped into her lap—or, rather, her lap sort of dropped into it.

"But I could—"

"I could—"

They both spoke at once. When she stopped, he started again.

"What I meant was that I'd be happy to wait while you do your research. Actually, I was just taking a break. I have at least two more hours to put in myself, reading back issues of the *Times* for a sentencing class."

"You're a law student?" She did some quick math in her head. The most he could be was twenty-four, maybe twenty-five. By comparison, her own twenty-eight seemed positively ancient.

"Yes. I finally managed to finish a B.A. and get into the NYU law program after four years in the Navy. I'm afraid you're looking at one of those long-on-the-vine Gen-Xers who couldn't decide what he wanted to be when he grew up . . . until he was pushing thirty," Jeff said ruefully. "On the plus side, though, if I graduate in the top ten percent of my class, Bradford, Trent and Lange have an opening in criminal law. Very, very snotty outfit, but it would be quite a coup if they made me an offer." *Not that I'd accept it, but damn, it would—will—be sweet.*

He wasn't too young for her! Gilly brightened. But his next question caught her off guard.

"You said you were editing a book? Do you work in publishing, then?"

"Yes." She paused then. This was always the hard part for her, explaining that she edited historical romances. Most people took romance editors about as seriously as they did romance writers, which was to say, not at all. She had heard more than her share of condescending remarks. *Just what kind of research are you doing? Wouldn't it be better to conduct it someplace a teensy bit less public than the library? Say, like your bedroom?*

"I have a cousin who works in marketing for Houghton Mifflin. Where do you work?" Jeff asked.

"FS&G. Farrar, Straus & Giroux, that is." The words tumbled out before she could stop them. Then, to make matters worse, she found herself adding, "I edit history and literary fiction. Right now I have to do some research on the Spanish-American War for a book I'm working on." Well, that much was true.

"History, huh? My undergrad work was in American Studies. I even did a senior thesis on Roosevelt's Rough Riders. We have something in common, Gilly."

"Uh, yes, I guess we do."

"Then we'd better get right to work," he said with another heart-stopping Colgate smile, taking her tote and gently leading her up the icy steps to the library doors.

Chapter Two

When they entered the reference room, Abbie Kunsler, the librarian, greeted Jeff by name. Obviously, he had used the facilities often over the course of his academic career. Gilly felt reassured. After all, this was New York, and she was by nature cautious. They both went to work on their separate projects, he scrolling through reams of old newspapers while she took careful notes from the antiquarian, non-circulating tome she had found to be an excellent resource to draw upon when correcting Gwendolyn's historical vagaries.

Within two hours she was finished. Jeff was still deeply engrossed at his computer terminal. Gilly walked over to Abbie's desk. The older woman smiled and adjusted her sharply delineated trifocals so she could make out Gilly's face. How to say this? Gilly cleared her throat nervously.

"Uh, Abbie, I was wondering . . ."

"About Jeffrey Brandt?" The reference librarian didn't exactly smirk, but there was a definite look of amused smugness on her angular, horsy face. "He's such a nice young man. Studious and polite. Been using our facilities ever since he was an undergraduate. I believe he lives somewhere down in the Village, not too far from NYU." Abbie paused to see if Gilly needed more data.

The information she had given Gilly was reassuring. The rest of what Gilly wanted was a little stickier.

"I was wondering, Abbie, if you would do me a favor—well, not so much *do* a favor as . . . er . . . well, *not* do something." At Abbie's puzzled look, Gilly sighed and confessed quickly before she lost her nerve. "You know I work for Leisure Books, but I'd really appreciate it if you didn't mention that to Mr. Brandt. He's under the impression that I work for FS&G."

"Oh?" One thinly penciled eyebrow rose above the trifocals.

Abbie wasn't going to help her out here.

Gilly struggled on, knowing her face was getting as red as the wild rosebuds on Gwendolyn's milky sea of white velvet. "Well, I sort of gave him the wrong impression—not that I don't plan to correct it, but . . . well, I'd rather do it in my own time." *Like by getting that job at FS&G.*

"I never gossip, Gillian," Abbie replied primly.

Before Gilly could speculate whether or not that meant the librarian would keep quiet, Jeff came ambling over to them. "All done?"

"Yes. I have my notes complete."

"Good. Then do you want to get that coffee, maybe a sandwich?"

They thanked Abbie for her help and left the cavernous library. Once again braving the icy streets, they walked quickly to a nearby greasy spoon on Forty-second Street.

The place was small and crowded. Here, too, everyone seemed to know Jeff. The waitress, a frowsy, mid-fortyish blonde, handed them laminated menus that looked only slightly newer than the Dead Sea Scrolls.

"The cheeseburgers are very good, but the chili dogs are my personal favorite," Jeff said while the blonde scribbled his order.

"I've always had a weakness for cheeseburgers—with Swiss, if you have it?"

The waitress looked at her as if she'd asked for fois gras, then nodded curtly and wrote up the order, adding the two cups of black coffee they requested. Gilly was careful to place her tote with the Gleeson manuscript on the floor where Jeff couldn't see it. Gwendolyn's working title was *Cuban Ecstasy*.

"So, when will you take the bar exam?" she asked.

"My coursework should be wrapped up by the end of this year. I'm planning to take a few months to review everything, then go for it."

"Got to make that ten-percent cut." She nodded, sipping the steaming coffee the waitress had deposited on the chipped Formica table a moment earlier. "It must be very exciting to have a top-level law firm interested in you. I imagine your family is really proud."

He looked down into his cup, then took a swallow before replying. "Yes. BT&L has always been my father's dream."

Was there something in the tone of his voice, a faint hint of irony? Gilly couldn't be sure, but she was curious. No more involvement with mystery men who had relatives—like wives and children—about whom she knew nothing. "Do your parents live nearby?"

"Scarsdale," he said dismissively. "I don't see them often. It's much more . . . convenient to stay close to school. I live in Manhattan, near NYU in the Village."

"I know," she blurted out, then blushed. "Er, Abbie mentioned it. Tell me about your family. Any brothers or sisters?" *Any wives or children?*

"One sister. Older, married. Two kids and a husband who's a broker on the Street."

His answers might have been a little on the laconic side, but it was quite apparent that he came from money. "Let me guess. Your dad's a lawyer, too?"

"Definitely yes, but retired now. He and my mother travel a lot. Right now they're in Bermuda."

"Sounds wonderful on a dreary Manhattan day like this. I'd love to travel if I had the time." *And the money.*

"It's greatly overrated. I saw a lot of the world during my tour of duty. Everyplace from Taiwan to Rio. The rich play, and the poor starve. Just like home."

Gilly cocked her head and smiled. "Do I detect a strain of social activism here? It may be passé now, but I like it. Sort of fits you."

He grinned. "How so?"

"Goes with the long hair and wire-rimmed glasses, not to mention the beat-up old Adidas and the necklace." She eyed the tooled leather with elaborate beadwork hanging partially revealed at the open collar of his shirt. Swallowing, she looked away before the sight of the dark chest hair peeking out around the odd piece of jewelry had her any more flustered. *God, I'm acting like one of Gwendolyn's virgins!*

"This?" He held up the small pouch, smiling. "It was a gift from a friend, David Strongswimmer, an Iroquois construction worker. His father is a shaman. He makes these to keep the wearers safe from harm."

"If they work high iron, I can see the need," Gilly said, shivering. "Personally, I get a nosebleed on the observation deck of the Empire State Building."

Jeff was not too keen on heights either, and he had given up a really well-paying job with Dave and his dad because of it. But he didn't want to talk about his jobs any more than he did his family. Instead, he switched the conversation back to her. "Tell me about Gilly. You aren't a native New Yorker."

"My Midwestern accent gives me away, doesn't it? I graduated from Oberlin six years ago and came to the Big Apple to set the publishing world on its ear."

"Seems like you've done a pretty fair job so far," he said, taking a huge bite out of his loaded chili dog.

They'd agreed jokingly on ordering onions ahead of time, since he loved them chopped on his hot dogs and she couldn't imagine a cheeseburger without a slice. It was a mutual passion, he'd said, laughing as they trudged through the slush to the coffee shop. Gilly took another bite of her burger, using her fingers to catch the stringy wisps of Swiss cheese before they stuck to her chin. "I want to be an editorial director someday."

"You'll make it," he replied, lifting his coffee mug in a toast to her.

When he asked her about her family, she debated. Then, remembering that his father was an attorney from Scarsdale, she reverted to the story that made life a little easier for her. The story she'd told everyone in New York. "My parents are dead now. I have a sister living out on the West Coast. I'm afraid we're not very close." No lie about her and Liv, that was for sure. "I was born and raised in a little town in northwest Ohio—you know, picket fences, apple trees, and Fourth of July parades. Pretty dull stuff to a native New Yorker."

"Oh, I don't know. There is a certain appeal to living a quiet, traditional life. And Scarsdale's not all it's cracked up to be." His dark eyes studied her intently over the rim of his cup, noting the way her pale reddish-blond hair curled in spite of the heavy woolen hat she'd pulled off when they entered the warm coffee shop. Probably natural curl and color. It fit with her light green eyes and the faint sprinkle of freckles across the bridge of that adorable little dumpling of a nose. "Any current relationships?" he asked, surprising himself.

"N-no." She cleared her throat. "I broke up with my fiancé six months ago."

"And haven't replaced him?" He looked dubious.

"No time." Not to mention no heart, since

Frank had pretty well fractured what little was left of it.

"So, a lady married to her career." His smile could have melted the polar ice caps.

Her heart did a funny little flip-flop as she raised her mug in return. "Here's to passing the bar." *Gilly, girl you're in deep, and this barely even qualifies as a first date!*

"So, he's a real babe," Charis mumbled through the mouthful of bagel she was wolfing down.

Self-consciously, Gilly looked around the crowded deli where she and her friend usually grabbed a bite before they went to work in the next block. Once they were at their desks, there was seldom time for lunch. She still found it disconcerting that New Yorkers could sit two feet from a person and completely ignore the most private conversations. "No, he's not a 'babe.' I don't go for the 'babe' type."

"Remind you too much of cover model hunks, huh?"

Gilly rolled her eyes in disgust. "Just because I mentioned that he had longish hair. Believe me, he bears not the faintest resemblance to 'The Blond One.' He's going to be an attorney. His family's from Scarsdale, for Pete's sake. He's scholarly and . . ." She groped for the right word.

"Sexy," Charis supplied helpfully.

Gilly sighed. "He's too good to be true, Charis.

We talked for hours in that coffee shop. He's sweet, very bright, ambitious, and has a great sense of humor."

"Must be fate."

"I don't know. My track record with men has pretty much stunk my whole life."

Charis nodded. She knew all about Gilly's family background, as well as her ill-fated love life. "I'm not saying fall on the guy and grope him after one date. Just give him a chance. Get to know his family. It's a real plus that they live so nearby. No wives or fiancées hiding in the closets if he takes you home to Mama."

"We're hardly at that stage. He only asked me to take in a movie tonight."

"Hey, it's a beginning. Lighten up, Gil. This may be the one."

It looked as if he was. Over the course of the next few weeks, Gilly and Jeff went to see films and plays and ate dinner in ethnic restaurants. They discovered they both loved old Bette Davis movies, Robert Browning's poetry, and tandoori cooking.

On the first Friday night in December, they saw *The Barretts of Wimpole Street* at a small art theater on Second Avenue. The city remained unseasonably windy and bitterly cold, although the snow had finally melted. They found a small Italian restaurant more notable for its dimly lit corners than for its food, but neither was hungry . . . for food. They lingered over glasses of Chianti, discussing the romantic old film, poetry, and history—everything but what was really on their minds.

"I know it's an old line, but candlelight does become you," he said softly.

"Isn't the line 'moonlight'?" Gilly was suddenly breathless when he took her hand and held it over the checkered tablecloth. His large fingers worked the pulse point of her wrist with maddening delicacy, slowly circling the slim expanse. She knew he must be able to feel her blood racing. Then he raised her hand to his lips and leaned forward to brush her knuckles.

"This table's too big," he murmured, even though it was tiny. He stood up and stepped from behind it, never relinquishing her hand. Then he slid in on her side of the secluded booth. "Now, where were we . . . ?"

"The table was too big," she replied helpfully, amazed that she could even remember his last words, much less repeat them. The heat of his thigh seemed to be searing hers. Their shoulders brushed, and Gilly was aware of how large and hard his frame was compared to her own slenderness. She could feel the tension coiled in that big body as he leaned nearer, but he pressed no farther, giving her the opportunity to withdraw.

"I think I want to kiss you now. What do you think?" His light caressing of her fingers continued, his thumb working that magic circle on her wrist as he drew her hand once again to his mouth.

The feeling of his warm breath on her skin made her practically salivate. "I think it's a great idea . . . absolutely sensational . . . brillian—"

His mouth moved closer to hers, and she raised her face, eyes closed, as their lips met. The pressure was light as gossamer at first, warm, very faintly moist. Every nerve ending in her body seemed to respond as he drew her closer in his arms and pressed her back against the wall in the dimly lit booth. Gilly's arms just naturally fit around those broad shoulders, pulling him closer, her fingertips kneading hard muscle.

His lips traveled from the edges of her mouth up to her blissfully closed eyelids, pressing soft kisses against the fluttering lashes, then moving over to one small ear. His tongue scalded it with a swift whorl, then retreated, moving downward to her neck. He was a devil for finding pulse points—should've been a doctor, not a lawyer. The thought flitted through her mind but evaporated when he returned his concentration to her mouth, which by now was open, breathlessly panting.

He tasted of the Chianti, spicy and mellow and male. She grabbed fistfuls of his hair and pulled him closer, giving him some tongue in return. When he growled low and intensified the kiss, Gilly felt her head spin. *Whoa! Too much wine . . . too much man,* the Ohio side of her brain reminded her. However, the New York side, a side she had until now never had much occasion to notice, utterly ignored it.

Gilly ran one hand through his hair, twining her tongue with his, darting it into his mouth, as her other hand glided down his neck to the open collar of his shirt. Her fingers sank into the thick black hair that had so tantalized her. Before she realized what she was doing, several of his shirt buttons were undone, and her hand slid inside. His skin was as hot as a tenement roof in July, and his heart pounded against her palm.

When he slid his hand up under her sweater and cupped one breast, she moaned and arched against him. Dark little restaurant or not, Gillian Marie Newsom had never in her life put on such a display. And she was loving it! They twisted and writhed with wild abandon until the obligatory wicker-encased bottle with the candle in it began to wobble precariously on the tabletop.

Jeff came up for air just as the waiter, an elderly Italian man with bushy white eyebrows and a sweet, gold-toothed smile, cleared his throat. He stood patiently with the bill in his hand while the young lovers quickly uncoiled. When he reached nonchalantly to steady the bottle, Gilly felt like slithering under the table with embarrassment. Her sweater was pushed above her waist, and her bra was unfastened! Damn, Jeff had clever hands. She could feel her face flame as he paid the check and the little old man disappeared.

"I think we'd better put ourselves together and leave so Signor Monserra can close up," he said, refastening his shirt buttons. All the while his eyes never left her face.

She could feel the scorching heat of them as she fumbled with her bra, then smoothed down her sweater. "Believe it or not, I don't usually get so . . . engrossed . . . at least, not in public."

He grinned. "I'm relieved to hear you don't rule out in private. Next time we decide to do this, let's pick a better place."

But since he lived with a roommate, they had no better place. Gilly's apartment in Yonkers was small, cheap, and dingy—all she could afford on an assistant editor's pay. She kept meaning to fix it up but never seemed to have the time. Even if it had been beautiful, like Charis and Bill's Park Avenue penthouse, Gilly was still wary of becoming involved too deeply before she found out more about Jeffery Brandt. Already he had far more control over her senses than any other man she'd ever slept with—of course, there had not been all that many.

Gilly didn't like to think of herself as a prude. Even if Charis said she was one. After all, she had been the only girl in her high school to reach her senior year still a virgin. Ken Planzer had taken care of that one night in the backseat of his father's Olds 98. That had been enough to get her to swear off sex until her sophomore year at Oberlin. The two guys she'd become involved with in college were no great shakes as lovers, although after Ken, they seemed better than they were by comparison. Then she met Frank Blane and knew, for the first time, sexual gratification. Oh, Frank had been practiced all right—with good reason. But he'd taught Gilly a valuable lesson. She wasn't going to fall for a guy again just because he sent her hormones into overdrive.

So she and Jeff had settled into a pattern of meeting when she got off work and he finished studying. Sometimes they spent evenings working in the library, then went for a quick bite at the coffee shop down the street. Whatever they did, the fiery interlude in the Italian restaurant was not repeated. Maybe Jeff, too, was having second thoughts about becoming romantically entangled. That thought did not console Gilly one little bit.

But what would happen if they really *were* right for each other? She'd told him a series of whoppers. Admittedly, they were the same sort of fabrications she'd resorted to with most people she'd met in New York. Frank Blane was the only man to whom she'd told the truth. The irony of that did not escape her. She would just have to wait and see what happened between her and Jeff.

One brisk, sunny Sunday afternoon Gilly and Jeff strolled casually along a path in Central Park when a jogger approached with two big rottweilers trotting obediently beside him. "I'd love to have one of those." Gilly sighed as the dogs passed by.

"You had rotties back in Ohio?"

"Not exactly, although I'm sure there was some rottweiler in Belvedere—he had a little of everything mixed in."

"Belvedere?" Jeff's tone was teasing. "You *are* a serious literary type."

She shrugged, kicking a pile of ice-crisped leaves. "I was twelve years old and had just finished reading *Morte d'Arthur*. I figured he'd be the last dog I had before I left home."

"You had lots of dogs growing up?"

"Three, counting old Rufus, who died when I was a toddler. I don't remember much about him except that he licked off the food smeared on my face. Then there was Spike. He liked to chase cars. What about you? Any pets allowed in Scarsdale?"

"My mother raised Afghans." She made a face, and he laughed. "Okay, so they aren't the brightest creatures, but I had an English sheep-dog that was smarter than some of my law professors. Come to think of it, Raleigh was smarter than most of them."

"I miss having a dog. That's one of the trade-offs for living in the Big Apple, I guess."

"Why? Surely you could get a small dog of some kind. Look around you. There are people with dogs all over the place," he said, indicating a sprinkling of various breeds, leashed and un-leashed, roaming around the park with their owners.

"True, but they don't have Danny DeVito in drag for a super."

Jeff burst out laughing. "This person I'd love to see."

"No, you wouldn't. She's just like Louie on 'Taxi,' only not nearly as nice. And she hates dogs. Says they bark and wake up the other tenants."

"Sounds as if the walls are as thin in your place as the shack where I live."

Uh-oh. Gilly had been very careful to evade any questions about her apartment. After all, what FS&G editor would be living in a dump in Yonkers like hers? Since he lived and went to school in lower Manhattan, she had insisted that they meet in the city for all their dates. And, for work and home, she had given him only her cell-phone number. "No, actually, the place is really cool—it's just Mrs. Kleinschmidt who's the problem."

"I'd like to see your place . . . one of these days."

His words were laced with meaning as he looked into her eyes. But since he shared his apartment with a fellow student who was almost always home studying, that left him no privacy to bring in a date, and there was no way she could invite him to her place in Yonkers.

They shared a smoldering look. There had been a lot of those since that first kiss. But what could they do? Come to think of it, they both knew what they could do. Just not where they could do it!

Chapter Three

"Bill and I will be in Monaco until December seventeenth. Of course you can use our place. . . ." Charis hesitated, then plunged ahead. "But Gil, do you really think it's such a hot idea to become this involved with a guy and not level with him? I mean, sooner or later you're going to have to tell him the truth." Charis watched as her friend sorted through the piles of manuscripts covering her desk. She knew Gilly was stalling instead of facing her question. Taking another bite off the end of the stick of celery that was her lunch, Charis grimaced. Raw veggies were all she'd allowed herself to eat for the past ten days. She simply had to drop ten pounds before she could wear that new bikini on the Riviera.

Finally Gilly shoved a manuscript across her desk and stood up, pacing across the crowded cubicle. "I don't know what to do about telling Jeff. I've tried to confess several times, but then I get to thinking about Scarsdale and Afghan hounds and—"

"Afghan hounds?" Charis put down her celery and gave her friend an odd look.

Gilly waved a hand dismissively and kept pacing behind her desk. "Jeff's mom raises them. Everything about his background is so . . . so perfect, and everything about mine isn't."

Charis walked over and took Gilly by both arms. "You won a full scholarship to Oberlin and graduated summa cum laude, kiddo. You're smart and good, and, frankly, I'd kill you for your body—if they could do full body transplants. Look, it's no crime to come from a poor family, and it's sure as hell no crime to work for a romance publisher either—unless this guy's a real snob, and if he is, who wants him?"

"I do!" Gilly's face reddened as Charis chuckled gleefully. "Oh, I didn't mean to imply that he's a snob. We don't go on fancy dates, and he wears old jeans and sneakers. He's never tried to impress me. In fact, I practically had to pry every bit of information about his family out of him."

"So, you're got the hots for the guy, but you're still not sure about him."

"That makes me sound awful."

"That makes you sound human, Gilly. And still insecure as ever. You've got to get over your past and enjoy the present." Charis's big brown eyes were filled with sympathy. "Look, sweetie, there is absolutely no reason this Jeff shouldn't love the real you. You have to believe in yourself."

Gilly sighed. "I'm trying, Char, honest."

Charis pressed a card key into Gilly's hand. "We're leaving Friday morning and won't be back for three weeks. The penthouse is yours. Live it up, sweetie!"

"You're a living doll, you know that?" Gilly replied, hugging her friend.

"Yeah, but by the time I eat all that wonderful French food, I won't be Barbie-sized, that's for sure! *Ciao,*" she said, tossing the remains of the celery stick in the trash as she headed for the door. *Maybe this guy will ground you in reality. Then again, it's hard to keep your feet on the ground when you're walking on cloud nine.*

Gilly straightened the magazines on the Ligne Roset coffee table, then fanned them out again. Her nerves were utterly frayed, she thought, gazing around the Lawrences' lush Park Avenue apartment. Some digs. The picture window directly facing her had a smashing view of the

Manhattan skyline, glittering like jewels in the
night. The living room was thirty feet long, an
unheard of expanse for most New Yorkers. On
one wall a huge stone fireplace soared all the
way to the ten-foot ceiling, gas logs giving off
cheery warmth. A long sofa of butter-soft terra-
cotta-colored suede stretched sinuously against
the opposite wall, flanked by two club chairs in
deep moss green. A painting that was either an
original Picasso or a darn good copy hung over
the sofa.

Gilly's feet sank into the thick pale gold carpet
as she made her way soundlessly to the kitchen
off one end of the living room. The terra-cotta–
tile floor was polished to a rich luster. Her heels
clicked over it as she checked the tray of canapés and crystal bowl filled with crushed ice and
boiled shrimp. A bottle of Stags Leap Chardonnay was nestled in its sterling ice bucket. There
was another bottle chilling in the Sub-Zero . . .
for afterward.

If only there's a before. Gilly hadn't been this
nervous since her scholarship interview with
the committee at Oberlin. She walked down the
hall to the big bedroom where a king-sized water bed sat enthroned on a raised platform, its
fluffy moss-green comforter inviting the viewer
to sink into the softness. How would it feel to
make love on a water bed? She hoped she'd find
out soon.

The floor-to-ceiling mirrors in Charis's dressing room reflected Gilly's slender figure. She appraised herself critically, smoothing an errant curl that kept slipping out of the French twist. Her sole extravagance on her modest salary had always been clothes. Although she shopped the sales at Bloomie's, the prices on Oscar and Anne, not to mention Gucci, were still steep. But worth it. She was glad she'd splurged on the Versace caftan. It looked casual and chic—and had the added benefit of being very simple to slip out of.

The security intercom buzzed, interrupting her critique. Breathlessly, she pressed the button, and the doorman announced that Jeff had arrived. "Send him up," she said with a catch in her voice. "Get a grip, girl. You're carrying on like one of Gwendolyn Gleeson's simpy heroines!"

Jeff rode up in the soundless elevator, admiring its dark walnut paneling and gleaming brass fixtures. Some class act. They must pay editors a lot better at the big houses than he'd imagined. For a fleeting moment he wondered if a woman as successful as Gilly would want to marry a struggling assistant district attorney, then quashed the thought with horror. Good grief, he'd met the woman barely a month ago! No reason to be thinking of anything as permanent as marriage. Just saying the word aloud normally made his tongue stick to the roof of his mouth. But then, he'd never met a woman quite like Gilly Newsom. She was funny and bright, wholesomely small town, even if her family was wealthy and she had a high-powered job in publishing.

The elevator stopped on the seventy-fifth floor, and the door opened silently. He walked across the marble foyer to apartment 7501 and rang the bell. Gilly opened the door the moment he buzzed, indicating that she'd been waiting on the other side. As he handed her the bouquet of white roses he'd bought from a vendor on the way over, his gaze traveled appreciatively over her body.

She was wearing something soft and flowing made of sheer silk in a dramatic tiger-stripe print. The neckline was cut in a low vee, revealing a sweet amount of pale flesh. The gossamer fabric faintly outlined tips of her breasts as she stepped back, inviting him inside. She buried her nose in the bouquet and inhaled. It was all he could do not to inhale her!

"How did you know white roses were my absolute favorites?"

He grinned. "I could claim ESP, but all I really had to do was watch you every time we passed a florist's shop."

"That's much sweeter than ESP," she said, noting the way his crisp white shirt stretched across those broad, muscular shoulders and contrasted with his naturally dark coloring. The sleeves were rolled up and the collar open. He wore age-softened jeans that looked as if they'd been spray-painted on. Her throat suddenly felt dry. No wonder. All the moisture in her body had moved south!

"Come in and make yourself at home—after you open the wine, that is," she said, taking his battered leather bomber jacket and hanging it in the entry closet.

He surveyed the huge living room. The soft sounds of Mozart's *Andante* surrounded them, floating through the vast space. "Wow. Even my old man would be impressed by that view, not to mention the painting. Hard to believe your super would give you grief about having a dog in a place this expensive."

"I'm glad you approve," she replied nervously.

"Not nearly as much as I do of you," he said, taking her into his arms. When she slid her arms up around his neck, the silk folds of her caftan rustled softly, and his nostrils were filled with the essence of vanilla. "Mmm, you smell good enough to eat," he murmured, nuzzling her neck.

Gilly chuckled. "Silly, you're smelling the flowers." The bouquet was draped over his shoulder, still clutched in her hand.

"That's what they say to take time to do, isn't it?" He continued his leisurely path of kisses and soft nips, running his mouth across the silky skin on her collarbone, then traveling up to the pulse racing at the base of her throat, sliding from there to her delicate jawline.

Her fingers combed through his hair, but she almost dropped the roses in her other hand when his mouth finally claimed hers. What began as a soft exploration suddenly turned to voracious hunger for both of them. Mouths open, tongues dueling, they pressed their bodies together, hips rotating and gliding in promise of things to come.

Jeff slid one hand from her small waist over her ribs to cup a breast, working the nipple with his fingertips until it stood out pebble hard. She moaned when he finally broke the kiss, but he continued to hold her pressed tightly against his lower body. "I'm going too fast, I know, but I've wanted to do this ever since you sat across from me in the coffee shop eating that damned cheeseburger."

"I wanted it, too . . . but a woman has to be careful," she murmured, stroking his jaw with her fingers. "You must've shaved really close tonight."

"There are places I don't want to give you whisker burn," he said wickedly. Then, stepping back, he lifted her arm and the roses over his shoulder. "I think you'd better get these into water before they wilt."

"Think *you* can wait?" she asked with a cheeky grin.

He looked down at the bulge in his jeans with

a rueful laugh. "Believe me, I've been in no danger of wilting since I met you!"

Gilly could feel the heat stealing into her cheeks. "You can make me blush like a schoolgirl." That fact did not induce her to take her eyes from his jeans, however.

"I find the trait endearing, but if you don't want me to ravish you right here on the entry floor, you'd better stop looking and blushing."

"Right. I think we should at least take advantage of the carpet in front of the fireplace." She turned in a cloud of gold and black silk and headed for the kitchen. "You can open the wine while I put these in water."

She picked up a Baccarat vase from the library table and headed toward the kitchen with Jeff following, admiring the way her hips swayed, faintly outlined through the sheer fabric of the caftan.

"Where's the corkscrew?" he asked as she filled the cut-crystal vase with water.

"Er, over there," she said vaguely, gesturing in the direction of a bank of drawers on the island in the center of the kitchen. She thought she remembered that Bill kept his wine paraphernalia somewhere in there. She prayed he did. *Stupid! Why didn't you search for the damned corkscrew when you brought the wine home?*

When she turned her attention back to arranging the roses, he rummaged through a couple of the drawers and located the implement, then opened the bottle with practiced ease. She turned and watched as he completed the task. Of course he'd know all about fine wines. She only hoped the man at the wine shop hadn't steered her wrong on the Chardonnay.

He inspected the vintage with raised eyebrows. "I'm impressed." When she picked up the bowl of shrimp and the beluga canapés and carried them into the living room, he thought, *I'm also in way over my head.* This woman was used to the finer things, no doubt about it. He pushed the troubling thought out of his mind and followed her, placing the wine bucket on the low kidney-shaped table near the fire.

Gilly arranged the food while he poured the cold golden liquid into two of Charis's Waterford flutes. They settled down on a big pile of pillows she had artfully arranged directly in front of the crackling fire. Handing her a glass, he raised his to salute her. When she responded, the clear ring of crystal sang in the air, air now filled with intense anticipation. As they sipped, their eyes never broke contact.

Then Jeff leaned forward and skewered a fat shrimp from the bowl. He held it out for her to take a bite. When she did so, he popped the other half into his mouth. Suddenly Gilly had difficulty remembering how to chew. He smiled at her, and she took his dare, picking up a canapé and offering him a bite. As he swallowed it, she watched the movement of his throat. Even the man's Adam's apple was sexy!

"I saw that once in a movie," he said.

"Tom Jones?" She watched him fork another shrimp and offer it to her, only this time instead of waiting for her to finish, he bit into the other end. As they slowly chewed toward the center, he slid the fork out and tossed in onto the table. Their lips met in the middle, tasting of sweet shellfish and salty caviar. After a quick brush that left every nerve end in her body zinging, he took her wineglass and offered her a sip. She drank. Then he turned the glass to the exact spot she'd sipped from and took a swallow, dark hooded eyes fixed on her lips.

"I guess some things are worth waiting for," she finally managed to whisper.

"Yes," he replied, placing the wineglass on the table and raising his fingertips to trace the bow of her lips. When her tongue darted out and caressed the pad of his index finger, he inhaled sharply. "I think we've waited long enough."

"Oh, yes," she breathed, but then her eyes grew round, her cheeks pink once more, as she pressed one hand to his chest, holding him off. "Do you have . . . that is . . . er—"

"I used to be a Boy Scout," he said, withdrawing a condom from his shirt pocket and laying it on the table beside them, charmed by the way she ducked her head shyly. "Now . . . where were we? Ah, yes." Jeff reached up and began unfastening the jeweled combs holding her hair, letting the long, pale copper strands fall heavily around her shoulders. He took one silky curl and raised it to his lips, rubbing it sensuously across his cheek. "You have lovely hair. Never cut it, please?"

"When you put it that way, how could I?" she replied as she melted into his embrace. They fell back on the pillows, hands and mouths caressing, exploring, devouring. Gilly could feel the warmth of his palm glide over her calf and the curve of her hip as he slowly pulled up the silk caftan, revealing her legs and the tiny bit of gold silk that comprised her panties. When his hand gently snapped the elastic, her hips arched reflexively.

"It's been so long . . ." Her words, low and breathless, faded away.

"Then we'll go slow," he murmured against the curve of her shoulder.

"But not too slow," she whispered, unbuttoning his shirt and nuzzling her way through the cunning pattern of hair on his chest.

When her tongue circled a hard male nipple, he growled low and his hands glided up to cup her breasts. "Mmm, no bra. I didn't think so."

"I used to be a Girl Scout . . . I came prepared, too," she said, pushing her breasts into the exquisite caresses of his fingertips and palms.

"Oh, you'll come, all right, over and over if I have my way."

"Do have your way with me, sir," she whispered, then added with a low chuckle as she began unzipping his fly, "and I'll have mine with you." He was as big and hard as the fireplace poker, as hot to her touch as the flames. When she pulled his erection from his jeans and began stroking it, he made a fierce sound deep in his throat that thrilled her.

If this kept up, he'd lose it before they went much further. Jeff remembered a cardinal rule and focused on it. "Shoes first," he whispered hoarsely, removing her busy hand. He sat up to pull off his loafers and socks. Then he gathered the soft folds of her caftan and pulled it over her head.

She raised her arms as the caftan floated to the carpet behind her, and he studied the slender perfection of her body. The pose emphasized the pert thrust of her breasts. They were not large, but neither were they small, just perfectly proportioned, high and firm, with nipples of palest pink, now crinkled into spiky little points, begging for his mouth.

The heat of his breath sent shivers of delight over her as he opened his lips to take one achy nipple, drawing it in delicately for the exquisite ministrations of his tongue. Then he moved to the other nipple and repeated the process, alternating between them while her fingers massaged his scalp, pulling him closer, arching into the pleasure.

"God, you taste sweet," he murmured, then gasped when her hand once more found his shaft. He let her stroke it several times while he continued suckling and teasing her breasts; then he rolled away and tugged the tight jeans off. He was aware of her eyes fastened avidly on his naked body, could tell she was pleased with how it looked. Women always were. . . .

Gilly opened her arms as he moved over her, wrapping them around his back, pulling him closer so their naked flesh pressed full length. Never had she been more aware of how small, slender, and soft she was. His body was hard, the muscles sleek and powerful. She buried her face in the curve where his neck met one broad shoulder and began kissing her way to his jawline. He had shaved very close, for she knew his beard was heavy. By morning there would be a dark stubbly shadow, and that, too, would be sexy as hell.

Jeff balanced his weight on his elbows and began kissing her, his tongue plunging and teasing, hers returning the caresses in equal measure. For all her blushes and shyness, she was a hot little thing, deprived of sexual pleasure for a long time. Not that he'd exactly had the time—or inclination—to be Don Juan himself the past few years. This was the time for them . . . together.

He reached back and grabbed the condom from the table, then quickly put it on and returned to her waiting embrace. He slid his palm over the concave surface of her belly, feeling the clenching need deep inside her, then slipped his fingers under the lacy wisp of her panties and cupped her mound. She arched up into his hand, crying out his name. When he began working the fabric over her hips, she raised her bottom and twisted smoothly so the tiny bit of silk slid off in his hand. He raised it to his face and breathed in the sweet musk.

"I've soaked them," Gilly whispered, shocked at her boldness, but it seemed to please him.

"Now," he murmured, positioning himself between her thighs and raising up so he could look at her as he slid slowly inside her body. Her legs went up, wrapping around his hips as she arched her back, waiting for his thrust.

"Now," she repeated.

It was heaven. Slick, gliding, undulating heaven. Every nerve in her body screamed with the unbearable sweetness of the pleasure. Never before had it felt so keen, so instantaneous, so effortless as it did with Jeff. This was more than the end of a long abstinence.

I'm falling for this guy!

The thought came out of nowhere, but before she could examine it further, he began to increase the tempo, and the mounting frenzy of her need drove every thought from her mind.

Like a wild woman she clung to him, her nails scoring his back, her thighs squeezing his hips, her back arching to meet each thrust.

"Little hellcat," he rasped, loving her wild, uninhibited response, waiting for what he could sense was fast approaching. She was so small and tight that he could instantly feel her orgasm begin, the hard, rippling contractions wringing from him an answering response. Jeff watched her eyes glaze over, the lashes fluttering down. Her body convulsed, flushing pink as she gave everything to her release.

He'd never seen a woman react so strongly, last so long. But his flash of male pride was quickly displaced when a wave of tender possessiveness swept over him. This could become habit forming, this woman, loving her this way. Not a thought he was expecting to consider the instant before the climax of his lifetime struck him like a tidal wave.

"Ah, Gilly, what have you done to me?"

The words were softly slurred into her hair as they lay in a welter of entwined arms and legs. She wasn't sure she'd heard him right or what the words meant.

Does he love me, too?

Chapter Four

Faint streaks of dim December sunlight climbed across the big rumpled bed where Gilly and Jeff finally ended up sleeping, but not until after they had spent most of the night making love, feeding each other shrimp and caviar, sipping wine before the fire, then resuming their passion. Gradually they worked their way from the living room into the king-sized water bed, although neither one could have said how they got from one room to the other.

Gilly awakened to the gentle motion of water when Jeff rolled over, placed one arm possessively across her breasts, then drifted back into deep slumber. Dreamily she recalled that last night with him gave a whole new meaning to

189

the term *motion sensitivity*. Jeff. She turned her head and studied him as he slept.

Thick black lashes veiled his eyes. Their rich brown depths had glowed like coals before the fire last night. What a waste to hide those incredible eyes behind glasses. He probably had to wear them in self-defense—to keep every woman he encountered from tearing off his clothes! She touched the abrasive stubble of heavy black beard on his jaw. Last night it had been shaven so smooth that he barely left a mark on her inner thighs. She grew taut and wet just remembering the way he had held her buttocks cupped in his hands and proclaimed in that low, sexy voice that the real feast was only beginning. Never before had she experienced such utter abandon with a lover. Never before could she have allowed one to take her that way.

This is it.

Charis had told Gilly that the first time she slept with Bill she knew he was the one. Gilly had secretly scoffed at the notion. She wasn't scoffing now. It had just happened to her. And the man who'd made her impossible dreams come true believed she was a high-powered hardcover editor from a wealthy family in small-town America. How could she ever justify her deception? Or tell him the truth?

Whoa, Gilly, she reminded herself. She was putting the cart before the horse. Just because she had gone bonkers over him did not mean that he reciprocated the feelings. Okay, he had said a few things in the heat of passion that could be construed as admissions that he cared. But he never said he was in love with her . . . in so many words. And even if he had, it had been in the heat of passion. Whew, boy, it had been a blast furnace of passion!

She wriggled up in bed and sat with his arm draped casually over her lap. Unable to resist, she let her fingers glide over his hair, thick and night dark, a bit tangled from their earlier exertions. He did look a bit like a book-cover model—not the bodybuilder type, but just as much a woman's fantasy. Her fantasy. Her hand ranged over his shoulder, stroking the sleek muscles as she studied the soft dark hair on his forearm. Without warning he suddenly rolled over and caught her hand in his, pulling her down on top of him.

"Good morning," he said in a low, sexy growl as his fingers tangled in her hair, bringing her face down to his. Between breathless kisses she returned the greeting, and he asked, "Sleep well?"

"You know I did . . . what little time I actually had to sleep."

"Now she's complaining," he teased, one hand roaming from her buttocks to the curve of her breast.

"I'll give you exactly a day or two to cut that

191

out," she said, arching into his palm.

"Mmm, think I may take a while longer."

He continued the slow, languorous caresses until she was half wild with desire. She straddled his hips, their legs tangled in the badly rumpled covers. She gazed down at him, watching as he continued making love to her breasts, cupping them in his palms, pulling the nipples and rolling them between his thumbs and index fingers. The world was spinning out of control. She placed her hands on his hairy chest, feeling the accelerating thud of his heart. Then she felt his straining erection brush against the crack of her buttocks.

"Think you can hold out longer?" she teased.

"Longer than you. Want to bet?" he murmured, seemingly engrossed in the way her nipples crinkled tighter and tighter under his ministrations. He raised his head, pulling her down so he could replace his hand with his mouth.

When she scooted back to accommodate him, she also reached down to grasp his stone-hard penis. His groan was muffled against her breast as she centered her body over it, guiding it very slowly inside. Then she stopped, breathless herself, and whispered, "Want me to stop?"

"My sweet little cock-teaser," he murmured, his hands now sliding over her hips, arranging them to his and her intense satisfaction.

When they again lay breathless and exhausted in each other's arms, he said, almost as if to himself, "It's amazing. I can't seem to get enough of you. You make me insatiable, Gilly girl."

"Hmm, I'm a cock-teaser, and you're a satyr. A match made in heaven?" she murmured with a chuckle. "I've never felt this . . ." *Go easy*, an inner voice cautioned. "This at ease with anyone before. It's comfortable with you—I mean, besides how we fit during sex."

He seemed to consider her words, then nodded. "You're right. And the way we fit during sex is a hell of a lot more than just comfortable, although I'm damned if I know an adjective to do it justice."

They lay in contentment for several more minutes, but suddenly he tensed and pulled away from her, looking over at the bedside clock. "It's nearly noon!"

"So? It's Saturday. You can't have classes on a Saturday afternoon, can you?" Gilly sat up, confused.

Jeff practically leaped from the bed and stalked naked down the hall, calling over his shoulder, "Not class, a . . . study session . . . with several other students. I have to run. I'm really late, Gilly."

By the time she grabbed her robe from the bathroom door and made her way to the living room, he was dressed and slipping on his loafers. He walked over to her and took her in his arms, pressing a kiss on her forehead. "I'm sorry, babe. I'll call you tonight when I get off—er, get finished."

Gilly had kept her phone by her side all afternoon and evening, several pencils and two manuscripts also lying beside her on the big sofa. She tried to concentrate on editing, but her heart just wasn't in it. Everything had been going so great . . . or so she thought. Had she done something to scare him off? She hadn't told him that she loved him or indicated that she expected some sort of commitment. Maybe she just gave off vibes that told men how she felt. Or, worst-case scenario, maybe now that he'd finally gotten her into bed, she'd lost her allure. Some guys were like that, but Gilly would have bet her life that Jeff Brandt was not one of them.

It was nearly ten that night when he called. He sounded beat. Gilly's heart nearly melted with tenderness when she heard his voice. They talked for half an hour, speaking of the kinds of inconsequential things lovers often do. He wanted to return to her place, but he had a big exam coming up on Monday and needed to study. He sounded disappointed. She was, too. But she had two edits to finish by Monday as well. They made a date for Monday night.

Jeff was going to pick her up at work. She figured she could make it from Leisure Books to the lobby in FS&G's building by half past five if she rushed. But at four-thirty her cell phone rang. Jeff had a "family emergency" and couldn't make it. They met the next night, and he was brimming with apologies, although not very forthcoming about what crisis had taken place in Scarsdale. He took her to a small Indian restaurant up by Columbus Circle, where the food was fabulous.

By the time they reached the Park Avenue apartment, Gilly had other things on her mind than family crises. He left her after midnight, saying he had an early-morning class. She had to be at work early, too. But sleeping in that big bed without him had become quite lonely. And, after all, they only had two weeks before Charis and Bill returned to reclaim their luxurious living quarters. Gilly didn't want to waste a single day.

Which led her to consider what she'd do when she was forced to return to her Yonkers apartment. How would she explain that they couldn't use her place any longer? She racked her brain for several days, trying to work up her courage to confess the deception, but every time she was on the brink of doing it, something would interfere. Either she'd lose her nerve or he'd break their date.

The abrupt breaking of dates was beginning to worry her. What if he was like Frank Blane after all? What if he had a wife or another girlfriend tucked away in his Washington Square apartment? When Charis phoned her from Nice, she laid out her misgivings about the relationship to the only friend she could confide in.

Charis didn't beat around the bush. "Arrange some excuse to go down to NYU and meet his roommate. But before you even waste time doing that, call the university and verify that they have a Jeffrey Brandt enrolled in the law program."

"But . . . that's so cold . . . as if I don't trust him."

"Well, why should you?"

"Yeah, he could be lying just like me, right?"

"You said it, sweetie, I didn't," Charis chided gently.

The next day Gilly did some detective work. There was indeed a Jeffrey Lyle Brandt enrolled as a third-year law student at NYU. Although his family had an unlisted number and Gilly had to ask a big favor from an old Oberlin classmate working for the phone company, she learned that a Lyle Bearsford Brandt lived in a Scarsdale. From another classmate practicing law on Long Island, she found out that Mr. Brandt was a retired attorney. Jeff was who he said he was. The only thing remaining was to check out the roommate and verify that he was a he.

"Would you believe the coincidence, Jeff—I'm going to be attending an afternoon workshop at NYU tomorrow. Can we meet somewhere for coffee—that is, if you have time?" Her voice sounded breathy and frightened; she had always been a terrible liar. *Except when you came up with that whopper about your job.* Ignoring the small squeak of conscience, she made arrangements to meet him on campus after his last class of the day.

The coffee shop was small and crowded, a favorite hangout for grad students. As they wended their way through the chairs and tables overflowing with a motley assortment of humanity, Gilly scanned faces. Long-haired hippie types with untrimmed beards and Birkenstocks argued vehemently with preppy-looking youths in button-down collars and Dockers.

"Does Karl hang out here?" she asked brightly. "I'd love to meet him."

Jeff shrugged, taking her coat, then pulling off his bomber jacket and piling them on what might have been the only unoccupied chair in the place. "Sometimes he's here. His schedule is pretty crazy."

"Whose isn't? This is the first time we've made contact in nearly a week," she replied.

He leaned down and brushed his lips across her neck as he pulled out a chair for her, murmuring, "We haven't made contact yet."

"Well, if Karl isn't at your place . . ."

"It's a student dump—two guys batching it, Gilly. Considering what your apartment is like—"

197

"You're a student. I was one once, and I remember what my place looked like—a mix of *Escape from New York* and *Angela's Ashes.*"

He studied her face for a moment as they sat at the small table with noise and people pressing in on them. "You are really incredible, Gilly. You're bright, beautiful, successful, you have everything you want—"

"Not everything, Jeff." Her fingers stroked over the back of his hand, tracing the pattern of dark hair delicately with her nails.

"Let me see if Karl's around." He squeezed her hand, then stood up and made his way to the bar, where he talked with a balding man sporting a belly that hadn't come from drinking expresso. As he served up coffees, he pointed across the room to a corner table near the window. There sat a tall, lanky man of indeterminate years who bore a remarkable resemblance to Jimmy Stewart, his concentration focused on an oversized textbook and papers spread out across the table.

Jeff motioned for her to join him as he wended his way over. "Hey, Karl. Dr. Oppermann laying it on again?" he asked as Gilly joined them. Placing his arm around her shoulders, he said, "I want you to meet—"

"You have to be the legendary Gilly Newsom," Karl said with a smile as guileless and open as a Kansas cornfield, which exactly matched his origins.

As he stood up and offered her a chair, they exchanged introductions. Jeff went off to bring them coffee. "Jeff says you're a Midwesterner. So am I. Ohio."

"I could tell by your lack of accent. Everyone on the coast has one. You ever notice that for all the kidding we get about being hicks and hayseeds, all the national newscasters talk like us, not New Yorkers, Southerners, or New Englanders?"

Gilly liked him already. "How long have you and Jeff been rooming together?"

Karl Mathis scratched his thinning brown hair and considered. "Let's see, I started law the term after Jeff, so that makes it about a year and a half now. With both our crazy schedules, we hardly ever see each other."

"Jeff says you really hit the books every night."

"Have to. I'm not as smart as he is."

Jeff rejoined them, and they talked for a while and sipped the scalding, inky brew. Gilly liked Karl—a plus, considering that she wouldn't have cared if he were an ax murderer as long as his name was Karl, not Karla.

Chapter Five

Everything should have been perfect after that. Gilly even thought up a stall for when the Lawrences returned to claim their apartment: the owners of the building were doing a massive repainting project, and she would have to vacate the premises for the holidays and stay with a friend up in Yonkers. That left her with a few more weeks to work up the courage to tell Jeff the truth.

But her confession to him had taken a backseat to other concerns. The broken dates were beginning to bother her. Bother her a lot. If he had to work the way she had to put herself through college, or if he'd had to really beat his brains out with the books, like Karl, she'd have understood. But Gilly knew better. Jeff was uncommonly bright. Karl had told her about his GPA and how effortless the law classes were for him. She also knew that no one with parents in Scarsdale's elite needed to hold down a night job. The hours during which he mysteriously disappeared were far too erratic for that anyway.

Gilly desperately wanted to confront him and ask point blank what was going on, but her guilt over her own deceptions held her silent. The strain in their relationship was telling on both of them. Just as she was leaving the office, her cell phone rang. "This is Gilly," she answered.

"Hello."

She could sense the hesitancy in his voice. "Hello yourself. We still on for dinner and a movie tonight?"

"That's what I'm calling about. Something's come up."

"This is the third time in the past week, Jeff." God, she sounded like a nag. Like someone who actually had a claim on him.

"I'm sorry, Gilly. Look, it's the end of the term, and I have all these projects to complete for my classes." Jeff racked his brain for something plausible. *Damn idiot, introducing her to Karl, so she knows enough to realize I haven't been studying all those nights!*

"But this is such short notice, Jeff." All his broken dates seemed to come that way—that, or he would simply be unavailable for days.

He could hear the chilly tone in her voice, and it fueled his guilt. "Professor Anderson has offered a chosen handful of the favored a chance to hear him expound on the New York State bar exam tonight. I can't pass up the opportunity."

"I thought Karl said Anderson had already left on sabbatical."

Now the tone of voice had shifted to decided suspicion. He cursed beneath his breath. "Sorry, Gilly, but I really have to go."

The next day, just as she was leaving for work, he arrived at "her apartment" with a big bouquet of white roses and a contrite expression. "Forgive me, please? I don't intend for anything to come between us, but you should understand how important finishing my degree is to me."

"How can I refuse when you put it that way?" She took the flowers and turned to reach for a vase. He slipped his arms around her and nuzzled her neck. "Enough of that or you'll make me late for work—and don't you have class this morning?"

He sighed theatrically. "You would have to remind me. Yes, I do, but we can at least take the subway together."

She put the roses in water, and they headed to the station, walking briskly in the chill December air. "There's something I've been meaning to ask you, Jeff."

He stiffened, faltering a step, covering it quickly "Shoot."

She forced a merry expression and teased, "Don't panic, it's not a proposal. Just a special occasion that I'd like you to share with me. My best friends are coming back to town next week and they always give a Christmas party at Windows on the World—you know, the restaurant at the top of the World Trade Center. Charis reminded me about it when she called last night. It would mean renting a tux. Although I know you'd look smashing in one, you might not want to, but—"

"You're babbling again, Gilly," he replied, interrupting her with a swift kiss on the cheek. "When is this stellar event?"

"On Tuesday, seven in the evening."

There was a hesitancy in her voice that puzzled him. Hell, she was right. He'd had enough of society events and monkey suits to last him a lifetime . . . especially monkey suits. But for Gilly he'd do it. "It's a date, kiddo. I just might be able to find an old tux buried somewhere in the back of my closet."

"Along with your sweaty gym shoes and that awful kelly green sweater?" Karl had taken to doing a lot of studying at the law library on campus the past few days—she suspected Jeff had asked him to allow them a bit of privacy—and Jeff had finally brought her to his apartment, which was really not as dreadful as he described.

"That's my lucky sweater."

"Why? You weren't wearing it the day you ran into me."

"Conceited woman," he groused, but before he could say anything more, Gilly gasped sharply. He, too, could hear the sudden screech of a dog in pain. It was coming from across the street, where a squat, muscular man was thrashing a rottweiler with the handle of the dog's leash. The cracking of leather striking the dog's snout and legs made Jeff wince. Gilly started across the street with fire in her eyes, but before she could get two steps off the curb he was beside her.

"Let me handle this." She did not protest, but neither did she stop following as he darted between cars to the other side. Jeff sprinted toward the guy flailing the hapless animal, a half-grown pup who cowered against the pavement. His tormentor now stood spread-legged over the rottie, ignoring the hard looks he received from a number of passersby.

"You stupid, worthless piece of crap! Trip me one more time 'n I'll kick yer brains in!" He started to raise the leash again, cursing loudly as he did it. He did not hear Jeff approach but was vividly aware the instant Jeff reached between his spread legs from behind and grabbed the front of his jacket, jerking it down roughly with one hand as he yanked the man's collar back with the other. Since the most delicate portion of his anatomy was now squeezed by his own coat, the abuser was forced to stand on tippy-toes, gasping for breath.

"What the f—"

"Is this your dog, you bastard?"

Gilly had never heard Jeff sound so street hard—a far cry from a scholar from Scarsdale. She paused on the curb, then reached out to grab the pup's leash when the thug dropped it. The poor beast was trying to crawl away. Gilly crouched to gather it in her arms, crooning to it as she listened for the reply to Jeff's question.

The man shook his head as best he could, bleating out, "N-no, I'm . . . hired . . . to walk it."

"Hired by whom?"

"Careful Canine Care Service." His rough bass voice was rapidly becoming a thin falsetto as Jeff's maneuver jeopardized the family jewels.

"Good," Jeff said, releasing the coat collar and driving his fist into the back of the man's neck, sending him sprawling facedown on the dirty concrete. "Then I'll see to it you're never paid to abuse another helpless animal."

By this time a crowd had gathered, watching the altercation. A small, dapper-looking man with a thin mustache stepped toward Jeff and extended a business card to him, saying in a crisp British accent, "Ever so glad that rotter finally received his comeuppance. He's been abusing that dog for days. He's received precisely what he deserved, but we do live in a rather litigious age. If you require a witness to testify on your behalf, please feel free to call upon me."

As he strolled briskly away, Jeff studied the card, which read:

Wentworth Flexner, Esq.
Labor Relations Consultant
I handle Union Problems
I handle Management Problems

In one corner was an address and phone number, in the other a picture of what looked like a chess piece. As Jeff was puzzling over it, an elfin little old lady in a nylon jogging suit gave her name and number to Gilly.

"I saw everything, dearie. That monster got exactly what he deserved. I hope your friend busted his nuts as well as his nose." She turned to the subject, who still lay groaning on the pavement. "Filthy offal!" She spit on him, then turned to Gilly and whispered, "That means *shit*, dearie."

Jeff walked over to them just as the elderly woman was departing. He knelt beside Gilly and stroked the pup's nose, which was bleeding from a cutting blow with the leash handle. He picked up the rottweiler and said, "Let's take him into the lobby of that building and call Careful Canine Care Service. I think they will be very interested to learn they hired a jerk who's been abusing their customers' pets."

"You were a real Sir Galahad," she said with a wide smile. "No one else had the courage to stop that brute."

"Hey, if I hadn't, you probably would've killed the guy. You should've seen the murder in those green eyes when you darted out into the street."

It took a half hour for the pet walking service to send a car to pick up Muffet, the rottie pup. The driver apologized profusely for the former employee's behavior and assured Jeff and Gilly that such an incident would never occur again. As the station wagon with the CCCS logo on it took off, they could see Muffet looking out the rear window at them.

"He's so sweet," she said wistfully.

"You really do miss having a dog, don't you?"

"Sure do, but lately there have been . . . other compensations," she replied with a teasing grin.

"Oh, great, now I'm in the same league as a puppy."

They laughed and teased as they resumed their walk to the station. Before they had to part for different trains, he kissed her tenderly and said, "I'll call you tonight, Gilly."

"Jeff?" She hesitated as he took her in his arms, oblivious of the rush-hour crowd bustling all around them. "About this party . . . it's pretty important. Charis and Bill are the nearest thing to family I have in the world, and I really want them to meet you." *Just like I want to meet your parents.*

They parted with his assurances that he would make the party, come hell or high water. Gilly tried to put her suspicions and fears out of her mind and concentrate on what she'd wear for the Lawrences' annual gala. Maybe that would be the best time to explain that she'd been staying in her friends' apartment and that she worked for Leisure Books, not FS&G. Maybe.

But why doesn't he want to take me home to meet his family? The thought had rankled ever since Thanksgiving. She had spent it with Charis and Bill as always, and Jeff had had his own plans, which she was certain involved his parents and sister. He hadn't invited her, nor had he made any mention of when he would introduce her to the exalted Brandts. Now Christmas was nearly here. She couldn't endure the thought of spending it alone or being baby-sat by the Lawrences again.

But Gilly held her peace. Time enough to worry about true confessions when Jeffrey Lyle Brandt made a few of his own.

Chapter Six

"Oooh, that dress should do it, kiddo." Charis Lawrence watched Gilly turn within the circle of mirrors outside the Bergdorf Goodman dressing room. They had been shopping for hours for the perfect gown for Gilly to wear to the big bash Tuesday evening. Down to the deadline as usual, they finally found it.

Gilly inspected herself critically. The dress was flaming orange red, a color she normally did not wear, but the dramatic shade did pick up the burnished highlights in her pale coppery hair and make her skin glow. The Grecian style left one shoulder bare. Diaphanous silk clung to her breasts and fell softly, whispering around her slender hips. The hemline was shirred up the right side, revealing the curve of her calf, even a bit of thigh.

"It's the most daring thing I've ever worn. And the most expensive," she said, turning again, unable to resist sliding her leg out and turning her ankle provocatively.

"You'll knock him dead. If that doesn't get a proposal, he's nerve dead from the waist down and you don't want him anyway."

"I'll settle for an introduction to his parents, Charis," Gilly replied wryly, then grinned. "Believe me, there is nothing whatever malfunctioning below his waist either."

"Bill did mention that the water bed seemed a little wobbly on its frame."

Gilly looked at her friend's big brown eyes, now crinkled with amusement. "You know I owe you big time for letting me use your place."

"Well, now that we have it back, how do you explain why you're living in Yonkers? You have to come clean with him, sweetie. After that you can name your firstborn after Bill or me."

"If only it was that easy, Charis."

"Read my lips and repeat after me: 'Jeff, I'm not an editor at FS&G. I work for Leisure Books editing historical romances.' See? It's not that difficult. If you confess the reasons you've always felt you needed to reinvent yourself—the *real* reasons, Gilly—this guy will understand. If he doesn't, he's a jerk and you're well rid of him. But if he's half the brilliant, sensitive, witty, charming, sexy gift to our gender you say he is, there's no way he won't come through for you."

Gilly hesitated. "I don't know, Charis. It isn't so simple. Why should I lay myself bare when he's keeping secrets, too? What the hell is he doing when he breaks all those dates with me?"

"I thought you established that Karl isn't Karla and that Jeff is a bona-fide law student at NYU with parents living in Scarsdale."

"Yes . . . but why all this mystery and the made-up excuses? I did some more checking. Professor Anderson *did* leave on sabbatical the week before Jeff said they were meeting to discuss the bar. He lied to me, Charis."

Her friend wore a troubled expression now, all traces of her earlier good humor gone. "It doesn't look good, does it? There's only one way to find out. You have to take the bull by the horns and ask him—but first you need to 'fess up yourself. No better time than when his guard is down. And you in that dress should sure do the trick."

In spite of Charis's words, the lovely gown seemed to lose its allure as Gilly stood looking at her reflection in the mirrors. "You're right. Tomorrow has to be the moment of truth."

Gilly put the finishing touches on her makeup, dusting sparkling powder across the bridge of her nose to hide her freckles. Were they still visible? She squinted into the small mirror on her dressing table. It was as dingy and cramped as everything else in the apartment. Jeff and Karl's place had a sort of Washington Square ambience about it, with Guggenheim prints on the walls, law books scattered on the coffee table, and multicolored beads partitioning the kitchenette from the living room.

"The only 'ambience' in this dump is the rhythmic clunk of the water pipes," she muttered as the kitchen sink gave another ominous gurgle. What would he think of it? Of her, for leading him to believe she lived in the lap of luxury? But she'd spent the last few days thinking things through and finally reached the decision that, for good or ill, she would tell Jeff the whole truth about her life. The deception was getting more and more complicated, the lies multiplying. How had she let things get so out of hand? Here she was, really gone on this guy, and the whole relationship was built on sand—with the tide rushing in.

Her guts were knotted tighter than old Mrs. Kleinschmidt's fists. As if she didn't have enough on her mind, the hateful super had left a note in her mailbox saying that starting next month, rent would no longer include heat. It seemed that some tenants were "abusing their privileges." Yeah, by renting out their bedrooms as meat lockers. Still, it was the least expensive place she'd been able to find in any neighborhood that was safe for a lone female.

Maybe she could fix up the joint before Jeff saw it. A little paint, a few bright scatter rugs over the worn carpet. She could even dig out those neat posters she'd saved from her stint working in that travel agency and hang them on the walls. The idea cheered her for a bit as she stood and began to slip into the dress. Buying it had maxed out her BG charge, not to mention the Ferragamo heels and matching bag she had splurged on to complete the ensemble. Charis had pronounced it "off the Richter scale" when they finished shopping.

Gilly glanced at the clock. The Lawrences were sending a limo for her in less than fifteen minutes. Just thinking of Jeff in a tux made her mouth alternately water with desire, then go bone dry with fear. What if he was furious with her? Or what if, after her heart-wrenching true confessions, he still refused to share the secrets of his life?

The sound of the buzzer brought her out of the cloud of angst. The limo was here to take her to Windows on the World in lower Manhattan, where Jeff would meet her. "This is it, Gilly. Show time."

"You simply must end this ridiculous feud with your father, Jeffrey. It's breaking my heart." The cultivated Vassar tone of his mother's voice was always underlaid with a petulant whine. If Clarissa Vandergriff Brandt had a heart, it was at least a ten-karat blue-white diamond. "Here; he wants to speak to you," she said, obviously signing off after delivering a ten-minute toll call's worth of guilt.

Jeff paced back and forth in the bedroom of his Village apartment. Damn, why did his parents have to pick this evening to break their year-long silence? He held the phone between his ear and shoulder as he fastened cuff links and slipped into the highly polished black shoes that came with the rental tux. The jacket hung suspended from the rod on the doorframe, waiting for him to slip it on and head out to meet Gilly.

He couldn't believe what it was costing him to please that woman. It must be love.

"Jeff, I won't beat around the bush," Lyle Brandt said in his best courtroom voice. "Keith Largent and I played squash together this afternoon." Largent was an old college pal of the district attorney. Jeff knew what was coming. "Are you still intent on throwing away a brilliant career?"

"If by throwing my legal career away you mean becoming an assistant DA, yep, that's my plan, Dad."

"In spite of your less than judicious choice of NYU instead of Harvard, you've achieved sufficient academic distinction to gain entry to a number of the city's most respected firms—with my connections, of course."

"We've been through all this a thousand times, Dad, from the day I came to you and told you I was enlisting in the Navy. I won't spend my life riding on your coattails." *And kowtowing to you like you did to Grandfather Vandergriff.*

"Damn my coattails! You possess enough hubris and intelligence to be a full partner in Bradford, Trent and Lange—if only you'd wake up and stop throwing away every opportunity. There's nothing to be gained in working in the bowels of the district attorney's offices. The prestige is in making partner in a fine firm, not to mention the crass matter of money. I'd surely think by now you'd have come to the realization that living without it can be . . . at the least, inconvenient."

"I've managed to pay my own bills for nearly eight years now. I like it that way." Nothing ever changed, Jeff thought dispiritedly. Why had he hoped his parents were finally going to offer an olive branch instead of a carrot attached to a very big stick?

"So that's your final word? You're going to throw your law degree away in the district attorney's office?"

"I'd rather put gangsters in three-thousand-dollar suits in jail than have them pay my retainer to keep them out," Jeff replied curtly.

"The self-righteous indignation of youth." Lyle's voice was sly now. "I was afraid our conversation would be as feckless as ever. Your mother really is distressed by your obstinacy, you know. That's why I decided on some rather, er, Draconian measures to bring you around. As you recall, before I retired, I sat on the board of the Blackthorne Scholarship Fund." Like the smooth trial lawyer he was, Lyle Brandt let the words sink in before continuing. "I still have friends on the board—those odious 'connections' you so disdain."

"Let me guess," Jeff said, fury rising with each breath. "You convinced them that my scholarship money should be cut off."

"Tuition is payable in advance, immediately after course registration, and this is your last term before graduation. It would be such a shame . . . almost as much of a shame as if you threw your life away prosecuting pimps and drug dealers."

"Like I said, Dad, I'd rather prosecute pimps than be one." Jeff slammed down the phone, then dug through a dog-eared Rolodex, found a number, and quickly dialed it. "Hello, Archie? Yeah, it's Brandt. That job you called me about the other day—is it still open?"

Gilly walked from the dance floor in a cloud of flaming silk. Heads turned, women's eyes hard with appraisal, men's with hunger. But she was as oblivious to the attention as she was to the stunning view of New York's skyline. The floor-to-ceiling windows showed off Manhattan to best advantage, glittering like a million winking diamonds spread on the black velvet of a December night.

She had danced with Bill Lawrence and a number of mutual friends, while her eyes eagerly scanned the doorway to the private dining room, waiting for Jeff to appear. It was well past eight, and dinner would soon be served. She had not been able to fit her cell phone in the tiny sequined bag and would not have carried the device regardless. *Is he breaking another date—this night of all nights?* The limo had been a little early. What if . . .

Gilly forced herself to push the horrible thought from her mind. But then worse ones flashed through it. Jeff lying bleeding on the pavement somewhere, victim of a mugger, or run over by a reckless cabbie.

"I'd say 'a penny for your thoughts,' but I don't have to ask," Charis said as Bill pulled out Gilly's chair and she took her seat at their table—next to the empty one reserved for her date.

"I don't know whether to wish him dead or call the hospitals to see if he's been admitted," Gilly said through gritted teeth.

"From the look on your face, I'd say it's a fair bet that he will be if he isn't already there," Charis replied.

When the messenger service delivered Jeff's

excuses at eight-thirty, Gilly alternated between sheer rage and hopeless tears, but pride kept her from resorting to a tantrum or a crying jag. She reread the terse message, then folded it up and placed it in her bag without further comment.

Dinner was served at nine. She shoved Belgian endive around on her salad plate, picked at her Lobster Newburg, and declined the Bananas Foster in spite of the ardent young waiter who dramatized his whole flambé act to impress her. When the dancing resumed, she made her excuses to her worried friends, feeling doubly rotten that she had put a damper on their holiday celebration because of Jeff's perfidy.

In the limo, she read the note over once more as icicles formed around her heart:

My Dearest Gilly,
No words are adequate to express how much I regret this. I would not willingly hurt you for the world, but I had no choice tonight. I'll call tomorrow and try to explain—if you'll let me.
Jeff

If you can explain your way out of this one, buster, either I have to be the most gullible fool since Eve ate that apple, or you're as slick as the serpent. Neither prospect appealed to her at all. But still her closet romantic's heart hoped . . . even as it ached.

Chapter Seven

Jeff sat bleary-eyed in his apartment, counting last night's take. He had made enough to pay the tuition—in one night. Of course, that still left the small matters of food, rent, and the loan payment for the better part of a year, but Jeff was far more concerned with how he was going to explain to Gilly why he had stood her up on her big gala evening. She had wanted him to meet her best friends, the nearest thing she had to family. He knew she also wanted to meet his parents, even though she'd been very careful not to say so directly. Gilly was the sort of woman who expected to be treated that way when a relationship became as involved as theirs had.

220

She was entitled to better than his last-minute retreats and unexplained absences. But was he ready for that kind of commitment? He honestly didn't know. What he did know was that Gillian Newsom scared him to death. She represented everything he had left behind after the last fight with his father when he'd left Scarsdale for good and went to see the world courtesy of Uncle Sam.

Although the Newsoms might have been from a small town in Ohio, they were clearly the same sort of socially prominent, hidebound conservative people as his family. And they were rich. Gilly surely made a very respectable salary working for a big publishing house, but that alone could not have paid for the way she lived. Family wealth must be kicking in to supplement her income. His career plans would put him in an income bracket barely above food stamps. And what about the way he worked his way through law school?

What would Gilly think?

Right now, she was his primary concern. He cared altogether too much for her. *But I won't be sucked into that kind of life. I hated it, and I'll never go back.*

Would she ask him to? They had never really talked specifically about where or how they would live. She probably assumed that he would fit in with her country club set. He had mentioned the idea of working in the D.A.'s office, but he doubted she realized what that would mean in terms of income.

Of course, he had never wanted to dwell on those sorts of long-term plans. They reeked of stultifying marriages. After observing nearly thirty years of his parents' life, then his sister and brother-in-law's, he was sure that was not what he wanted. But he was damned if he knew what he *did* want.

The telephone sat accusatorily on the bedside table. He started to pick it up and call Gilly. It was ten in the morning, and she was at work, even if she and her society friends had made a night of it. Of course, she might slam the receiver down the moment she heard his voice. "Can't blame her for that," he muttered under his breath.

He'd tried to phone her the moment he'd accepted Archie's offer yesterday evening, but her line was busy. He'd borrowed Karl's digital phone and tried again en route to the job, but he couldn't get through. All he could do was hire a messenger service to deliver his apologies.

Swallowing a considerable amount of pride, he picked up the phone and dialed.

Jeff's voice had sounded strained and tired. "Stop it. You're making excuses for him already!" she scolded herself. He could do that for himself, not her job, man. If he even deigned to try. All she'd ever gotten before was a simple apology with no frills added. Well, if you counted white roses, she guessed there were a few frills. But he couldn't buy his way out of this with flowers. Literally. He had no address for her place in Yonkers. He *couldn't* send flowers.

She stood glumly, watching the Christmas shoppers bustling all around her, carrying bags filled with gifts. Ice skaters glided across the rink at Rockefeller Center. The enormous tree, all bedazzled with lights, stood in the distance. A light snow was falling. And she was stalling.

Let him wait for me this time.

When he called, she had made a frosty agreement to meet him at a small Chinese restaurant near Rock Center at noon. It was now twelve-fifteen. Charis had walked into her office first thing that morning to check on her and offer advice. Gilly knew she had to confess her deception to Jeff, but there were some things that simply had to come first from him. Charis had agreed with her this time. In fact, her friend had urged her to really "kick his butt!"

Her footsteps came down hard on the snowy pavement as she made her way toward the small restaurant. He was waiting inside the dark interior, looking heart-stoppingly handsome. He wore jeans and that ratty old green sweater, his lucky sweater. *You're going to need a lot more than luck to get out of this one, bud.*

When she walked closer she could see in the dim light that he looked tired and haggard, with dark circles under his eyes. "Your night must've been even better than mine," she said without preamble, not letting her guard down.

He shrugged. A waiter glided up with menus and ushered them to a booth in the back. Although the room was crowded, conversations were muted, blending in a low hum. They removed their coats and hung them on the wall rack across from the booth, then scooted in opposite sides. As they looked across the table adversarially, the waiter took their drink order and beat a hasty retreat.

"I don't know how to start, Gilly. . . ."

"How about with where you were last night," she supplied, shoving the menu aside.

Jeff rubbed his eyes, which felt as if half the sand under the Coney Island pier was lodged behind the lids. "Look, I know you wanted me to meet your friends, and I fully intended to be there. . . ."

"Even if you didn't want to meet them? Look, Jeff, I guess I can see the handwriting on the wall. You're never going to level with me about who you are, other than that you're Lyle Brandt's son from Ridgecrest Drive in Scarsdale. I already know that. What I want to know—"

His head was pounding as he tried to think through how he was going to admit the truth to her when her last words hit him. Lawyerlike, he interrupted, "How do you know that?" At her

The Best in Love Spell Romance!
Get Two Books Totally FREE*!

An $11.98 Value! FREE!

PLEASE RUSH MY TWO FREE BOOKS TO ME RIGHT AWAY!

Enclose this card with $2.00 in an envelope and send to:

Love Spell Romance Book Club
20 Academy Street
Norwalk, CT 06850-4032

blank look, he continued, "I never mentioned my father's name, and I sure as hell never reminisced about fond childhood memories on Ridgecrest Drive."

Her face began to heat up. *Oh, shit!* "Well, I, er, that is, I sort of investigated to see if you were who you claimed you were. Charis said—"

"You society types sure do like to be certain of a guy's pedigree, don't you?" he lashed out before thinking. "What did you do, hire a discreet private detective to check up on me? That day you just happened to be on campus for a workshop—that was a setup, too, wasn't it?"

Guilt was written all over her face, but Gilly's own temper was beginning to simmer. In fact, it had just come to a full, rolling boil when he accused her of hiring a private detective. "I probably should've hired a detective to find out about you, since it was obviously the only way I'd ever get the facts straight. You never had any intention of taking me to meet your family, did you? All I was just some silly romantic fool to have a fling with, then walk away from, no strings! Well, let me help you out, Jeff." Abruptly, she slid out from behind the table, practically knocking over their approaching waiter as she whirled around to glare at Jeff. "I'm walking away first—no strings, no regrets."

Go after her, a voice deep inside him urged. He almost gave in to it but then sat back down with a sigh and cupped his aching head in his hands. Life was just too damn complicated.

The baleful-looking Chinese waiter seemed to agree. "You not order now, sir?" he said in halting English.

"Afraid not," Jeff muttered, pulling out his wallet and extracting enough to pay for the pot of oolong tea and a generous tip. "Never get involved with high society, my friend."

The waiter nodded gravely at the parting "fortune cookie" advice.

All afternoon Gilly thought she was going to die. By the time she left work, she was even more afraid that she was going to live. The rest of her life stretched before her, filled with endless Gwendolyn Gleeson manuscripts and no Jeff Brandt. She moped around her apartment without eating supper. Then a sudden fit of energy— or was it insanity?—sent her in search of Mrs. Kleinschmidt.

The super opened the door, her round face scrunched like a prune as she glared up at Gilly. "Yeah. Whaddya want? If you come to bellyache about paying yer own heat, find another place to live."

"I haven't come to complain, Mrs. K. All I was wondering was whether that paint was still in the basement and if I could look through it to see if there was a color I could use to paint my apartment."

"Yerself?" A look of intense suspicion crossed

her face. "You 'n' all them other troublemakers on the third floor always wanted me to hire someone to do it like I done the halls."

The halls had been painted three years before Gilly moved in, six years ago. Subway station walls were cleaner, but she forbore to mention that. "Yes, myself. I just wanted to spruce the place up a bit, sort of cheer myself up, since it's Christmas time."

Mrs. K made some sound between clearing phlegm and burping. The dozen or so hairs arranged over the top of her pink scalp jiggled as she nodded. "All right by me, I guess. KKK stored the stuff so anyone who wanted could use it. Themselves," she added meaningfully. KKK was the nickname tenants and super alike had bestowed upon Klinger & Kinsolving Consolidated, a slumlord corporation.

Half the night Gilly scraped, rolled, and brushed until she was ready to drop, then stood looking around at her handiwork. The once dingy place now had soft cream walls with celery-green trim. She hung some old prints from college and several travel posters. Tomorrow after work she'd go out and buy some new throw rugs, scatter pillows, and other accents to brighten up the oversized, garage-sale furniture.

She was turning over a new leaf, beginning a new life. *Yeah, and it's almost Christmas, and you're alone again.* Gilly made an early resolution. She would not inflict herself on her friends like some desperate orphan this year. She'd spend Christmas here in her own place and buy herself a real Christmas tree and surround it with presents—all for her. After what she'd been through, she had earned it.

"No way are you going to mope alone at home over the holidays!" Charis said. It was quitting time, and they were leaving the building. Gilly was loaded down with manuscripts she had not worked on because of her decorating frenzy the night before. "Look, girlfriend, I know this thing with Jeff hit you hard, but that's all the more reason not to be alone on Christmas."

Gilly pushed through the heavy glass door to the street and was greeted by an icy blast of wind. "That's all the more reason for me to learn to do just that. I know you mean well, Charis, but I have to stand on my own two feet. I've always been too . . . too needy, I guess."

"Given what you went through as a kid, you're entitled," Charis said as they trudged up Sixth Avenue toward the subway station.

"That's no way to go through life. Look at the trouble it's gotten me into."

"Man trouble, you mean."

"Yeah, I mean."

"Well, you need to meet somebody new, that's all there is to it."

"Give me a little time off to catch my breath

before you start fixing me up again, will you? I really need a break from this relationship thing."

Suddenly Charis stopped in her tracks, causing the woman directly behind her to veer around, giving her a dirty look. "So much for the Christmas spirit," she said, laughingly as they began to walk again. It was walk or be trampled in the holiday rush. "I have it, Gilly, the perfect ticket. It should be a blast. Bill will understand."

"It must be contagious. Now *you're* babbling, Charis."

Her friend chuckled, grabbing Gilly by the arm. "You and I, sweetie, are going to the holiday party the sales reps are throwing for Leisure and some of their other romance customers tomorrow after work. The entertainment should be exactly what you need. No relationships . . . but there should be a string or two involved." She giggled like a schoolgirl.

"I can't go through with it, Charis. Kathy Betterson just came up to me and positively leered when she described what goes on at these things. I can't believe the publishers actually attend it."

"Your Ohio roots are showing again, Gil. You're in the Big Apple now. A contingent from *RT* is coming. Rumor has it even Kathryn Falk and Carol Stacy are joining in the festivities this year, along with some of their staff." *RT, Romantic Times*, was the leading magazine in the romance genre, and getting its CEO and publisher to attend the party was quite a coup.

"It just sounds so . . . icky, Char. Remember, I'm a small-town girl at heart."

"You're from Cleveland, Gil," Charis reminded her. "Lighten up. It'll be fun."

Gilly had never approved of holiday office parties. They tended to be loud, raucous affairs where everyone drank too much and let loose inhibitions better kept in check. But Charis would give her no peace if she did not attend.

So that evening Gilly found herself entering the hotel suite where the party was being held. The big room was festooned with red and green balloons and holly wreaths. Mistletoe hung everywhere. There were a lot of faces she didn't recognize, mostly female. The sales reps, mostly men and far fewer in number, jovially obliged the laughing women who lined up to give them mock smooches.

A pair of bartenders stood at long tables covered with bottles and glasses, mixing everyone's requests while exchanging quips with the celebrants. Charis and Gilly made their way to the bar and ordered screwdrivers, then moved off to sip their drinks and join the revelry. After a while they got separated, and Gilly wandered to the room where the entertainment was scheduled to commence in a few moments. In the center of the room a large open area was surrounded by a circle of folding chairs about a dozen deep, all decorated with red satin bows.

"Take your seats, ladies and gentlemen—especially you ladies. The show's about to begin, and I know you won't want to miss a single thing." A big heavyset man with a microphone walked around shooing the revelers into the room. Gilly stood behind the door, wondering if he worked carnivals during the summer months. *Probably not much for him to do but this in the off season,* she sniffed to herself.

"C'mon, let's get front-row seats." Charis appeared out of nowhere, grabbing Gilly's arm and steering her forward.

Women were already swarming into the room like bees to a honey tree. "I don't think this is me, Char. I'd rather just stand in the back of—"

"No way, kiddo. You are going to sit up front, you are going to let down your hair, and you are going to have fun! Look, even the Lady of Barrow is taking a front-row seat, and so's Carol Stacy. If the CEO and publisher of the biggest magazine in the trade don't think they're too good to have a few kicks, why should you?"

Well, when Charis put it that way, it did make Gilly sound awfully stuffy. She allowed herself to be led down the aisle and took a seat in the second row, just behind the celebrities from *Ro-*

mantic Times. She noticed the editorial directors as well as various other high-ranking women employed by the publishing houses taking their seats. How bad could it be?

Chapter Eight

Then the music started—not the gyrating sort of hokum she'd expected, but a popular holiday song. The man who had been ushering the revelers into the room was now wheeling a low, wide cart down the aisle. On it sat a large package, gift-wrapped in red and white foil with a huge red satin bow on the lid. When he reached the center of the room, he stopped and set a hand brake on the very substantial-looking vehicle that had transported the "entertainment" into the room.

"Ladies, I give you Gentleman Johnny Jackson!"

With that, the emcee stepped away, and all eyes in the room fastened themselves on the big box stage center. Slowly the lid began to rise and slide ever so slowly over to one edge. Every female in the room seemed to hold her breath, Gilly included.

It must be the screwdriver. I never could drink without getting giddy.

Her eyes were glued to the top of that box just like everyone else's. When the lid began to fall, a female sales rep sitting in the front row jumped up and caught it in her arms, peeking inside the box with a squeal of delight. A red satin top hat appeared first, tossed casually over the rim of the box by a white-gloved masculine hand. Now every woman leaned forward on her folding chair. The top of his head emerged, followed by a pair of broad shoulders encased in a form-fitting red satin tux. He was facing the opposite side of the room as he slowly stood up, revealing . . . "Buns of steel!" a copyeditor sitting next to Gilly breathed in awe as the aforementioned tush began to move, ever so slowly, ever so sensuously, to the beat of the music.

The red satin tux pants looked spray-painted on his body as he stepped over the edge of the gift box and jumped lithely to the floor. He scooped up the top hat with one hand and placed it on his head at a rakish angle. Everyone was hypnotized by Gentleman Johnny.

"I never thought I'd say it, but I think this guy has a better bod than Bill—oh, God, don't you dare tell him I said that!" Charis whispered without taking her eyes off the long-legged man in red satin. She did not notice that Gilly was sitting very still, making no reply, her eyes wide and glassy as she stared at the tall man with the shoulder-length black hair.

It can't be. . . .

Her mind simply shut down. He did not have to turn around. She knew every inch of that gorgeous body—the broad shoulders, the long legs, the "buns of steel," and the graceful hands. Especially the hands—those slim, powerful hands, which he was now divesting of their gloves. Hadn't she studied the pattern of hair on their backs as he slept beside her? She knew the way he moved, the way he held his head, every nuance of his appearance. Even when he spun around and faced her side of the audience, Gilly could not fully take it in—Jeffrey Lyle Brandt, a male stripper!

Good grief! He's coming closer. She slid down in her seat, deathly afraid that he would recognize her amid the throng of eager women who were by now growing increasingly raucous as he began to shrug the shiny red satin jacket off one muscular shoulder. Gilly couldn't seem to tear her eyes from him and the incredible exhibition he was giving. *If I don't quit staring, he'll sense that it's me!* The surge of panic gradually subsided as a bitter thought stung her: She was hardly significant enough in Jeff Brandt's life for him to feel any special bond that would allow him to pick her out of a crowd, especially a crowd like this.

Flexing his knees and ever so subtly moving his hips to the music, he swung the jacket over one shoulder and strode across the floor like a devil-may-care hitchhiker, Clark Gable in *It Happened One Night*. When he lowered the jacket around the shoulders of Leisure's contracts manager, she nearly swooned before he whisked it away and sent it flying into the box. Then he pulled off his tie and tossed it to the back row. There was a veritable feeding frenzy as women clawed each other for the small piece of red satin.

Like those of every other woman in the room, Gilly's eyes followed avidly as he popped the rhinestone cuff links from his shirt and put them provocatively into one tight pants pocket. Then he started flipping the rhinestone studs from the front of his shirt into the audience. Joan Rivers might have said that if God had intended women to get down on the floor and exercise, He would have strewn it with diamonds, but in this case rhinestones worked even better. A dozen women were on their hands and knees, seizing the faux gems as he unfastened the cummerbund at his waist and used it playfully like a back scrubber, all to the beat of the music. He applied the sash to a few other more imaginative places, then tossed it, too, into the box.

By the time he had the shirt peeled open, revealing a dark thatch of hair that narrowed enticingly at the waistband of his pants, the women were shrieking and stomping like Greek maenads. Cries of, "Do it, Johnny baby!" "Bare your soul," and, "Yesssss!" echoed around the room, almost drowning out the music.

He left the shirt gaping open and turned his attention to his shoes. How the hell could a man taking off shoes and socks be sexy? Oh, it was, it was. "Oh, God, even his feet are gorgeous!" a young billing clerk whispered breathlessly to her companions.

Gilly watched the rhythmic balancing act as he stood on one foot, the other in midair, all the while moving with the music. He tossed one shoe over his shoulder into the box, then the other. She remembered watching Jeff go through his Tai Chi exercises, never imagining how much the discipline would help with the contortions he now performed. The roar of the crowd grew deafening when his hand moved to the fly of his pants.

At the rear of the room several high-ranking publishing executives stood in the shadow of the door. None were certain whether to be horrified or amused by their employees' enthusiasm. Deciding to go with the holiday spirit, they exchanged a few hearty chuckles and ordered more martinis.

"Omigod, he's going to do it!" Charis whispered to Gilly as Jeff began slowly lowering the zipper. But then, before she could notice her friend's frozen demeanor, he stopped, raising it once more.

Charis, like every other woman in the room, groaned . . . every woman but one. He teased them again and again as he made his way around the circle, playing the largely female crowd for all it was worth. There was a palpable sigh of satisfaction when the zipper finally stayed down. He let the fly gape open, revealing the pattern of black hair arrowing past the navel in his washboard abdomen to disappear tantalizingly below. His narrow hips gyrated in slow sync with the music, emphasizing the way the skintight red satin pants clung to his lower body as he shrugged off the white silk shirt and flung it onto the growing pile of clothes inside the box.

"I wouldn't have to do any Christmas shopping for my boyfriend if I could get my hands on that box," one editor said to another. "But then again, I'd a hell of a lot rather see Johnny wearing those clothes than Sam."

"I'd rather see Johnny *not* wearing them," her companion replied, eyes glued to the man as he began to ease the pants down with excruciating slowness, letting the women work themselves into an even greater frenzy.

The tips were better that way.

When he finally peeled them completely off and threw them into the box, one shiny red pant leg dangled over the edge, swinging to the music. He was six feet, two inches of lean, sinuous muscles and looked lightly tanned . . . everywhere. The tiny briefs didn't conceal much.

Now the money-making part of the event began in earnest. He gave them several minutes to look but not touch, dancing smoothly around the circle, almost but not quite daring them to make the first move. Someone always did.

It was an assistant art director, with a twenty-dollar bill and her business card. She boldly reached out and stuck both into the elastic band around his hips, whispering, "We simply must have you for a cover model. You're utterly perfect. Call me, darling."

He smiled and moved on as women began flinging bills of all denominations at him. Aware that two of the most influential women in the romance industry were sitting in the front row, he paused in front of them. They watched with rapt attention. Kathryn Falk, Lady of Barrow, stared up into the most fathomless brown eyes she'd ever seen, saying breathlessly, "I never carry cash. I suppose you're not equipped to process a credit card . . ." Her attention again moved down to his undulating hips and the scanty covering thereon. "Hmm, foolish of me to ask. Would you by any chance take a check, darling?"

"Gentleman Johnny" nodded with a blindingly white smile. Kathryn whipped out her checkbook and began to scribble, all the while darting glances at the stunning entertainer. She had to tear up two checks before finally completing one that was legible.

As she jammed it into his G-string, Carol Stacy continued rooting through her Louis Vuitton handbag like a demented squirrel searching for a cache of acorns. All she could find was a crumpled twenty-dollar bill. She stuffed it into his G-string and said apologetically, "I'm sorry it's so little. Oh, no! That's not what I meant—I meant the money . . . really . . . you're . . . fine . . . very fine."

He grinned at her and gave her a wink, then moved on. Kathryn leaned toward Carol and said, "We have to get that hunk for our next cover-model pageant. Would he ever be an asset!"

Enjoying the retreating rear of "Gentlemen Johnny," Carol only murmured, "Mmm . . ."

"Carol, are you listening?"

"I am, Kathryn, I am. He has a very fine asset . . . a superlative asset!"

Gilly sat near enough to overhear the exchange. So did Charis, who giggled and looked over at her friend. "At least I'll say this— he isn't some cheap bump-and-grind gigolo who shaves his body hair and lives on steroids. Everything this guy's got, he's got for real, no additives needed."

Then, for the first time, Charis noticed the

way Gilly was slouched down in her seat, practically cowering, her eyes wide with stunned shock. "Say, sweetie, are you all right? I mean, I didn't intend to gross you out . . . although I guess every woman in the place has already done that. I'm sorry. I—"

Charis stopped short as Gilly's eyes began to focus and narrow. Gilly's mortification at the chance of being recognized was finally beginning to shift to boiling fury. "How dare he do this to me! The hypocritical, conniving, sneaky, slimy, deceitful, wretched . . . did I say hypocritical?" Charis nodded dumbly. "He tricked me! He . . . he . . . he told me he was from Scarsdale. His mother raised Afghan hounds, and he was supposed to be a lawyer."

"Then all of the adjectives are appropriate," Charis said dryly, realizing with an irrepressible urge to guffaw that "Gentleman Johnny" was really "Gentleman Jeffrey." "This is too rich!" The whoop of laughter burst out before she could stop it.

Gilly turned to glare at her, then returned her narrowed eyes to Jeff. "I suppose you'll say I deserve it for telling a few fibs myself."

"A few fibs? C'mon, girlfriend. You told some whoppers."

Gilly ignored the still chortling Charis, whose attention had also returned to Jeff's body. He had made almost a complete circle of the room, working his way through the chairs, which

241

were now askew at all angles as the women jumped up, yelling, clapping, and throwing everything from cash to clothing. They blew kisses at him, the bolder ones going so far as to reach out and touch those "buns of steel" or tangle their fingers in his hair.

Somehow he always gracefully disentangled himself without ever seeming to put off a single woman. Now and then he would pause and reach out a hand to women who were shy or not particularly attractive, drawing them up for a light buss on the cheek, then carefully letting them down, collapsed in bliss on their chairs. By the time he'd worked three quarters of the crowd, his skimpy briefs were literally stuffed, front to back, with money . . . and slips of paper with phone numbers on them. The cash he'd keep, the other he wouldn't.

He was almost ready to call it a day and signal Archie to take down the lights so he could make his exit, when he saw her. It couldn't be. But it was. Her pale green eyes were blazing with wrath as they collided with his startled dark ones. *Shit!* How in hell did a literary editor from FS&G end up here?

Nothing to do but brazen it out. Struggling to maintain his professional persona, Jeff made his way toward her. Maybe now that she knew his dirty little secret, he could explain everything, and she would understand why he'd stood her up the night of her friend's party.

Then again, maybe not. She looked mad enough to chew nails and spit fence staples, as David Strongswimmer's dad used to say. He proceeded cautiously, aware as he had not been for several years, of the effect his act had on women. It was like trying to walk through a wall of limpets.

Jeff had thought after the first few months that he'd gotten over the acute embarrassment, but it came rushing back now. When she realized that he was trying to reach her, Gilly jumped up and practically climbed over the bodies of the people who were in her way, just to escape him. By the time he called out her name, she was down the aisle and out the door. He collected himself enough to give Archie the signal. The lights went down and the music rose to a crescendo as Jeff backed into the open circle and took a bow, then bounded up the aisle and disappeared to the roaring cheers of his fans. Archie followed with the gift box. One woman tried to snag the pant leg still dangling over its edge, but he foiled her by grabbing it first and tossing it inside.

Jeff raced through the suite and down the hallway, darting glances into the empty rooms, calling Gilly's name. She had vanished. Then he came to the ladies' room door and paused.

"Don't even think it, chum," Archie said, lighting up one of his Swisher Sweet cigars in spite of the NO SMOKING signs.

"She's probably gone anyway," Jeff replied, more to himself than to Archie.

"You gonna chase after her, ya better put a little more on first. If the cops don't getcha, the cold sure as hell will."

"Merry Christmas to you, too," Jeff replied with a snarled oath, then turned and headed into the men's room, where his street clothes were waiting. He knew there would be no Gilly waiting. Ever again.

"Dames is nothin' but trouble," Archie philosophized as they walked toward the elevator. "But they pay like hell won't have it if you got the right stuff. You could go for the big time, Jeff."

Archie had delusions of managing Jeff's "career." "No way. We've been over this before. I'm only doing it until I finish my law degree."

Charis Lawrence had lost Gilly in her headlong flight, so she regrouped and went looking for the man in her friend's life—or out of it, for the time being. Genuine concern tempered her raging curiosity about Gilly's mystery man. She staked out the men's room and waited, then followed at a discreet distance as he and his assistant loaded their gear into the freight elevator at the end of the hall.

"Well, Char, my girl, it's now or never," she whispered, steeling herself as she walked up to them and extended her hand in what she hoped was a calm, professional manner. *God, what if he thinks I'm going to give him my phone number—or a pair of panties!*

Chapter Nine

Christmas Eve afternoon. Gilly reached for the phone, almost desperate enough to call home. Home. As if she'd ever had one. Oh, there was the shabby old shotgun house just off Superior Avenue on the east side of Cleveland. Mill hand houses—that's what folks used to call them. Endless rows of narrow frame buildings, soulless in their austere similarity. Her family had lived in one, bought with the money Whalen Newsom had once earned before the steel industry started closing down and her dad became a brutal drunk. Her mom had stuck it out stoically, living with grinding poverty and abuse, unable to see any other possibilities.

She and Liv had. But that was where the similarity ended. Gilly had struggled for scholarships, while Liv had dreamed of Hollywood and instant stardom. Her older sister had dropped out of high school and run away with a sleazy actor, turning up drugged out and pregnant when Gilly was a freshman at Oberlin. She'd lost the baby but not the drug habit. It was the final thread to snap in Clarissa Newsom's life. Their mother slipped away that year, and Liv returned to the West Coast. She and their father heard from Liv occasionally, when she wanted money. Gilly sent what she could at first. Whalen used what little he had to buy Four Roses.

He was still alive, her dad. It was Christmas, and he was the only man in her life. A hell of a note. She dialed his number and let it ring half a dozen times before he answered. His slurred speech indicated that he was already celebrating the holiday, although it was only mid-afternoon. "Whaddya want?"

"Dad, it's Gilly. Just calling to wish you a Merry Christmas."

"Whozit?" a high-pitched female voice whined through the wires. Gilly listened as her father and his current floozy exchanged drunken curses, ending with the all-too-familiar sound of a fist hitting flesh. "Gilly, that you, girl? Hardly recognize yer voice after all this time. You never come around anymore.

Whatzamatter, too hoity-toity for an old steel-worker?"

"You know that's not true, Dad. I have a really tough job here in New York, and I don't get much vacation time. I—"

"Well, if you can't come, least you could do is send me a few bucks once in a while. I got another notice from the gas company." His voice was wheedling now.

Her stomach clenched. She knew he'd never given a damn about his daughters, any more than he had about his wife. "You have enough between your mill pension and Social Security to live on, Dad." *If you didn't drink it up.* "The house is paid for." *Thanks to Mom's working all those years at Kmart.*

"I don't need any of yer smart lip. I got expenses—medical expenses." He faked a cough.

Gilly knew he was as healthy as a horse in spite of having a liver the size of The Flats. Every dime she'd ever sent him went directly to the liquor store. "Have you seen Dr. Raymond?" She'd learned years ago that the best way to foil his manipulations was to check with their old family physician. Unlike Whalen, the doctor told her the truth.

The conversation deteriorated from there, ending with him yelling at her, "Yer just like yer no good sister and that bitch that spawned ya. Ain't no daughters of mine. Prob'ly the mailman's."

As he laughed drunkenly at his own witticism, Gilly quietly set the receiver back on its stand. She rubbed her eyes and leaned back in the overstuffed chair, which had now been covered with a moss-green throw. The room no longer looked like a hovel. In fact, her redecorating frenzy had wrought wonders. Warm earth tones dominated, with terra-cotta and cream-colored throw rugs brightening the dull neutral carpet, and melon and celery-green scatter pillows piled on the sofa. She stared at an immense poster of a southwestern desert scene, courtesy of Delux Travel, which hung over the faux fireplace mantel. She'd even splurged on new lace curtains in celery green and bought a small Christmas tree. After that she'd run out of energy. There were no presents under the pine.

The charming, cozy atmosphere did not lift her spirits. For a place to feel cozy it had to have more than one lonely, morose, self-pitying person in it. "Get a grip, Gilly. You'll survive. Lord knows you've already lived through worse," she muttered to herself. "If only I could have a dog for company, to hell with 'Gentleman Jeffrey'! There I go again, feeling sorry for myself."

She walked into the apartment's tiny kitchen—really an alcove off the living room—and opened the fridge. A carton of eggnog sat on an otherwise bare shelf. Hmm. Well, why not? She poured a cup two thirds full and topped it off with a generous swig of bourbon, then eyed it. "Better watch it or I'll end up like my father." The thought made her shudder. She took a swallow. Not bad. But she knew she had to be careful. After all, look what had happened when she'd imbibed only one screwdriver at that ghastly office party.

She had been ready to cut loose and act just as nuts as the other women. Even Charis had been wild. Whatever had possessed either one of them to go see a male stripper in the first place? It just wasn't their style. But her friend had sure gotten into the spirit of the thing. Jeff seemed to have that kind of effect on women. At first she hadn't noticed it so much because of the low-key way he dressed—the wire-rimmed glasses, the impoverished-student facade. But gradually she'd begun to see that all women—even ones as seemingly impervious as Abbie at the library—were suckers for a guy with those soulful chocolate eyes and that guile-less grin.

Gilly tried to think of something else—like why her best friend hadn't called since that ghastly debacle at the office party. All she had wanted to do was go home and lick her wounds, but she had at least expected Charis to phone and see that she was all right. "You told her you didn't want to be a burden on their holiday plans this year, so what are you bellyaching about?"

The question seemed to hang in the air. Maybe she hadn't intended for Charis to take her so literally. Maybe she wanted to see Jeff again. No! Who was she kidding? His face floated in her mind, haunting her awake just as it did in her dreams—actually, nightmares last night. He'd worn red satin again, only this time it was a devil's costume, not a tux, and he'd been leading her down the flaming path to hell. Not that she needed to be led—she was already there.

The phone jangled, interrupting her morose thoughts. When she picked up it was Charis. Gilly sighed. "Look, you're my best bud in the world, but I'm not coming over to foist my gloom on your holidays. Final word."

"Good. I don't want you to."

That had Gilly's attention. "Then why—"

"Listen, after you went storming out into the night, I tracked down 'Gentleman Johnny' and had quite an interesting talk with him."

Gilly almost dropped the phone. "You did what?"

"Now, calm down. Hear me out. You of all people should know I'm no pushover. In fact, after we talked, I had Bill do some checking . . . just to be certain everything Jeff told me was on the up and up."

"What, pray tell, did he tell you?"

"Enough to convince me that he deserves another chance." She waited a beat, and when

251

Gilly did not respond, she continued, "I convinced him that you do, too."

"Big of you—and him," Gilly replied sourly.

"Don't blow it, sweetie. This is your big chance. I think this guy's the one for you. He's going to call you. Give him a chance, and tell him *everything*." She stressed the last word.

"Living it was painful enough, Char. I don't know if I can."

"You know he's working his way through school by stripping. The least you can do in return is confess you're from Cleveland."

"It's a hell of a lot worse than that, and you know it."

"Yeah. So should he."

So should he. Gilly mulled over Charis's words as she paced around the apartment. Dusk brought fat white snowflakes, as if the ice-bound city needed more White Christmases. Bah, humbug! She dropped the curtain back into place and continued wearing out the new area rug in front of the sofa. If Jeff was so eager to have a mutual baring of souls, why hadn't he called by now?

The doorbell buzzed, and she practically jumped out of her skin. When was the last time someone besides Mrs. Kleinschmidt had come to her door? Frank had. Not a good answer. Not a good question. It was probably the old harridan with some sort of complaint.

Just as Gilly was about to turn the deadbolt, she remembered that Mrs. K had gone to spend the holiday with her sister in Hoboken. She squinted through the cracked glass of the peephole. Jeff stood outside. Or what looked like two Jeffs, each holding a stack of holiday packages. She really had to have that glass fixed, she thought inanely as she struggled to make her vocal cords work. Suddenly they seemed glued together.

"Who is it?" Brilliant, after looking through the glass!

"It's Jeff, Gilly. Please, let me come in. Did Charis call you?"

"Yes . . . but . . ." But what? What was she waiting for—for him to get down on his knees and beg? Come to think of it . . . Gilly opened the door with clumsy fingers, and there he was. Just looking at him made her knees go weak. A light dusting of snow frosted his glasses and glistened on his black hair and brown leather jacket. His smile was dearly familiar yet tentative as he held out the packages.

"Peace offerings?"

She opened the door wider, and he walked in, carefully depositing the packages on a chair—all but one, a large box tied with a big red bow. That he placed on the floor beside the end of the sofa. Then he looked around as he shrugged off his jacket. Gilly had always been aware of how extraordinarily graceful he was, even in the simple act of taking off a coat. Now she understood why. Lots of practice. "Charis said you wanted to talk." She walked over and reached for the damp bomber jacket. The moment she picked it up and felt his heat in the leather, smelled his scent, she knew it was a mistake. Ignoring her racing pulse, she went to hang it in the closet, waiting for him to make the next move.

"I wondered what your place would be like."

"Not a knockout like Charis and Bill's, is it?"

"I like it better. It fits you, Gilly. Warm, comfortable . . ." His eyes met hers, and the words faded. "Charis told me a lot of things about you—about how you grew up—that I needed to understand." He paused for a moment, then plunged ahead. "Now I want to explain about me." He searched her face.

Deliberately, she had not come close to him. She stood across the room, afraid that if she so much as touched him, she'd melt into a puddle like the snow off his sneakers. "Okay. Have a seat, and let's talk." She gestured to the sofa behind him. When he started to sit down, she said, "You look cold. How about some coffee first?"

"No, no thanks. Please, let's just talk for a while."

He waited while she warily took a seat on a chair across from him. "I did check up on you, Jeff. You caught me at it. I know your family is

well enough off that you shouldn't have to . . .
to do what you do for money."

"I sure as hell don't do it because I like it." His
voice was grim.

She could sense the tension in his body as he
leaned forward and combed his fingers through
his hair, then clenched his fists. "Why, then?"
she asked softly.

"It all began when I was a kid, I suppose. My
father and I were always oil and water. I'm Jeffrey Lyle Brandt the Fourth, you know."

"I never knew anyone with a Roman numeral
in his name before."

He chuckled at the artless way she said it.
"You are the real deal, Gilly. That's what I love
about you . . . among other things." He paused
and cleared his throat, then plunged ahead.
"Charis described your childhood—the poverty
and your dad's abuse. I guess growing up in
Scarsdale isn't so bad by comparison, but I always felt like an outsider. Let me rephrase that.
I wanted to be an outsider. I felt suffocated by
the way my family lived. And, yes, poor little
rich boy, my mother and father did leave me
and my sister with hired help a lot of the time.
I was sent to prep schools in part to get me out
of their hair.

"One summer, my sophomore year, I fell in
with a kid on the yard crew at our country
place. David Strongswimmer—you've heard me
mention him. It was quite a revelation—a

bright, ambitious guy who was working his way through school—high school. We became good friends."

"And your family didn't approve."

"That's putting it mildly. In addition to being the wrong class, he was the wrong race—Native American. Iroquois. And his father, who worked high iron here in the city, was a shaman."

"The medicine man you told me about." Gilly was fascinated, unaware that she was leaning toward him.

Jeff could hardly concentrate on what he had come prepared to say when the butter-yellow velour robe she was wearing gaped open and he could see the swell of her breasts. He nodded, then continued, "Yes. He had a way with people. Almost as if he could see inside them. Whatever he saw inside me, he must've liked, because he practically adopted me after that."

"He's the one who gave you the beaded necklace you wear so often."

He tugged the leather strap out from beneath his sweater. "When things got really bad between my father and me, the Strongswimmer family was always there for me, especially after my father issued his ultimatum—go to Harvard or he'd disinherit me. It wasn't only that Harvard was his alma mater and a Brandt tradition, sending me to Cambridge was also a way of separating me from my friends."

"And you refused."

He nodded. "I enrolled at NYU. Worked my way through a couple of years, but it wasn't easy. Unlike one very smart lady I know, I hadn't exactly applied myself during my high school career. No scholarships. Dave worked high iron with his dad, and they got me on. Money was damn good, and I figured I could save enough over the summer to pay for the next year's tuition. But then . . ."

Gilly could see that he was struggling with what came next. "Something awful must have happened." She shivered just thinking about those men walking on girders sixty stories above the ground.

"I almost got Dave killed. I'd only been on the job a couple of weeks. Never had a fear of heights before that, thought I could handle it. But one day I panicked when I made a misstep and grabbed Dave's arm. He went over, while I managed to catch hold of the girder we were on when I fell. He dropped six stories before he broke his own fall by catching an electrical line." He started to sweat just remembering it. Uncertain how long he'd been sitting there swamped by the horrible memories, he was surprised when Gilly handed him a cup of steaming coffee and knelt by his feet on the rug.

"He didn't die." She prayed his friend hadn't been permanently injured.

"No. He was able to hang on until they

reached him and hauled him back up. Neither he nor his father blamed me. Said that kind of thing happens to beginners all the time. Dave went right back to work the next day. I couldn't. I was broke, guilty, and confused as hell . . . so I joined the Navy and tried to find myself.

"Dad had always pushed me toward the law, and I'd always resisted, but after the service, I decided it wasn't the law that was the problem. It was my father. I was able to scrimp by on GI Bill money and finish my bachelor's in history, then enroll in the law program at NYU with grades good enough for a scholarship."

"But not enough money in it to pay for tuition plus food and rent." Gilly had been there, done that. "I worked all kinds of jobs while I was going to Oberlin, too."

"But not stripping."

"No," she conceded. "No one ever offered me the chance."

"But you graduated anyway. I might have, too, but Ira Strongswimmer developed arthritis and had to quit work. Then he contracted heart disease and ran up some pretty substantial medical bills that the family couldn't handle."

"So you stepped in."

"I tried to bargain with my dad for a loan—I'd go to Harvard if he'd cough up the money for Ira's surgery. I honestly thought he'd go for it, but he knew by then that I'd never spend my life the way he wanted. He refused. So I told the

Strongswimmers that my rich daddy had given me the money and then took out a loan to pay off their bills. They've been repaying me as best they can afford, but with tuition, living expenses, and loan payments . . . I had to drop out.

"That's when I met Archie Kolcheski. He offered me a chance to make really big bucks for only a few hours a week, leaving me time to study. The catch was that I had to go to work whenever he called me. Since it was mostly nights and didn't interfere with my class schedule, I agreed. I didn't like it, but I did it.

"Then I met this woman from small-town Ohio, society family, posh job, luxury digs . . . and, what can I say? I fell for her even though she seemed to be everything I'd wanted to get away from my whole life." He gave her a lopsided smile that melted her heart. "Must be love, Gilly." Then his expression turned grave, and he took her hands and held them between his, massaging them as he spoke. "I never meant to hurt you, Gilly, least of all at the Lawrences' bash or at your publishing party. But my father pulled another rug out from under me financially, and I was really in a bind."

"I can imagine what you must've thought when you saw me in the audience at the publishing party. Oh, Jeff, I told you the same lies I told everyone here, inventing the perfect family, the perfect hometown, the job I always dreamed of. All so I could keep the real past, and how bad it made me feel, at a distance. The only thing I told you the truth about was Mrs. Kleinschmidt. Can you forgive me?"

"Gilly, when you look at me with those big green eyes, I can barely remember what my name is, much less hold a grudge. I'm glad you aren't high society, but I'd love you even if you were. I did love you, but I was too wrapped up in my own guilt to realize it until I thought I'd lost you for good. If seeing me like you did at that party . . . if you can forgive me for that—"

"Shh," she said, touching his lips with her fingertips as she knelt between his thighs. "I'm glad you aren't high society anymore either, but I'd love you even if you were. I'll be more than happy to settle for an assistant D.A., if you'll settle for a romance editor."

"Why not? That way, a happy ending is guaranteed," he whispered, reaching down to pull her into his arms.

Chapter Ten

Jeff just held her close to him, inhaling the sweet vanilla scent that was Gilly—soft, warm, vulnerable. She had been hurt so much in her life already, and he vowed that she never would be again. His hands slowly traveled down the back of the fluffy yellow robe, feeling the delicate indentations of her spine, the delicious curve of her buttocks. Then he lifted her up against him, kneading her soft flesh, listening to her sigh of contentment.

Gilly raised her arms, encircling his neck, pulling him closer to her as he lifted her. Their mouths met in a light, brushing kiss that built slowly. She traced the sculpted contours of his lips with her tongue, flicking it into one corner,

261

then the other, loving it when he growled low and opened his mouth. She received his tongue, matching him thrust for thrust until they were both breathless.

His fingers splayed over her back, then moved up to her head, framing her face as he kissed her eyelids, nose, cheekbones, and temples tenderly while he pulled her up on the sofa to lie on top of him. He massaged her scalp, taking the pins from her hair so that it fell in a coppery curtain, veiling them. "You have such beautiful hair," he murmured against her throat, lapping with his tongue at the furiously beating pulse point between her collarbones.

She chuckled low. "So do you. I like being able to grab hold." She demonstrated, taking a fistful of his dark hair in each hand and pressing a deep, sealing kiss on his open mouth.

"Ravish me," he whispered.

"Like in a romance novel?" Her voice was muffled in his mouth.

"Yeah, just like."

"How would you know? Ever read one?" she asked between kisses.

"You can show me."

She propped herself up on his chest and looked down, loving the game. "Well, first I think we'll have to begin with 'divesting me of my garments.' "

"My pleasure," he replied, rolling up and flipping her down on the opposite end of the big sofa. "Am I allowed to ad-lib now and then?"

"Absolutely." As she spoke he slowly untied the sash of her robe and pushed the heavy lapels back, revealing the swells of her breasts. The cool air instantly contracted the nipples, which ached for his touch.

She arched them toward him, saying, "Now you'll have to 'tease my twin peaks of desire with your mouth.'"

He swooped down and did exactly that, eliciting a sharp gasp of pleasure from her. "I never thought I'd owe so much to Gwendolyn Gleeson," she murmured as he kissed his way across her collarbone and down each arm as he freed it from the robe.

She looked up at him, straddling her hips, then let her hands glide sinuously up his thighs until she reached the edge of his sweater. She started to raise it, but he quickly reached up and yanked it over his head and threw it to the floor. "No fair. The heroine gets to undress the hero, too."

"Sorry. What next?" he asked, looking down expectantly to where her hands rested on the waistband of his jeans.

"Not so obvious," she murmured, letting her fingernails graze his belly as she ran her hands up over the contours of his chest, tracing the patterns of body hair, then circling two hard dark male nipples. It was his turn to gasp with pleasure. Her fingertips feathered around to his back, then returned again to the snap on his jeans. She hesitated, licking her lips, then smiled seductively and began to lower the zipper. "I seem to remember..." Her hands slowed, stopped, raised the zipper, then lowered it again. "Think I'll suggest that trick to Gwendolyn."

As she teased, he hardened and swelled until he thought he would burst. "Who the hell is Gwendolyn?" he growled, reaching for her hands. But she was quicker, sliding the zipper down and reaching inside.

"Ah!" she exclaimed softly, stroking his hardness, rubbing it against her naked belly.

He swung his legs off the sofa and stood up, pulling her with him. Her robe fell away. She wore nothing beneath it. As his eyes swept down her body with appreciation, she whispered, "I just got out of the bathtub a little while ago."

"Do you hear me complaining?" He began nibbling kisses across her neck and shoulder as she tugged at his jeans, shoving them down his hips. "One thing I learned the first time I went onstage," he murmured between kisses, "shoes first."

"Oops." She giggled, watching as he untied his sneakers and pulled them off, then his socks. The jeans still hung provocatively around his hips. "Now, where was I?" She reached out and yanked the jeans down with one hand.

He kicked the pants away and scooped her up in his arms, turning toward the bedroom. Gilly's bed was not a luxurious water bed like the Lawrences' but neither of them cared as he lay her on the fluffy gold comforter and stretched out beside her. She went eagerly into his arms, and their bodies pressed close, hard against soft, rough against smooth, dark against pale. When he slid inside the silky warmth of her, they both sighed with the rightness of it, the perfect bliss. And it was very much like a romance novel, Gilly decided as he began to move and she with him.

Then all thoughts were obliterated as the languorous tempo accelerated. They rolled across the double bed, not hearing the creaking springs or feeling the cold air because the room's radiator never worked right. This was their perfect night, on an old, lumpy mattress in a dingy flat in Yonkers. And it didn't matter one bit.

In the dim light filtering in from the living room, they could see each other's faces, look deeply into each other's eyes. When he sensed her begin to climax, he rolled her on top and held her hips cradled in his hands, feeling the sensual brush of her hair against his thighs as she tilted her head backward, arching into her release. He watched the delicate pinkening of her fair skin. The flush spread from her belly upward, bathing her breasts in a rosy glow, but by then the contractions of her body sent his spinning out of control.

Gilly looked down through a haze of ecstasy at his beloved face, watching his jaw clench, feeling his big, hard body give in, joining hers in a fierce, breathless rush that sent her into another deeper orgasm, seeming to merge them soul as much as body.

Perspiration sheened their flesh in the chill evening air as they lay spent and panting, renewed and at peace. His hands traced with wonder the pinkness slowly fading from her skin. Then she reclined on his chest, inhaling his unique male musk, a scent she would never tire of should they live to be a hundred.

Jeff buried one hand in her hair as she snuggled her head against his shoulder in utter contentment. "I love you, Gillian Newsom. Will you marry me?"

She raised her head and looked up at his serious expression. A slow smile bloomed on her face, curving her lips and making her eyes glow in the dim light. "If you don't mind that I'm a poor assistant editor living in Yonkers, yes, oh, yes, Jeff."

"All I'll ever be is a struggling attorney in the D.A.'s office. If you don't mind, I sure as hell don't. In fact, one of the things I worried about was your high-powered job and rich family. I didn't like the idea of living off a woman."

"Male chauvinist," she said with a pout that was anything but serious.

"Not that I don't believe you can become an executive editor at the biggest press in New York if you set your mind to it," he said, starting to nibble on her shoulder.

"Mmm, love the vote of confidence . . . love what you're doing even more. . . ."

A chorus of high-pitched squeals suddenly broke the silence. "Another county heard from," Jeff said, chuckling.

Gilly groaned. "Could that be those damn mice? I've never heard them so loud before. Maybe we should look for another apartme—"

"Those aren't mice."

"They aren't?" she asked, dubious, watching him as he swung his legs over the side of the bed and padded naked into the living room. She admired the view in spite of her puzzlement. Buns of steel, indeed.

He returned, carrying the big box wrapped with the red bow that he'd set so carefully on the floor beside the sofa. She could see now that there were small holes all around the sides of it . . . and tiny furry arms sticking out of them! Gilly sat up in the center of the bed as he placed the box on it and sat down himself.

"They fell asleep after I fed them. The vet said they'd sleep a lot for the first few months." Jeff slipped the ribbons off and lifted the lid, revealing two fluffy little balls of fur. He scooped one into each hand and held them up for her inspection. "Gilly, meet Rover and Fido."

"Kittens!" she said with pure delight, taking the pumpkin-orange one from him, then the black one with white feet, nuzzling them against her face. Their shrill little mews had quieted as soon as they were removed from the box. Now loud purrs filled the room.

"Kittens? Don't be insulting, madame," he said, feigning indignation, turning one purring fluff ball this way and that, as if examining him. "Rover and Fido are merely, ah . . . unusual-looking dogs who happen to have defective barkers. However, they might catch those mice you mentioned—once they get bigger than the mice, that is."

Gilly looked at Jeff's tender expression and offered him the little black and white kitten. Her face was radiant as she said, "What you will, Petruchio. Thank you for such a wonderful Christmas present."

"You're the best Christmas present I'll ever have, Gillian Newsom."

"In case I never mentioned it before, I love you, Jeffrey Lyle Brandt the Fourth."

As the snow fell outside the lace curtains, they exchanged a kiss while each held a kitten snuggled between them.

Man With A
Golden Bow

Nina Bangs

*For the past and present members
of Houston Bay Area Chapter Thirty,
thanks for all your years of support and encouragement.*

Chapter One

She wanted a bad man in the worst way. Bad as in hot and hard. A man able to steam up car windows with his kisses and make her dance naked in the street. A man with wicked hands who'd touch her in places that would make her scream.

Unfortunately, he wasn't here. She'd already checked under the couch. All she had was this video Carole had loaned her.

Jenny Saunders wasn't too sure about the video. She chanced another glance at the couple on the screen, then picked up her phone and called Carole.

"Carole's Baskets and Gifts. How can I—"

"Carole, about this video—"

"Jenny! You're watching the video? Is it seriously hot or what? Puts you in the mood, doesn't it? I love it when they—"

"I don't believe real people do it in those positions. Okay, maybe in New York, but not here in South Jersey."

"Listen, girlfriend, you've gotta get into a different mind-set. Anything is possible when two people are carried away by passion. Billy and I did it five times last night. That video inspired us."

"*Five* times?" She was twenty-eight years old and missing out on one of a woman's greatest experiences while her friends left her in their dust. What if she died tonight? She'd never *know*.

"Of course, maybe things'll settle down after we've been married a few more weeks. Wait just a sec." Jenny could hear Carole talking to a customer. She watched the video while she waited. Hmm. That position had possibilities. "Okay, I'm back. Look, if you're going to lose the big V, then you have to be willing to experiment."

"The big V? Virginity isn't a disease, Carole."

"Don't know about that. Anyway, it's all set with Sloan. He's on his way, and he doesn't suspect a thing. The rest is up to you. Are you wearing that little black bra I bought you?"

"Sure." She'd *never* wear that bra. There wasn't enough of it to wear. "Are you sure Sloan will show up?"

"Hey, have I ever lied to you? I can't believe you don't love that video."

"If I were a chiropractor, I'd love it." She turned her head sideways to see if she could catch any fleeting expressions of passion on the faces of the couple now in a new pretzel position. Nope. No passion. A little pain, but no passion. "I don't know about this plan, Carole. A lot could go wrong. I haven't seen Sloan in ten years. We've exchanged a few letters, a few phone calls, but that's it."

"So whose fault is it you were away the other times he came home? Sloan's my cousin. He's family. Nothing will go wrong."

"But—"

"Don't you dare back out. I will *not* let them carve 'She Died a Virgin' on your tombstone. You think too much."

"That's what I do, Carole. I'm an accountant and accountants think. And right now I think I might've made a—"

"Uh, gotta go. Another customer just walked in. Talk to you later."

Jenny stared at the phone. Just like Carole. Her friend set the trap, then ran for the hills before the tiger arrived. Not that Sloan was a tiger. He was a comfortable friend from high school, someone she'd grown up with, someone who wouldn't make her nervous. *Someone you haven't seen in ten years.*

She flicked off the TV. Carole was right. She

couldn't back out. She wanted this. Jenny Saunders wouldn't spend another Saturday night alone with only her lustful thoughts for company. And no way would she come home one day to find the state putting a historical marker outside her door—The Last Living Virgin in New Jersey.

Besides, no one would ever believe it. She could talk the talk, think the thoughts, but she'd never managed to walk the walk.

It wasn't as though she hadn't tried. She'd scoped out men until her eyes crossed. Sue her for being picky, but Lenny who owned the bagel shop down on Broadway and whose date conversation centered around which cream cheese tasted best on his raisin bagels did *not* make her heart beat faster. Besides, she couldn't get physical with a guy who was as soft and doughy as his bagels.

Jenny smiled. Sloan had called after that horrific date. He was funny, comforting, and talking with Sloan was a laser light show compared to the Lennys of the world. Maybe he wasn't long-term-relationship material, but . . .

Jenny's doorbell interrupted more in-depth analysis.

She put her eye to the door's peephole, but all she could see was a giant basket. *At last*. Her Christmas basket, delivery man, and the possibility for one glorious life-fulfilling fling had arrived.

Jenny opened the door only as far as her security chain would allow. "Yes?" The basket was beautiful. Now if she could only work up the courage to look at the delivery man.

"I have a basket here for Jenny Saunders. Are you Jenny Saunders?"

She looked at him. He smiled. *Yes*. They should distribute protective glasses with that smile.

"I might be." Something was wrong though. She'd bargained on her good old high school buddy, Sloan. Someone she could feel comfortable with on her fling. Someone attractive, but not *too* attractive. Someone sexy, but not *too* sexy. Someone who wouldn't intimidate the heck out of her. This was *not* Sloan Mitello. This was intimidation with a capital "I."

"You're not the delivery man I expected. I don't open my door to strange men carrying baskets. Look what happened to Little Red Riding Hood. She ended up with a wolf in her bed." *Stupid, Saunders*. She must have bed on the brain.

"I think Little Red was the one carrying the basket, not the wolf. And it was her grandmother's bed."

"Whatever. It's the concept."

"Don't you remember me, Jenny?" His eyes gleamed with laughter and a promise that he'd be well worth remembering.

"Nope." She would swear she'd never met

him. This man was tall, with broad shoulders, lean hips, muscular thighs, and shoulder-length black hair. He also had a wicked grin that suggested he was on good speaking terms with sin. She wouldn't forget someone like him.

"Sure you do. It's me. Sloan. Carole said she had baskets backed up to here." He pantomined a line on his throat.

Nice throat. She had this crazy urge to put her lips on the spot where his blood pulsed hot and strong. Jenny frowned. Crazy urges could be dangerous. As dangerous as the man standing on the other side of her door.

"Anyway, she asked me to help out by delivering a few of the local orders. So here I am with this basket from—" he glanced at the card—"a secret admirer."

"Sloan Mitello?" She narrowed her gaze. Tall and gangly Sloan Mitello? Short hair, semi-geeky? No, Sloan Mitello never looked like this man. "I don't think so."

He shifted the basket onto one hip and pulled his wallet from the back pocket of well-worn jeans that showed every muscular curve of thigh and hip. Wonderful jeans. "Okay, here's my license." He held the wallet up to the crack. "And just to make sure, how about a trip down Memory Lane?"

"Memory Lane?" *Sloan?* Absolutely, positively not. No way could she have a wild fling with this Sloan Mitello. He was too . . . too *much*.

"Your couch. Senior Week. We'd gotten bored with the people we were with, so we ended up together watching an old movie, *The Man with the Golden Gun*. You said you'd rather have a man with a golden *bow*." He leaned closer. "Would you have opened the door if I showed up wearing nothing but a big flashy gold bow, Jenny? Would you have let me in?" His voice was dark seduction.

"Umm . . ." *Say yes, you wuss*. The woman she wanted to be wouldn't hesitate. The woman she was couldn't make up her mind.

"I *really* wanted to wear that bow, but I ran into a couple of problems."

Sure. Problems. "Sloan Mitello. I can't believe it." She was smiling. The same silly smile Sloan had always drawn from her, back when she'd allowed herself silly smiles.

"I know, I know. The bad penny." He grinned at her.

She drew in a deep breath. She'd forgotten. His body might've changed, but he'd always had that killer smile. And once she got past the way he looked, he still sounded like her old high school buddy.

"First problem. It's cold outside. I could throw a coat over the bow and me, but what if I got in an accident on the way over? How would I explain to the cops why I'm just wearing a bow?" His grin widened. "I've changed, Jenny. Time was when I wouldn't have given a damn what anyone thought."

"Changed? You?" One of the things that had separated them. He'd been a brilliant free spirit, a never-has-to-crack-a-book kind of guy.

She'd had to work after school to help her family make ends meet after Dad's latest money-making scheme crashed. And she *hadn't* been brilliant. She'd had to study long into the night. She hadn't had time to think about . . .

Okay, so she'd thought about him, but she knew too much about the Sloans of the world to risk more than friendship with him. Besides, in high school it had been hard to imagine making love with someone who, in third grade, had given her a dead spider neatly nestled in a Godiva chocolate box he'd found.

"Next problem. How do I get the sucker to stay right *here*?" He backed away from the door so she could see exactly where *here* was. "Hey, I'd have to cover up the gift part so it'd be a surprise. Know what I mean?"

The visual had her gulping in another life-saving supply of oxygen. Okay, no more of the virgin-who-would-be-bad routine. She'd wanted a hot and hard man, so here he was. Now what was she going to do with him?

"Besides, you have a nosy neighbor downstairs. She'd be punching out 911 before I even got up the stairs." He moved close to the door again until only one vivid green eye was visible. "I'm cold out here, Jenny. Let me in."

Said the wolf. Jenny unhooked the chain, then opened the door.

He swept into her tiny living room bringing cold air and memories.

"So you're back in town?" *Well, duh*?

"Yep. I have some unfinished business."

All motion and energy, he looked out of place next to her calm ivory furniture.

Placing the basket on her coffee table, he swung in a circle, glancing briefly at her furniture, at her few tasteful bought-to-fit-with-the-decor pictures, at her neat and perfect *everything*. And judged. She knew what he'd say before he said it, because despite the years they'd been apart, she remembered Sloan.

He turned back to her, his long dark hair sliding across the shoulders of his short leather jacket. "You need some red in here, Flame."

Flame. Some dusty corner of her memory smiled at the almost forgotten nickname. He'd said if he had hair her shade of red, he'd grow it down to his butt. Looked like he was working on the butt thing while her hair was a short smooth cap.

"I don't need red. The decorator said this living room was me." She didn't *need* Sloan back in her life either—all the colors of the rainbow wrapped in shades of intense emotion.

But she *wanted* him. Give her a few days to

adjust to the new Sloan and he'd be a perfect fit for her brief-encounter-of-the-sexual-kind. For the first time in her life she'd walk the walk.

His glance slid across her hair, lingered. "You've got red whether you want it or not, Jenny. Make the most of it."

He moved close. Close enough for her to smell the promise of snow on his open jacket, the scent of warm male on his black T-shirt, to watch the swell of chest muscles as he took a deep breath.

Close enough for all of *her* breath to leave her in a startled whoosh as he ran callused fingers over her hair, then continued until he touched the spot where her pulse beat a tom-tom response.

"You need long hair, Jenny. Long ribbons of fire rippling down your back, over your shoulders, down to . . ."

His husky murmur died away as his fingers traced a path down the vee of skin exposed by her blouse, paused where the vee ended, seemed bent on traveling to new and unexplored places.

She was sweating even though she knew darn well she'd set her thermostat at a perfect seventy-two degrees. But her body's thermostat was measuring a different heatwave right now. One with long dark hair, hot green eyes, and a hard, beard-shadowed jaw.

The Sloan Mitello she'd known had never

messed with her personal heat indicator. What was he doing? She stepped back, then sank onto her decorator-approved couch. Hard. Her bottom didn't even make a dent in it.

Hard. There was nothing soft about the new and improved Sloan Mitello.

Mental picture. Position four on Carole's tape. Jenny draped over her ivory couch, Sloan's dark hair trailing between her thighs. His lips . . . Jenny smiled. *Bring on the chiropractors*. A new woman was about to be born.

"Thanks for delivering the basket, Sloan." Time to get back to the mundane so she could regroup and plan her strategy. She wasn't used to impulsive. She'd spent her whole life thinking things through carefully, weighing all the angles, making informed decisions.

"Mind if I catch the end of the Flyers' game before I leave?" He turned to search for her remote.

"Sure, go ahead." *Think*. What to say? *Wow, I was just dreaming about Mr. Hard-and-Hot, then I open the door and there you are*. She might be the queen of flip, but her lips wouldn't form the words. Perhaps something a little more subtle.

He located the remote and reached for it. "It's a week until Christmas and Carole's business is booming. I'd barely gotten in the door when she handed me some baskets and told me to deliver them. Couldn't believe the coincidence when I saw your name on one of the baskets."

"Right. Coincidence." How about orchestrated with all the finesse of a bulldozer.

"How's life been treating you, Jenny?"

"Life's been good." She frowned as he turned on the TV. "My accounting business is growing and I—" Ohmigod! She'd forgotten about the video. She'd turned off the TV, but not her VCR.

Too late. She was toast. Her life flashed before her eyes, but Sloan didn't notice. He was gazing raptly at the screen.

The silence stretched on . . . and on . . . and on.

"Uh, you can catch the end of that game if you hurry."

He didn't look at her. "Nice camera angle there."

"I don't believe real people do those things."

He finally looked at her. His gaze trailed over her body like Little Red's wolf planning his day's menu. "Believe it." His eyes lit with laughter. "Want to try?" He hit the stop button.

As the baddest virgin in Jersey, she should've swiveled her hips, winked at him, and murmured, "Thought you'd never ask."

Instead, she resorted to babbling, a skill she'd honed to an art form. "A friend gave me that tape. It's not mine. I was just sorta glancing at it when you came."

Silence.

"Look, I don't need to watch tapes. I know

about things like that."*Say something before I gag on my own foot.*

"Really?" He looked intrigued.

"Sure. First there's the come-on." *Let me do your tax returns, and I'll find so many loopholes and write-offs Uncle Sam will be paying you for the next twenty years.*

"Then there's foreplay." *Come to my office and we'll do the paperwork. Bring your receipts.*

"Finally, there's the climax." *My refund check came! I love you.*

"Sounds impressive." He rose to put the remote on top of the TV.

Numbers were her game. What was the probability of another man having buns exactly like Sloan's? Firm. *Male.* One in ten thousand, one in a million? Interesting research question.

"It figures you'd end up as an accountant."

"What? What figures?" Suppose he *had* shown up with just a gold bow? He'd need a way to keep it from sliding off. Of course she hadn't gotten a look at his . . . If *that* was big enough, nothing would slide off.

"It figures you'd work with numbers."

"What's wrong with numbers?" She wondered if they sold stick-on bows with a Post-it backing. Something that wouldn't be an owie when you pulled it off. She thought about pulling it off and licked her lips.

"They're safe. Always the same."

"I prefer reliable. Reliable's important." A ribbon thong had possibilities too. She could picture the gold ribbon snaking down between those amazing buns, separating, delineating.

"What about exciting, fun. Isn't fun important, too?"

"Exciting and fun can't be counted on. If I add a column of figures, there's only one right answer. Exciting and fun can have an infinity of answers. I wouldn't know which was the *right* answer. How would I know which way to go?"

Go? Where would the ribbon go next? Hmm. It would slide between those yummy thighs and come out . . .

"It's hot in here. Does it feel hot to you? Feels hot to me." She bounced off the couch and reached the thermostat in record time. Without looking, she flicked it down to what she hoped was Arctic Zone level.

Turning back toward him, she met his gaze across the room. "What were we talking about?"

"Haven't a clue." His grin touched her, swept away the ten years he'd been gone along with the strangeness that had frozen her brain cells.

Relaxing into the remembered familiarity, she walked back to the couch and sat down. "I'm surprised you thought of that gold bow thing."

Abandoning the remote, he moved to the couch and sat down beside her. She fought to retain her old-friends-meeting-again attitude. But he didn't feel like an old friend. She wasn't sure what he felt like, but it definitely *wasn't* an old friend.

"I have a great memory, Jenny." He edged closer.

"Right. Great memory. Gee, I wonder what's in my basket?" Reaching out, she lifted the basket from her coffee table and plunked it down between them. Not exactly the Great Wall of China, but it'd do in a pinch.

Hello? You're supposed to be encouraging up-close and cozy. But she needed some time. Her decision to have a fling had been a cerebral decision. She was a cerebral person. The man sitting next to her appealed to a completely different body area, and she hadn't had enough time to make the move from penthouse to basement.

The laughter glittering in his green eyes mocked her puny effort. "Are you telling me you don't remember the movie?"

She removed the red cellophane wrapping from around the basket. Concentrated on the satisfying crinkling sound. "Nope. I don't remember a thing."

"That's because you'd chugged four beers."

"I *never* drank four beers." She carefully removed the first item from the basket. Lavender bubble bath.

"Sure you did. You were fun that night." A line formed between his eyes as he studied the bubble bath. "Looks like your secret admirer's in touch with his feminine side."

She stopped to stare at him. "*How* much fun?"

His grin widened. "Not *that* much fun. Anyway, it was close to Christmas, and you said you'd rather have a man with a golden bow any old time."

"I remember. Vaguely. Doesn't sound like me, though." She lifted out the next item. Peppermint foot balm.

"Exactly. That's why you were so much fun." He peered at the foot balm. "Wow. A clue. Know any men with a foot fetish?"

She paused in the midst of pulling out a soothing vanilla candle. "I was fun because I wasn't me? Correct me if I'm wrong, but that sounded like an insult."

He shrugged, and for the first time looked a little uncomfortable. "Hey, everyone's more fun when they lose a few inhibitions." He took the candle from her. "You know, if you drip candle wax on a man's bare chest—"

"You'll set his chest hair on fire?" *Now* she was getting mad. "I guess you were never more fun then, because you didn't have any inhibitions to lose."

"Yeah. Hot wax would burn like hell. Warm chocolate syrup might be fun, though. Have any in the kitchen?" He reached across the barrier of the basket and tugged at a piece of her hair.

She jerked her head away and smoothed the hair back into place.

"Getting a little ticked off, are we?" He didn't try to hide his laughter.

"Never." She yanked a bag of potpourri from the basket and slapped it down on the couch with such force the cellophane split. Unidentified dried vegetation drifted around her on a sea of flowery scent strong enough to clog her nasal passages. "I never get upset."

"What the hell is that?" She'd finally found something to put him in full retreat. He slid to the end of the couch and eyed the bits of leaves with suspicion.

"Flower Garden of Desire." Lord, what a mess. She'd have to drag out the vac after he left.

His bark of laughter startled her.

"You're kidding. No man in his right mind would give that kind of junk to a woman."

She narrowed her gaze. "A sensitive man would."

"Who is this secret admirer?"

"I don't know. If I knew, then he wouldn't be a secret admirer anymore, would he?" Uh-oh, time for a shift in topic. "So what've you been doing with your life lately, Sloan? Last I heard, you were working for some electronics company. And before that it was public relations. I've lost track of the others."

He shrugged. "Oh, this and that."

A dreamer. Sloan Mitello has been a dreamer in high school, would always be a dreamer. Just like her dad.

"Anything permanent?" Dreamers might be great men, but they made lousy providers. Always moving onto the next big dream, then when that failed, moving onto another, then another.

"Sorta."

"So let's hear about it." Dreamers dragged their families along for the ride, getting up hopes that the next venture would be the big one. It never was. She knew. Been there, done that.

"I have a business, Jenny." He edged closer again.

"Where?" Maybe she'd misjudged him.

"On the internet."

Not substantial enough. A business should be something you could touch, go to each morning at nine o'clock.

She gave herself a mental head-slap. *He doesn't have to own a Fortune 500 company to be great in bed.* "What's the name of your business?"

He glanced at his watch. "Sorry, I didn't realize how late it was. I have two more baskets to deliver. Look, I'll get back to you."

Oh-no. She couldn't let him go yet. They hadn't worked out a fling arrangement. If she wasn't such a wimp, they'd be in her bed by this time. But she was a wimp, and she couldn't abandon completely the habits of a lifetime. She had to work up to things slowly.

Okay, relax. Carole said he was staying till after Christmas. You can just order another basket. Lucky she was on vacation from work till after Christmas. She'd have plenty of time to orchestrate this fling.

Her panic eased. But before he left, she wanted to know something. "What's the name of your business?"

He'd risen and was already at the door. Opening it, he glanced back and smiled. "Desiresfulfilled dot com." Then he quietly closed the door behind him.

Jenny sat amid the clutter of the basket she'd ordered for herself. Desiresfulfilled dot com? Sounded like a porn site to her.

Chapter Two

Sloan shifted the candy-cane shaped basket onto one hip so he'd have his other hand free to ring Jenny's bell. Her secret admirer had struck it lucky this time. When Sloan had seen the garbage the guy had ordered for this second basket, he'd dumped it and filled it with really great stuff. He hoped Carole never found out.

What kind of guy would send a woman something called Flower Garden of Desire? A loser, that's who. He didn't deserve Jenny.

Jenny. He closed his eyes, remembering every expression in those big blue eyes, the slide of her hair over his fingers, the scent of warm woman. Yep, Jenny Saunders had changed.

He'd been interested in high school, but he'd

seen past her smart mouth and known she wasn't ready. Besides, he'd had worlds to conquer. He'd gotten a scholarship to Berkeley and headed for California. Between study and work, he'd been too busy or too broke to make many trips home. And when he had, Jenny had been away. But things were different now.

Even though he hadn't seen much of Haddonfield in ten years, Carole had kept him in touch. She'd told him every time one of Jenny's boyfriends bombed. Sloan smiled.

He glanced down at the basket balanced on his hip. He *never* did baskets. Now if you had a desire to own a castle for a day or to go diving for the Loch Ness Monster, Sloan Mitello was your man. But this once . . .

This basket was a winner. He'd slaved over a hot stove making Jenny's favorite cream-cheese-and-olive sandwiches. Okay, so the stove had been stone cold, but anything he did in the kitchen that had more than two steps—take out of fridge, then nuke in microwave—was hard labor.

He rang the bell. He had time on his hands, and the holidays were for fun. Besides, someone had to save her from this secret admirer jerk.

He shifted the basket. She was probably checking him out through the peephole now, trying to decide if she'd pretend she wasn't home. *Come on, Jenny, open the door.*

A minute later, he huffed out on a puff of impatience, and started to turn from the door. Probably better to walk away now. Besides, why give some loser credit for those cream-cheese-and-olive sandwiches?

She opened the door.

He didn't question his spurt of gladness. "Secret admirer basket number two. Special delivery."

"This late? I thought it'd be . . ." She cast him a startled glance, then bit her lip.

"Thought it'd be what?"

"Nothing." Her leopard-print robe stopped at midthigh, and her red hair was tousled. She gazed at him with sleepy uncertainty. He eyed the leopard print. Maybe there really was a wildcat in there somewhere. Hey, a guy could hope.

Her bottom lip was full, moist, and he drew in his breath on the sudden desire to taste that lip, trace it with his tongue, explore the sweetness of her mouth. Body parts responsible for signaling approval applauded wildly.

"Don't you believe in calling, Sloan? It's eight o'clock at night."

Jenny's words said one thing, but her glance said another. Her gaze slid past him, never quite making eye contact. Nervous? Why?

"I'm glad to see you, too." He walked in without her invitation. "I'm the king of impulse. One of my endearing qualities." He set the basket in the exact middle of her couch so she wouldn't have to build a barricade between them.

He sat down beside the basket. "Come look at your basket."

"Mine?"

"Sure. Says right here, from your secret admirer. Hope he had better taste this time." Wow, would you look at those legs? Long, smooth, forever. He watched her walk to the couch and sit down.

"Look, it's eight o'clock, and I was in bed."

His mental video fast forwarded. *Her bed*. A tangle of white sheets. She'd have white sheets because Jenny was a white-sheet sorta woman. A life-was-real, life-was-earnest kind. But she'd look great on those white sheets, her nightgown riding up those incredible thighs to . . . He hit the stop button. *Whoa tiger*. "In bed? You were in bed at eight o'clock? No one's in bed at eight o'clock."

She shrugged. "I'm a morning person. I like to get a head start on my work."

"Break the rules for once, Jenny. The night is young. Open your basket. I want to see."

She sighed. "You're not going to go away, are you?" No matter what her mouth said, her eyes said "stay."

"Not a chance. Let's see what's in the basket."

She sat down on the other side of the basket. Her robe hiked up another few inches. He didn't notice, but his body did. His body passed on the information.

He watched her gingerly pull a gold box from the basket.

"Godiva Chocolates? Chocolate is bad for you."

"Godiva is good for you. Trust me." This wasn't the Jenny he'd known. The Jenny he'd known could be bribed with chocolate to do any number of things, like research papers . . .

He tried to ignore other, more interesting possibilities. What kind of woman thought Godiva wasn't good for her? Godiva was desire, sex, and orgasm wrapped in one gold foil package.

Then he remembered. Third grade. The spider. He grinned. "Relax, Flame. No spider this time. Besides, you broke my young heart. That spider was my most prized possession, and you rejected it. Loudly."

She returned his grin as she reached into the basket and lifted out his bag of sandwiches. "Cream-cheese-and-olive sandwiches? Ohmigod, real cream-cheese-and-olive sandwiches!"

"This guy must know you pretty well."

"I guess he does." Her voice was husky as she looked up from the sandwiches.

This was *not* feeling too great. It didn't make sense. He was mad at this secret admirer jerk who *hadn't* sent the basket that was making Jenny all emotional. Go figure.

"What else is in here?" She rooted around and pulled out his homemade ticket with the word "fun" scrawled across the top. Frowning, she read it. "A ticket to the West Street Holiday Light Show?"

"Wow. Imagine that. The guy has good taste after all. Remember? That's the neighborhood where everyone decorates their houses with lights and makes the electric company happy for a whole year. We went there at Christmas during senior year."

She shook her head. "I don't have time for that kind of thing anymore."

He stood. "Get dressed. Let's go."

"No." She bit her lip. "We could just stay here and . . . talk."

"No?" Some women *really* had a tough time having fun. "Here this guy spent time making the ticket and you won't even use it."

"It was a waste of his time." She stood, probably signaling he'd used up his allotted ten minutes of her life.

"It was only a waste of time if you don't use it." Sloan wondered about her nightgown. He pictured short and sheer, clinging to full breasts, flat stomach, and curving hips. He'd always pegged Jenny as a pj type of woman.

She picked up a piece of chocolate and absently unwrapped it. "If I go with you now, I'll be tired in the morning."

Exasperation made him want to storm out of

her apartment, but something held him in place. Maybe it was the past, the memory of them watching an old movie together, having fun together.

Cut the sentimental crap, Mitello. Admit it. She's a beautiful woman, and you want her. Simple.

He stood. She backed away. He moved forward. She backed away. Finally, her back against what he assumed was her bedroom door, she held the chocolate between them like a small talisman.

His body tightened with his need to reach around her and open that door, to back her across her bedroom, to fall with her onto those white sheets. "Take a bite, Jenny." Anywhere would be okay. Well, almost anywhere. Love bites were an accepted precursor to . . .

"What?" Her eyes were wide, her lips slightly parted. He leaned toward those lips, pulled by a force stronger than gravity.

"Take a bite of the chocolate, Flame. It'll put you in the mood." Suspicion flickered in her gaze, but he caught a flash of excitement too.

"The mood for what?" He didn't mistake her breathless tone as she raised the chocolate to her mouth and bit off half of it.

A chocolate smear on her lower lip became a holy grail. "For having fun. What else?"

He braced his hands against the wall on either side of her head to help him withstand the pull of her lips.

No good. He was a goner. Lowering his head, he kissed her.

What was it about the taste of chocolate on a woman's lips, on *her* lips? The sweetness drew him. He ran his tongue lightly across her lower lip, savoring the promise, and when she parted her lips slightly, he didn't hesitate to taste more deeply.

Lost in the kiss, he drew her closer, and felt her still clutching the piece of chocolate between them, the soft pressure of her breasts, the hard pressure of his growing enthusiasm.

And knew he had to let her go. He sensed her hesitancy, her confusion. Knowing where he wanted this kiss to lead, Sloan darn well needed Jenny clear-headed and willing when it happened. Drawing back, he grinned. Okay, maybe not so clear-headed.

Jenny stared at the slightly flattened piece of chocolate she still held, then set it down. Not even Godiva could compare with that kiss.

Now. She could have her fling tonight. He was interested. He'd gone to the trouble of filling her basket. *He'd kissed her*. He'd invited her to look at Christmas lights with him. *He'd kissed her*.

All she'd have to do was open her bedroom door and invite him in. *No*. It was too soon. She always planned things carefully, allowing for all eventualities. She hadn't planned for tonight. He wasn't supposed to deliver the basket until tomorrow.

You are such a coward, Saunders. She'd been backpedaling since the moment he'd walked in, but she needed a little more time. After all, she hadn't seen him in ten years. He took a little getting used to.

Noticing the chocolate smudge on his shirt, she rubbed at it with her finger, felt his sudden intake of breath at her touch, and smiled. "Sorry about your shirt."

She wouldn't mention the kiss. *But she'd think about it.* It was the joy of a windfall profit, the excitement of tax time. Hmm. Both great things, but they didn't quite compare to *The Kiss.*

"So will you go with me to the light show?"

His voice still held the huskiness she imagined it would have just after waking, or just after making incredible love. *With her.*

Don't blow it now. "I'll . . . change." Reaching behind her, she opened the door, slipped into her bedroom, and slammed the door shut. *Making incredible love with her.* The thought took her breath away.

Ten years ago, had it occurred to her? Sure, but she'd been smart enough to realize Sloan Mitello was a dreamer, and she didn't want any kind of emotional involvement with a dreamer.

But a fling? A fling didn't need a lot of emotional involvement.

Pulling on her jeans, she let her thoughts drift back to his kiss. It was . . . the tartness of just-squeezed lemonade, the sweetness of saltwater taffy.

Both things that were bad for her. Lemonade gave her heartburn, and saltwater taffy was pure sugar. She avoided them.

But what could it hurt to go out with an old friend? Besides, she needed time to plan every step of her fling. She ignored the jeering cluck clucks from her personal truth monitor.

"I don't know, Sloan. Looks like an awful lot of work, putting up all those lights." She snuggled against the warmth of Sloan's side as they stopped to admire another house covered with thousands of fairy lights. "And the electric bill will probably settle the national debt." Sloan's arm across her shoulders was nice, but she would *not* miss it when her fling was over. And her truth monitor was *not* at this very minute writing up a lying ticket.

She felt his frustrated exhalation. "Just enjoy it, Jenny, then walk away. You don't have to pay the bill."

Glancing up at him, she wondered. Someone had to pay for all the flash and beauty. And what if you couldn't walk away? "I pulled up your website last night. Fulfilling people's dreams must be a pretty tall order."

"Desires, Jenny. I fulfill people's desires."

"Same thing."

"Uh-uh. Dreams are what you have when you sleep. They're soft and blurred around the edges. Desires are grounded in reality. They're hard and passionate. Challenging."

"But how reliable are they? What if one month people decide they don't want any desires fulfilled? Who pays your bills?" She could feel his growing frustration, sensed a pending explosion.

"*I* pay my bills."

"But suppose you wanted to get a loan. No loan officer I know would pay out a penny to someone who made desires come true. Besides, if you make people's desires come true, then they don't have them anymore. They're worse off than before. Sounds cruel to me." Any minute now he'd blow. She could feel his tension in the clenching of his hand on her shoulder, knew she was purposely goading him, and hadn't a clue why.

Her truth monitor pulled out a fresh pack of tickets and began writing up a bald-faced-lie citation. Fine. She'd liked his kiss, realized it was driven by frustration, and wanted to experience it again.

Besides, she'd finally figured out what his kiss was. It was . . . *summer*. Warm sand, blazing heat, crashing waves that took your breath away, and a dangerous undertow that would knock you off your feet if you weren't careful. Yep, definitely summer.

Of course, summer was bad for her too. Scratchy sand on neon-red sunburn. Waves and undertow that conspired to drown her. Guess she'd have to avoid summer . . . after her fling.

"People never run out of desires, Flame. I bet even you have some."

"Even me? That was meant as an insult, but you know something, it wasn't. Dreams, desires, whatever, are hope-builders. They're not for me." She'd been about ten when she vowed never to follow any of life's yellow brick roads.

He'd stopped to gaze at a huge house that would've put Buckingham Palace to shame. Cost? Probably in the obscene range, with the same number of twinkling lights. She felt like shielding her eyes from the glare. "Now I know why my lights have been flickering. This place is one giant power drain."

Sloan shrugged. "So the guy likes Christmas. What can I say?" He turned to face her, his powerful body silhouetted against the massive light display, his dark hair whipping in a sudden gust of cold wind.

And for a moment, she allowed herself a desire. Sloan bending over her as she lay on her white sheets, his long hair falling forward, strong tanned arms braced on either side of her as he moved closer and . . .

She smiled. That was one desire she intended to come true, as soon as she had everything planned with no chance of anything unexpected happening.

"Christmas is driven by merchandising. It's just an excuse to spend money." She gazed past him at the house. "This? This serves no purpose."

"This serves *my* purpose. I had this house built, Jenny. Ever wonder why I never invited friends over to visit when we were kids? Mom and I lived in a small apartment. Had to turn sideways to get around the one bedroom. I slept on the couch. And we never had Christmas lights. Most of the time we didn't even have a tree. No money." He allowed her to hear the edge in his voice.

His? She'd never guessed about his life. Carole had never said anything. "You're joking. Dreams don't buy this kind of place. Dreams don't buy much of anything."

Sloan dropped his arm from her shoulder, and she mourned the loss. "What do you have against dreams, Flame? The truth."

He wanted truth? She'd give him truth. "Dad is a dreamer. He filled my childhood with dreams. Next Christmas he'd get me a horse. After this deal came though we'd move into a nice house. And I believed him because he was my daddy and he'd promised. Until I got old enough to realize Dad's deals never came through, and I was never going to get that horse. We lived in dumps with barely enough to eat most of the time until we moved to Haddonfield and Mom got a pretty good job."

"There're worse things than not getting a horse."

"Sure." Like not believing in promises anymore. "Do you know how many Christmases I stood at my window waiting for that dumb horse?"

"So you signed off on all dreams?"

"Right." She narrowed her gaze on his house. "Of course, getting your desire might not be all that sensational."

"Hey, insult me, but leave my house alone."

She sighed. "Sorry. It just seems like an awful big place for one person to be rattling around in . . ." Uh-oh. Maybe he had plans to fill it with a wife who could fulfill all his desires.

He grinned. "Nope. Just me for now."

"Oh." Now there was a well-rounded response. "I guess I sound like the Scrooge of dreams, but you know, I really think dreaming is an addiction. After a while, the dream itself became Dad's fulfillment." She looked away. "I even wonder if dreaming might be hereditary. There're times when I want . . ."

"Want what, Jenny?" His voice. Warm, *tempting*.

"Nothing." She looked back at him. "Nothing at all."

"Hmm." He didn't sound convinced.

She glanced at the fairy-trail of twinkling lights, and knew there was nothing left to say. Nothing left to share. They didn't have a darn thing in common. *Except that incredible kiss and the fling she intended to have with him.*

His huff of resignation formed a small cloud in the frigid air. He put his arm around her and turned her to face him.

She noticed a few stray snowflakes drifting around him, and when one settled on his lips, she reached up and touched it with her fingertip, felt it melt beneath her body heat, felt the softness of his lip.

Before she could withdraw her finger, he clasped it and drew it into his mouth. With hooded gaze, he watched her. The moist heat of his mouth threatened to turn her whole body liquid, like spring's first hot assault on winter's last snowman.

She could feel the rhythmic stroke of his palm up and down her back, her nipples' sudden sensitivity. And when, for a moment, he pulled her against him, the hard thrust of his body between her thighs assured her he felt the same.

He released her finger, and she backed away from him, her breaths coming in quick gasps that had nothing to do with exertion. *This is what you wanted.*

His hard face creased into a smile that would've convinced Little Red Riding Hood and all her extended family to climb into bed with him.

He drew his bottom lip between his teeth, and she wanted him to kiss her so badly she felt the ache all the way to . . . She clenched her thighs to hold the ache in.

"It's funny. We come from the same kind of background, but you settled into a nose-to-the-grindstone job and I—"

"Settled into a life of drifting." Oops. Maybe she'd been a little too blunt.

Placing his arm across her shoulders, he forced her to face his house. "You know, sweetheart, you've given me a reason to stop my no-account drifting for at least a week. I'm going to be the guy who brings Christmas back to you."

He leaned close. "Ever lived inside someone else's dream, Flame?"

Chapter Three

"Why would I want to do that? Living inside your dream could be real scary." Amazing. She was shivering in the cold, but the place where his arm rested was toasty warm. "Besides, I thought you said they were desires."

"For the experience. If you don't have any dreams of your own, you might enjoy living someone else's secondhand." Lifting his arm from her shoulders, he reached beneath the collar of her coat and gently massaged the base of her neck. "And you're not ready for desires yet. Dreams become desires."

If he thought that would relax her, he was mistaken. Neck nerves screamed "He's touching me!" then galloped off to spread the news to her brain. Her brain was a notorious gossip. Details would be all over the neighborhood in seconds.

"One week till Christmas, Flame. Live my dream with me. Why not? It might be the only one you ever have."

He'd moved close, and his warm breath fanned her neck; his husky murmur fanned her imagination. This was it. Her moment of truth. She swallowed hard. Okay, maybe she could put if off for a few more moments. "I guess you really must be settling down, Sloan. When're you moving into your house permanently?"

He looked as though her question had surprised him. "Soon. I came here this week to make sure everything's ready. Then I'm flying to California to—"

She couldn't stand it anymore. "Exactly *what* are you offering?" If she was jumping out of a plane without a parachute, so be it. But she had to know.

He shrugged, then smiled. His smile was the promise of all things dark and delicious. "Whatever you *want* me to be offering, Flame."

That was pretty clear. "Okay, let's get this deal straight. I live in your energy-efficient castle for a week, enjoy your dream, however misguided, then go home. End of experience."

"Bare bones? I guess that's it."

"But what will I *do* for a whole week?" *Besides*

*have hot sex with you as soon as I get up the
nerve to suggest it.*

He exhaled sharply. "Right. You need a job
description. How about decorator? I need some
feminine input for the color schemes in a few
of the rooms." His lips curved up in a take-me-
to-bed smile. "Do a good job and you might
even get a visit from Santa."

"Bribery? Sounds like bribery to me, Mitello."
She'd *really* rather do this in the familiarity of
her own apartment, but Mrs. Clark downstairs
would be whacking her ceiling with a broom
handle at the first sound of a banging headboard.

*Besides, after this week is over, do you want to
go to bed each night with the image of Sloan's
body beside you, the remembered warmth of his
hand on your breast, the scent of him clinging to
your dreams, the sound of his breathing haunting
the silence of dark nights?*

This was supposed to be a fling. Short, sweet,
and over. She didn't want to climb into bed with
his memory every night. It would be better if
she stayed at his house.

He shrugged. "It's all about incentive, Flame.
What do you have to lose? You might even learn
something about desires. For example, mine
paid for this house." He pulled her against his
side again as another cold blast swirled around
them.

For a moment, she allowed the flex of his hip

to distract her. "What do I have to lose?" *My virginity.* A hoped-for outcome. "Nothing, I guess."

"Afraid, Flame?" His words were soft, almost lost in the whistling wind. "Afraid you might like it too much here? Afraid that deep down where the real Jenny Saunders lives there's a dreamer? Someone whose dreams could turn to desires?"

"Of course not." She *wasn't* like her father. She'd never be like her father. *But are you sure?* "I don't have anything to prove to you."

"When was the last time you had fun? I bet you haven't done anything just for the hell of it since the mud puddle."

She smiled. She'd forgotten all about the mud puddle. A warm June afternoon after a heavy shower. It was still Senior Week, and everyone was still crazy. A walk in the woods where they'd found this big muddy spot. She'd caught him off balance and pushed him in. He'd stripped down to his shorts, then he'd taunted her. "Afraid of getting dirty?" His tactics hadn't changed much.

She hadn't stripped off her shorts or top, but she couldn't resist his dare. They'd laughed and rolled in that mud until she couldn't laugh anymore. If she closed her eyes she could almost breathe the heavy humid air, feel the slickness of his skin beneath her fingers. *His skin.* Strange she'd remember that.

"Well?" He sounded a little anxious.

Good. She wasn't finished thinking about that mud. *Admit it. The thought of rolling around in slippery mud now with Sloan Mitello is . . . dangerous ground. Literally.*

"You gonna walk away from it?"

She smiled. *Not until I can tell Carole I did it six times in one night.* "Okay, but you might live to regret this." She cast a speculative glance at all his lights. "Make sure you show me where your ciruit breakers are."

He hugged her close. "Will do."

Her moment of bravado oozed out all over the sidewalk. She'd agreed. She was committed. By the time she walked away from Sloan's house, she'd be a woman of the experience that worried her.

They'd gone back to Jenny's apartment, gathered her things together, and were now climbing the stairs to her room in his house. And Sloan still wasn't sure what this was all about.

Sure it was physical, but physical didn't have to be in his house. Physical could be anywhere.

Question. Why had he fed her that hokey line about bringing Christmas back to her? He didn't want to be *involved.* So now he was trucking up the stairs of his house loaded down with her stuff. *That* sure seemed involved to him. Didn't make sense.

At least she wouldn't be getting anymore secret admirer's baskets for at least a week. He smiled as he opened her door.

"*This* is my room?"

Sloan nodded. He'd looked forward to her expression of horror. Jenny didn't disappoint.

"Santa's behind is sticking out of the fireplace. I can't believe you got *all* twelve days of Christmas in one room. I hope that's an artificial partridge. Why is Rudolph standing on the mantle? I can't sleep with twinkle lights around my bed and a tree next to me. I *never* liked camping out." She twirled in a circle looking for new complaints.

"Oxygen."

"What?" She focused her outraged gaze on him.

"The tree will supply oxygen so you'll be able to breathe between complaints."

"Look, this was your idea." Her gaze was now focused on the top of the tree. "This whole house is frenetic. Don't you yearn for one spot that isn't overflowing with holiday spirit?"

He shrugged. "Not really. I have a whole childhood of holiday spirit to catch up on."

She still stared at the tree top. "Well guess what? This room is going to be your calm spot in a sea of celebration, because first thing in the morning I'm going to ban all holiday spirit from this room."

His muttered "Scrooge" didn't break her concentration on the top of his tree.

"You know, that's a really unusual ornament."

He glanced at the top of the tree in time to see a small whiskered face emerge from the branches. He breathed out a sigh of growing impatience. "That's Toby." Reaching up, he snatched the tiny white kitten off the tree. "Sorry. I'll try to keep him out."

Sloan shifted his gaze away from Toby in time to catch Jenny's transformation.

Her expression softened, her lips tilting up in a smile that turned his insides to mush. Why couldn't she look at *him* with that expression? Okay, maybe not that exact expression. He'd like a little more lust in it, a little more I-want-you-naked-in-bed-with-me.

"He's cute. Yours?" Her tone suggested surprise.

"Yeah. I came across this box of abandoned kittens yesterday, so . . ."

"You took him in."

He would've rescued a thousand kittens to have her look at him with exactly the expression she had now.

"That was sweet, Sloan." She moved to his side and reached out to stroke the kitten.

Her stroke didn't end with Toby, but continued up his arm until her fingers reached his hair. She smelled of cold air and warm woman.

Sloan couldn't help himself. Placing Toby on her bed, he reached out and traced the line of her jaw. Smooth. Determined. *Clenched*. He was making her nervous. But he couldn't help himself. Even if he sent her screaming into the night, he had to taste her one more time tonight. That was his immediate desire, and he rarely left desires unfulfilled, especially his own.

Transferring his hand to the back of her neck, he pulled her to him. As she turned her head against his shirt, he could hear her mumbling something about adjustment time and ahead of schedule. Made no sense to him.

He fingered the short strands of hair at the base of her neck. What a waste. He longed to run his fingers through silken flame, but he'd have to make do with something else tonight.

Gently, he kissed the soft skin beneath her ear, then ran his tongue the length of her neck to where the pale silk of her blouse stopped him. It would take no effort to lift the edge of the blouse and continue his journey. His body was already making travel arrangements, and his bags were packed. He shifted to relieve the pressure.

Her soft sigh moved against his chest, warming him from the inside out. He gently turned her face up to him and kissed her forehead, then the end of her nose, then . . .

Then he moved away from her.

She wasn't ready. Her cheeks were flushed and her eyes bright, but he sensed her inner trembling, her tenseness. She hadn't been ready in high school either, and he'd walked away from her. Not this time. He'd give her some space and his own personal brand of attention, and by the end of the week . . . He smiled. She'd be ready.

"I guess I'd better unpack, then get some sleep. It's been a long day." She bent down and unplugged the twinkling lights. "Talk about sugarplums dancing . . ." Absently, she pulled her blouse away from where it clung to her breasts. "I guess you have things to do, so you can leave."

The outline of her breasts, which no amount of blouse adjusting could hide, didn't say "leave." The flick of her tongue across those luscious lips didn't say "leave." *Nothing* about her said "leave."

"Right. Leave." *Relax.* But he wasn't in relax mode. He had to get out of here before he did something that would definitely prove *his* readiness. "Sleep tight, Jenny."

As he shooed Toby out, then shut the door behind him, he got a final glimpse of her bemused expression. Was there a little bit of regret in her gaze? A little bit of sexual frustration in her clenched fists? He hoped so.

Because his whole body was vibrating with sexual readiness, with heat and want and *denial*. Incredible. No matter how often he reminded his body that this was Jenny, his old *pal*, his body ignored him. Its chant of "Sex, sex" was getting to be a real pain. Literally.

Sloan Mitello wasn't into pain. He was into fulfilling desires, his own as well as other people's. Even though Jenny wouldn't believe him, he had quite a few unfulfilled desires. Now might be the time to check off one of them. A minor one, granted, but one with tantalizing possibilities.

Sloan walked to the back door, flung it open, and stepped outside. He glanced at the ten-foot high wood fence surrounding his property, then strode along the path that wound between now-bare oaks and maples to the cleared area with the frozen pond.

He should be freezing, but his body's memory of Jenny was heated need. Snowflakes fell faster as he looked up at the night sky. He grinned. Showtime.

Methodically, he stripped off his clothes, then stood naked as the freezing crystals touched his body then melted, running in rivulets over his chest, his stomach, his thighs. Bracing his legs, he inhaled raggedly as needle-sharp pricks of coldness settled on the part of him that needed it most.

He pictured Jenny here beside him, her smooth body bare and gleaming in the snow's false light. She'd laugh and raise her arms to the drifting flakes. He'd watch the lift and thrust of her breasts, the flakes settling on each nipple, her nipples hardening. He'd reach for her, but she'd dance away as she reminded him, "Not ready, Mitello." Damn!

Closing his eyes, he wondered why the flakes didn't hiss as they touched him, forming a cloud of hot steam. Opening his eyes, he held out his hand to catch the flakes, then smoothed the coolness over his body. Flinging his head back, he felt the snow touch him everywhere like tiny fingertips.

Exhaling sharply, he glanced down. Nothing short of an ice bath would affect his body's hot-and-hard mind-set.

The slam of a closing window shifted his attention.

Jenny.

He turned the thought over in his mind, enjoyed the possibilities. Hmm. Maybe she wouldn't dream of sugarplums tonight. A man could hope.

Gathering up his clothes, he carried them back to the house. No use putting them on when he was going straight to his shower. His *warm* shower, then to his hot dreams.

Just before going inside, he glanced up at Jenny's window. Dark. He smiled.

Chapter Four

Jenny crept from the window. She'd opened the darned thing to cool off her hot thoughts of Sloan. But after what she'd seen, she might never have a cool thought again.

When she was sure he'd gone inside, she plugged in the twinkle lights. She didn't want the bright light of a bedside lamp to draw his attention if he went outside again. Mesmerized, she watched the blinking little lights do an uncoordinated dance around her bed.

Sloan had changed her concept of "snowman" forever. In the shifting shadows cast by the lights, she could still see him standing naked in the falling snow, his head thrown back, hair a dark halo framing a face etched with need. For *her*. His hard body gleaming against a white background. Aroused. For *her*.

For the first time since this new Sloan rang her doorbell, she felt confident. She could do this. She *wanted* to do this.

With renewed determination, she picked up the phone to call Carole. She needed to let her friend know where to reach her.

While Carole's phone rang, she sat down on the bed facing away from the door and window, but that did little to erase Sloan's image from her mind. Finally, Carole answered her phone with a sleepy hello.

"Sorry, Carole. I didn't realize how late it was."

"Jenny?" Carole's voice lost its sleepiness. "So what happened? Did it work?"

"The basket was perfect, and I'm staying with Sloan this week. He's interested and I'm ready. If everything goes as planned, I'll have my fling by the end of the week. Then I can go home and get on with my life." A breath of cool air played across the back of her neck. She mustn't have closed the window tightly.

"This could lead to greater things, girlfriend. Maybe you and Sloan can work on a longer relationship."

"Not likely." Jenny smiled. Since her marriage, Carole had turned from confirmed single-forever-and-proud-of-it to dedicated match-maker. "Sloan's a great guy, but he's fling material, not a long-term relationship kind of man."

"You don't know that for sure."

"Sloan's a dreamer, just like Dad. He might be successful right now, but a dreamer's world can collapse at any moment." *She knew*. "No, I'll have my fling with Sloan, then down the road a while I might meet a nice stable guy with a dependable nine-to-five job and I'll marry him."

"Boring, Jenny. Really boring."

She didn't want to get in an argument with Carole when she had plans to make. "Anyway, I'm ready for my fling. Talk to you after it happens." She hung up before Carole could mount another defense of Sloan.

"To paraphrase an old Hanes commercial, you're not ready until *I* say you're ready."

Ohmigod. She turned slowly. Sloan leaned casually against the frame of the open door. "Why didn't the door squeak? Every door should squeak."

"That's quite an opinion you have of me, Flame."

He wore only a towel wrapped around his waist, and despite her horror, Jenny's gaze was drawn to the muscular length of him. Obviously her optic nerves were *not* in sync with her brain.

He dropped several towels on a chair near the door. "Thought you might need these."

"I'm sorry you heard that, Sloan. Do you want

319

me to leave?" She didn't *want* to leave, not when she was so close.

He raised an eyebrow. "Did I say that? Besides, where else will you find such a convenient *fling*?"

Jenny winced. He was right. She'd never find someone this right again. "So where do we go from here?"

He shrugged away from the doorframe. "When I feel you're ready, I'll give you your 'fling.' "

"So you're saying you'll call the shots?" She didn't like it, but she'd have to agree if she wanted to stay.

"Pretty much." He smiled. Not a nice smile. "One thing I need to know. Where'd you get your opinion of me?"

She drew in a deep breath. He deserved the truth. "I went to school with you, remember? You always had some wild scheme that never panned out. And as far as I can see, you've drifted from one thing to another since you graduated. This house is great, but it could be gone tomorrow." *So could you*. She'd never give her heart to someone she couldn't depend on. "I know you, Sloan Mitello."

For the first time, she glimpsed anger in his eyes. "You don't have a clue who I am, who I *really* am. You're too busy with your preconceptions to find out." He turned from her. "See you tomorrow, Flame." He was gone.

Jenny lay down and closed her eyes. What a mess. But things would look better after a good night's sleep.

She fell asleep on her side, one hand clenched between her thighs. Protection or invitation? Her last thought left things open to discussion.

The decorations were falling off the tree. She refused to open her eyes when the first one bounced off her chest, then crawled to the side of her neck and curled up against her. Even when the second one landed on her head, then tangled itself in her hair, she didn't open her eyes. It was the third one, the one that landed on her feet, then bit her big toe, that did it.

She forced her lids open. Three pairs of big eyes in little fuzzy faces peered at her. None was Toby. One was orange, one was gray, the last was calico. If the old tale of each color standing for a different daddy was true, then mama cat had been a very busy lady. No virginity issues there. "Go away and leave me alone, fuzzies."

"I'm afraid that won't be possible, madam."

"What?" She bounced to a sitting position and came face to face with the Ghost-of-Christmas-Best-Forgotten.

"Mr. Mitello called this morning and employed me to take care of you during your stay here. I've cooked breakfast. Eat it." His nose gave new meaning to patrician, and his eyes were almost crossed from looking down it at her.

"I don't eat breakfast, and who're you?" She hugged her jammies tightly to her and slipped a tentative toe to the floor.

"You do now, and I'm Ridley." He was a caricature of all the uppercrust servants that ever lived. Or died, in Ridley's case.

She glanced at the tray he'd set down on her bedside table. Ugh. Oatmeal. "I don't like oatmeal."

"You will drink the orange juice and eat some of the oatmeal before you set one tootsie out of this bedroom." He glared at her. "Madam."

"Now just a minute . . . Ridley. I don't have to—"

"Mr. Mitello won't be pleased to learn I made something you don't like. He might even fire me. I have twelve grandchildren." He paused to let the number sink in. "All expecting gifts for Christmas."

"Oh." Emotional blackmail. She was a sucker for it. No matter how she felt about her own dreams, she didn't have the heart to stomp on Ridley's. "Well, maybe just a bite."

She was on her fifth spoonful of sticky oatmeal, trying for six, when Sloan appeared. He filled the doorway, bringing with him the scent of snow and woodsmoke, and the memory of what they'd said to each other last night.

Dressed in white T-shirt and worn jeans, he

was every woman's fantasy of a bad man who'd make it good for her.

And he would be *her* fling. He'd promised. When she was ready. Of course, she was ready now. She was sure of it.

"How's it taste, Flame?"

"It'll be delicious." Position ten on Carole's video. She could hardly wait.

"Ridley, make sure you cook oatmeal every morning for Jenny." Sloan smiled, his gaze cool and knowing.

"I live to cook, sir." Ridley cast Jenny an innocent glance, picked up her abandoned tray, then made a dignified exit.

Sloan walked over to Jenny's bed and sat beside her. After depositing the three kittens on the floor, he cast her an amused glance. "So . . . you love oatmeal, do you?"

When would he mention her fling? "I hate oatmeal. I was eating for Ridley's twelve grandchildren."

"Ridley doesn't have any children, *or* grandchildren." He glanced at the kittens, who were making a determined effort to scale the comforter.

She couldn't see his expression. Should she apologize for what she'd said last night? *When would he mention her fling?* "He lied to me? I can't believe he lied to me. Why did you hire someone who lies like that?"

He finally looked at her, and the wicked slant

323

of his grin made her almost believe in the possibility of dreams. *Almost*.

"He told me he had to support his old and sickly parents."

"And?" She noted that his gaze had shifted to the top button of her pajamas.

"His parents died thirty years ago."

"And you still hired him?" Why were they talking about Ridley, and when would he mention last night?

"What can I say, his references were great." His gaze slid over her. "A person might lie to me, but if they have good references I could be persuaded to give them a second chance."

Come on, Sloan, get to the point. Jenny frowned. "Employers probably gave him good references so they wouldn't have to eat any more of his oatmeal." She cast him a suspicious glance. "He said you hired him to take care of me. Why?"

He loved it. The way she pushed out her lower lip when she frowned. The way she'd tried to be kind to Ridley. The way she thought she'd have her fling and walk away from him. "Since you don't have any dreams of your own, I thought I'd fulfill a few you *would* have if you believed—"

"Okay, okay." She put her hands over her ears. "Here's a dream you can fulfill. Get Ridley to order take-out for dinner."

"Done." He gently pulled her hands from her

ears. "So, you think you're ready to have sex with a stranger."

"No." She averted her gaze, staring at the twinkling lights by her bed. "I mean, yes. You're not a stranger."

"Sure I am. It's been ten years, Flame. Do you know all the places I've been, all the things I've done? Or do you only know what Carole told you, what I told you the few times we communicated? Maybe you should run back to Lenny and his bagels. He'd be a lot safer."

"No." Her gaze never wavered from the lights. "Does Brinks deliver your electricity bill payment?"

"Let me worry about the electricity bill. Are you ready to do it right now?" Those pj's had to go. Since he'd done the naked-in-the-snow desire last night, he needed something new to replace it. How about a Jenny-hot-and-naked-in-my-bed desire? No, that wasn't new.

"Pretty blunt, aren't you, Sloan?" She finally looked at him.

"And you weren't? Could've fooled me."

"Okay, I'm sorry for some of the things I said, and I shouldn't have plotted behind your back. So consider yourself apologized to." She cast him a disgruntled look. "This is hard for me. You could be a little more subtle."

"Well hell, afraid I'm not a subtle kind of guy. If I'm going to be part of your fling, maybe you should tell me what kind of man I'm supposed to pretend to be." He probably shouldn't have given her that opening. He didn't like the glitter in her eyes.

"You have to be sensitive. I'm into sensitive." Her gaze turned thoughtful. "I like poetry. Maybe you could send me poems."

Cripes. She wanted a man who sent her poems? He'd never gotten past the "Mary Had a Little Lamb" stage in poetry. He'd thought a lot about Mary. *Without* her lamb.

"And you have to be a good dancer. I'd definitely want that."

Great. Some of the women he'd danced with had ended up needing foot surgery.

Her expression brightened. "Oh, and I'd like you to be thin and ascetic-looking with big soulful brown eyes."

Hmmph. A dead-ringer for the old hound dog he'd rescued when he was a kid. Sloan could starve himself for months and never qualify as thin and ascetic-looking. "Sounds like I'm a real fun guy."

"Yeah, and we could listen to chamber music on cold winter nights." She pursed her lips. "Do you like chamber music?"

"Depends on whose chamber we're doing it in." So he was a rhythmically and musically challenged, insensitive, over-muscled jerk. He'd deal with it. "Of course, as Mr. Perfect I won't have any dreams."

She didn't even blink. "None."

"Right." He watched her climb from bed, walk to the closet, then pull some clothes out. "Look, I have a few things to do. I won't be tied up long. Hope you won't be bored."

She shook her head and smiled, the first natural smile he'd seen this morning. "I have to check my e-mail, then I'm going to do a little redecorating here." She cast him an impish grin. "You did say you wanted some help with color schemes, didn't you?"

"Redecorate away." He rescued the kittens, who were stranded halfway up their own personal Mt. Everest, then turned and made his escape.

Jenny watched him close the door behind him. Why had she fed him that nonsense about what she'd want him to be? *Because you didn't have the guts to tell him he's perfect just like he is.* Wow, was she into self-honesty or what?

Fine. Three seconds of painful introspection were enough for one morning. She gazed around the room. Beautiful but busy. Sort of took after its owner.

She'd have to create her own island of serenity in this room if she expected to survive the week. Besides, calming down the bedroom would take all her concentration. Wouldn't give her time to draw mental pictures. Like his bare legs tangled with hers on the bed, his bare body covering hers.

Passion led to dreams of more passion, and she had a suspicion that Sloan Mitello's love-making wouldn't be like a library book that you could renew if you weren't done with it.

Jenny glanced around the room. She'd worked her buns off, but it was worth it. Much better. She felt calmer already. She gazed at her laptop. No interesting e-mail.

She was about to shut everything down, but then she decided to take just one peek at Sloan's site. What damage could just one peek do?

Fascinated, she stared at the empty box on her screen. *Let us fulfill your desire*. No discussion of money, of contracts, just type in your desire. Made it sound so easy.

Of course, she wouldn't get sucked into something like that. Only a fool would believe you could make dreams come true so easily. Her fingers moved on the keys.

Surprised, she realized she'd typed something. "I remember the mud puddle." She felt a little embarrassed, and she hadn't a clue why. There was no reason to be embarrassed. Defiantly, she hit enter. She hadn't really voiced a desire, she'd just reminded him of old times. "So what's the big deal?"

There was no one to answer her question.

Leaving her room, she spent time scoping out the rest of the house. Wow. She'd never realized there were that many holiday decorations in the world.

And why did he need an indoor garden room complete with mini-pond and waterfall? Sloan wasn't a sit-by-the-pond-and-ponder-life's-secrets kind of guy.

What did she expect? The Sloan she'd known ten years ago had been an ordinary guy. . . . Okay, so Sloan had never been quite *ordinary*. But this Sloan was larger than life, so she shouldn't be surprised when his house was over the top.

Where was he, anyway? Maybe she'd go back to her room and read for a while, get her mind off of where and when *it* would happen.

Deep in her book, she was startled by a knock. Dragging herself from the chair where she'd curled up, she pulled open the door.

"Hi, Flame. I thought you might . . ." He glanced into the room. "Sonovagun." Striding past her, he stopped and stared. "Who needs the Grinch when you have Jenny Saunders, Terminator-of-Holiday-Cheer?"

Maybe she'd gone too far. This might call for some soothing. A neck rub? It'd always worked on Mom when Dad had come home with a new scheme for making a million. Besides, she needed to get used to touching him in an impersonal way before . . . *Just do it*.

"Sit down, Sloan." She pushed him to a sitting position on her bed, then knelt behind him.

Placing her hands on both sides of his neck, she gently massaged. Tight, very tight. And those were *her* muscles. His were even tighter.

"Relax and feel the calmness, the peace of this room," she murmured against his neck. "I didn't really change that much. The comforter is reversible. The ivory is much more calming than red and green. And I got rid of the tree and lights and Santa and—"

"Right. No big change." He moaned as she massaged down his back to the base of his spine. "Damn that feels good."

No joking. Her hands were doing some serious shaking as she stroked his body, felt the bunch of muscles beneath her fingers. "I can feel you relaxing already."

"Sure. Relaxing." His breathing didn't sound relaxed. "I'm so relaxed, I think I'll lie down."

She moved out of his way as he lay down on his back. What to do?

He watched her out of half-closed eyes. He smiled. "Keep going. I can feel those muscles tightening again. All this white stiffens me right up."

She huffed. "All that white snow didn't stiffen you up last night," She considered her statement. "Okay, maybe it stiffened you a little." *Foot-in-mouth disease strikes again.*

His smile broadened, grew wicked. "What're you afraid of, Flame? I thought you said you were ready."

"I *am* ready." And Little Red Riding Hood thought *she* had problems with wolves in beds. But he'd given her the opening she'd been hoping for, permission to work her wiles on him.

Fine, so she didn't have any wiles, but she could learn. She straddled his hips. His growing interest in her relaxation technique was obvious, and she slid back and forth over it to make sure she was right.

Yep. Very interested. She must be working harder than she'd thought because she was gasping for air.

He closed his eyes, and his grin vanished.

Reaching under his shirt, she worked her fingers over his stomach, his chest, then paused when she reached his nipples. Gee, couldn't forget his nipples. Had to relax them too. Rolling them between thumb and forefinger, she clenched her thighs at his groan of pleasure.

She didn't know how much more relaxation she could stand before she ripped his jeans off and planted herself on top of his—

"Dinner is served, sir."

No, no, no! She collapsed onto Sloan's heaving chest and completely agreed with his grunted four-letter appraisal of the situation.

She started to climb off, but he held her in place. "Get out, Ridley."

"As you say, sir."

She twisted her head so she could see Ridley. A Ridley who was the picture of expressionless calm. A Ridley who had a dirt smudge on his nose. She took courage from this small sign of human weakness.

Ridley backed from the room. "I'll see you in the morning, sir. And madam, your oatmeal will be ready at precisely eight o'clock." He closed the door on her reaction.

Arrgh. "If that man tries to con me into one more bowl of oatmeal, I'll—"

"Shh." Sloan put a finger to her lips, effectively silencing her.

Amazing, but any part of him touching her resulted in a complete loss of rational thought patterns. Now, what had she been saying?

"Guess the oatmeal killed the mood, huh?" He allowed her to climb off him, then stood.

She couldn't quite meet his gaze. "Umm . . ." Think. She knew thousands of words. So why couldn't she remember even one?

"Hope you like hoagies." He pulled down his shirt, then strode to the bedroom door.

"Hoagies?" Good. One word was better than none.

"Yeah. I had Ridley order them from Mario's. I told him to put everything on them. That okay?"

"Sure." Whoopie! She'd remembered another one.

"Then guess what, Flame?" He grabbed her hand and pulled her out the door.

Oh, no. She'd forgotten about the mud puddle. *Please don't let him say anything about the mud puddle.*

"After we eat, you're going with me to make someone's desire come true."

Thank you, God.

Chapter Five

"Ready to go, Flame?"

"Mmm." She closed her eyes as she savored the last bite of her hoagie. Not much on earth could compete with one of Mario's hoagies. The salami, the cheese, the peppers, the—

"Here's your coat." Sloan stood behind her chair.

"Hmm." She felt sort of guilty. Sloan had wolfed down his dinner, then gone off to change while her taste buds had wallowed in unrepentant gluttony.

"We can walk to Mary Kelly's place. Great exercise."

She swallowed, then narrowed her gaze as

she turned to confront him. "Are you suggesting that . . ."

Her voice trailed off for lack of oxygen. *Santa Claus*. He was dressed as Santa. A very sexy Santa, pillow-enhanced stomach and all. If he crawled down her chimney she wouldn't be waiting with just milk and cookies. "Why are you dressed—"

"I'll explain while we're walking." He bundled her into her coat, then carefully buttoned her up. One button at a time.

His knuckles grazed between her breasts. Lingered. She felt the pressure as though there was no flesh, no bone separating her heart from his touch. Her heart's pounding seemed to grow with each second his warm hand remained against her.

And when his fingers slid down to the button over her stomach, she almost gasped with relief. For a moment she'd thought she'd have to put her hand over her heart to keep it in.

Her stomach wasn't much better though. He slid his fingers under her blouse and laid his palm flat against her skin. She knew the sensation, had felt it this summer when her roller coaster car had hovered for what seemed like eternity above an endless drop. It was excitement, frightened anticipation, the need to scramble from the car before the plunge, the knowledge there was no escape. And as his fin-

335

gers glided lower, scraping the top of her jeans, sliding between skin and cloth, she felt the earth drop from beneath her.

"I . . . I can finish that." Her fingers fumbled at the last few buttons, while he moved away from her.

"Right." His voice was rough as he strode to the door and yanked it open, letting in a blast of frigid air.

He didn't look to see if she followed, and she had to trot to catch up with his long strides. "What's Mary Kelly's desire, and why're you bringing me along?"

He kept distance between them, not glancing her way. "Mary can tell you her desire. And I brought you along to show you that desires *do* come true. Maybe not exactly when we want them, but more like when we *need* them, when it's *right* for them."

He laughed and shook his head. "Doesn't make a hell of a lot of sense, does it?"

She cast him a cautious glance. "Not exactly." She had to know something. "Did you make your desires come true at the right time? Wouldn't it have been better if you'd had all this when you were a kid?"

He finally looked at her. "Maybe, maybe not. If I'd had all this when I was young, I might not have worked so hard, fought my way up to being a success. My desires were my incentive. What's your incentive, Jenny?"

She tugged the collar of her coat higher around her ears. "I don't need an incentive."

"Wow, what a woman. No dreams, no incentives. Self-motivated to the core." His glance mocked her. "But wait, there's a crack in your armor. Your dream about having a fling with some man."

Only with you, no one else. The truth leaped out and bit her before she could run. She wanted to squirm away from it, deny it, but it held on and tightened its grip. "You're good at twisting words, Sloan."

He ignored her comment. "What about happy, Flame? Are you happy with your life?"

"Sure, I'm happy. What's not to be happy about?" Her words came out in little white puffs of defiance.

"Hey." He held up his hand. "Just asking."

Strange, he was still fuming over the plan she'd cooked up with Carole and her assumption he was a doing-what-feels-good kind of guy. Sure, he wasn't into long-term relationships. And sure, any man would jump at the chance to have a fling with Jenny. So what was he so ticked off about? Damned if he knew.

But no matter how angry he was, he still wanted her to be happy in her life, not just in his bed. And it seemed to be getting more important by the minute. Why? The personal happiness of a woman had never driven his past relationships.

He cast her a sideways glance as she stomped along beside him. Didn't look like she was thinking happy thoughts right now.

Exhaling a breath of resignation, Sloan reached out and clasped her hand. He was rewarded when she turned to him with a brilliant smile. She certainly had no trouble making *him* happy.

He kept her hand warm in his all the way to Mary's house. "Okay, go up, knock on her door, then when she answers, tell her you're Santa's helper, and he's on his way down."

She blinked. "Santa's *helper*? Down? Down where?"

He leaned over and kissed her on the nose. "Down the chimney. See you in a few minutes."

Sloan turned and strode toward the back of the house, where a ladder awaited him. He hoped to God Mary had had them build that chimney wide enough.

Jenny didn't give herself a chance to stand and ponder. Climbing the steps to the big old Victorian house, she rang the bell. No matter how crazy this whole thing seemed, she had to admit it was more fun than sitting in front of her computer looking for tax loopholes that Smith Inc. could crawl through.

The small gray-haired woman who opened the door was everyone's image of a grandmother. She offered Jenny a kind smile. "Yes, dear?"

Jenny waited expectantly for her next words which would obviously be, "Have a cookie." Nope. No cookie offer.

Okay, she could do this. Jenny opened her mouth and forced the ridiculous words past lips that hadn't uttered a ridiculous word in years. *Until Sloan Mitello rang your bell.* "Umm. I'm Santa's helper, and he's on his way down."

The small woman actually clapped her hands, and Jenny muttered a mental *Oh boy*.

The woman reached out, grasped Jenny's hand, and dragged her into the house. "Come in, come in, dear. I'm Mary Kelly and this is so exciting."

Jenny allowed herself to be led into a large living room that looked like it had been lifted from a Currier and Ives print. Large overstuffed chairs, doilies, knickknacks, a gigantic tree decorated with what must be hundreds of balls, and a huge fireplace that was blessedly, at least for Sloan's sake, unlit.

Now, how to phrase her question in a diplomatic way. "And what is Santa bringing you tonight?"

Mary laughed. "Oh, he's not bringing me anything tonight. I'm just going to sit on his knee and tell him what I want."

Jenny forgot about diplomacy. "Sit on his *knee*?"

Mary's smile widened. "Let me guess. Santa got you from the Santa's-Helpers-for-Hire temp service, and he hasn't had time to fill you in."

Jenny was past words. She nodded and cast a nervous glance at the chimney. If the scrabbling sounds on the roof were any indication, Santa was about to make a dramatic appearance. And not a minute too soon.

Mary laid a comforting hand on Jenny's arm. Jenny noted the boulder-sized diamond in Mary's ring and did some readjusting on her grandmother image. No flour-covered hands fresh from baking Christmas treats for the grandkiddies here.

"I'm not crazy, dear. Sit down, sit down." She pointed to the nearest chair. Jenny sank into the soft cushion and wondered if Mary would be interested in a trade for a designer couch. "I come from a family that didn't believe in filling children's heads with useless dreams. When my friends were standing in line at Wanamaker's to see Santa, I was being told there was no such person, and you only got in life what you worked for."

She sat down on the chair's arm and peered at the chimney where grunts and muttered curses echoed.

Jenny bit her lip to keep from grinning. No ho-ho-ho's. Maybe Santa shouldn't have chowed down on that last hoagie.

Mary sighed and glanced back at Jenny. "My parents were good people, but they didn't understand that everyone needs dreams, even if they're just small ones." Standing, Mary moved to the fireplace, knelt down, then peered up the chimney. Satisfied that Santa didn't need rescuing yet, she came back to Jenny's chair.

"By the time I was old enough to do what I wanted, I was also too old to sit on Santa's knee. Clients wouldn't have much confidence in me if they saw me sitting on Santa's knee in some mall." She patted Jenny's hand. "Their trust is so fragile."

Jenny was getting more and more concerned. *Come on, Sloan.* "What do you do?"

"I'm a corporate lawyer." Mary straightened the doily on the chair's arm.

Corporate lawyer?

Mary smiled. "My colleagues call me The Shark. A silly title, don't you think?"

Jenny gulped. "Right. Silly." Luckily, she was saved from having to make further comment as Santa's feet, legs, hips, and buns slid from the chimney. Then stopped.

"Where's the rest of Santa?" Mary sounded aggrieved. Half a Santa would probably be grounds for a breach of contract suit.

Jenny jumped to her feet and hurried to the chimney.

"Ho, ho, ho! Santa's stuck. Santa's helper needs to give Santa some help *now*." Santa did *not* sound amused.

Jenny felt she would explode with the effort to hold back her laughter.

341

"I had that chimney built specifically for Santa. Obviously the company didn't get the dimensions right. I'll talk to their lawyers tomorrow."

Somehow, Jenny felt sorry for the chimney builders. But she didn't have time to worry about anything right now except getting Sloan out of that chimney.

Wrapping her arms around his hips, she pulled. Nothing. Well, almost nothing.

Her cheek was pressed against his buns. Firm buns. Muscular buns. She could feel them clench. *A woman of experience would rub her cheek against them, maybe even indulge in some appreciative purring.* All she could manage was a rise in heat at the point of contact.

"Jenny?" His voice was husky, almost strangled. She hoped the sides of the chimney weren't pressing on any vital organs.

"What?" *A woman of experience would place her lips on one mouthwatering bun and slide her tongue across the rounded contour.* Too bad. There would be no Santa bun for Jenny. On the up side, she wouldn't have to worry about getting rid of the cotton taste.

"How're you doing, dear?" Mary's voice sounded anxious.

"Fine. Just fine." Snuggling her face against his bun, she gave another ineffectual yank. Darn, bun-lust had made her weak.

"Jenny!" Sloan's voice sounded desperate.

"Hmm?"

"I can't come out like this."

"Why not?" She was having a real hard time concentrating. She'd refocus. In a minute. *A woman of experience might gently nip his bun.* She considered it.

"Dammit, Jenny, move your hands up."

She blinked. What did her hands have to do with anything? But obediently, she slid her fingers up to his groin. She widened her eyes at the same time she reluctantly dropped her hands from him. Wow. That certainly refocused her. She knew the many things an experienced woman would do with *that*. After all, she'd seen Carole's tape.

"Jenny, get Mary to pull me out." His words came in gasping breaths as though he'd just finished a race. "By the legs."

"Sure." She hadn't *wanted* to let go. She'd wanted to fill her hands with him, fill *her* with him.

She sure hoped Sloan decided she was ready soon. Not only was she ready, she was overripe and on the verge of falling off the vine.

"I . . . I can't budge him, Mary. You try."

Mary nodded. Taking Jenny's place, she wrapped her arms around Sloan's legs and yanked. He popped from the chimney like a champagne cork.

Keeping his back to them, he dusted himself off, then grabbed a pillow from a nearby chair.

"Ho, ho, ho! Come sit on Santa's knee, Mary, and tell him what you want for Christmas."

Dropping into a chair, he plopped the pillow onto his lap, then patted his knee. Mary sat on his knee, then waited expectantly.

"Have you been a good little girl, Mary Kelly?" Sloan's breathing had returned to normal.

"Oh, yes." Mary frowned. "Except for maybe that hostile takeover, but that's not important."

"Well, tell Santa what you want him to bring."

Mary's eyes took on a predatory gleam. "I want a new Lexus. Black. I want a condo in Atlantic City near the casinos and with a water view. I want stock in Dell, Microsoft, and Amazon. Oh, and I need someone good to organize my home." She blinked. "I'm not being greedy am I, Santa?"

"Santa thinks you *deserve* those things. I'll be making my list and checking it twice, Mary, and I'd just bet you'll have a very merry Christmas."

A Lexus? Jenny wondered how *she* could get on Santa's list.

Mary cast Jenny a sly glance. "Santa, there's someone else waiting to sit on your lap. I want her to go next."

"Me?" Jenny glanced behind her. Yep, no one else around. "I don't want anything for Christmas."

"Of course you do, dear." Mary's gaze sharpened. "This is part of my dream. I want someone else waiting to talk to Santa."

"Part of your dream, huh?" Jenny glanced at Sloan, who was frantically shaking his head. "Since you put it that way . . ."

Mary slipped off of Santa's knee, and Jenny sidled over to stand in front of him. No time like the present to start on this experience thing. If she was going to do it, she might as well do it right.

Jenny tried to control her smile. It wasn't her regular one. She could tell from the way her lips felt that it was a cat smile. If a cat could smile.

She drew her tongue slowly over her bottom lip and watched Sloan's eyes widen, then narrow. While he was busy interpreting the meanings of her cat smile and lip licking, she whipped the pillow from his lap and planted herself firmly in its place.

"Oh, my. Look at the time." Mary bustled toward the doorway. "I have to make a business call. Don't do anything important without me."

Jenny didn't even notice when Mary left. She was too involved with wiggling her bottom deeper into Santa's lap.

"That might not be the safest position, Flame." Sloan's low growl signaled the end of his Santa persona. "Could lead to a growing problem."

"It already is." Jenny couldn't control the breathless sound of her voice.

"Maybe we need to examine our option."

"Option? Singular? Maybe we need to enlarge our choices." She couldn't stop herself from sliding her bottom across his lap.

"I already have." He moved beneath her, the thrust of his hips strong. "And if you don't stop rubbing that tempting bottom against me, I'll exercise my option right now and disgrace the Santa image forever."

She opened her eyes wide. "And would that be your Option Claus?"

He buried his face against her neck and groaned. "That was awful, Jenny."

She breathed out, the sexual tension broken for the moment. "I guess I need to tell you what I want for Christmas."

"Hey, Santa's my name and gifts are my game. Let's hear it."

Okay, she wouldn't be greedy. She'd only ask for a few things. Nothing big or expensive. She *did* need a new couch.

"I want . . . a horse and some chocolate syrup."

Chapter Six

Sloan was attuned to her every breath, every movement as they walked back to his house. She probably regretted her impulsive wishes already, but it was too late. Much too late.

The snow muffled their steps, but nothing could muffle the pounding of his heart, the surge of blood gathering in one strategic area, the desire that built with every white puff of breath he breathed into the cold air.

First things first. Reaching out, he took her hand into his. He felt the slight tremble of her fingers.

He said nothing, allowing the warmth to creep back into her hand, allowing the trembling to still. She had to sense the need that churned in him, that urged him to lay her down in the snowy bank beside that old maple tree and make love to her until the snow turned to steam.

"So, do you do those things often, Sloan?"

She wiggled her fingers in his hand, and he tightened his grasp. *No escape, Flame.*

"I *never* do those things. My assistants take care of the warm fuzzies. But Mary's a friend and lives close by, so I made an exception. I just do the interesting stuff." *Ask me what the interesting stuff is.*

She didn't ask. "Those were some pretty big promises you made to Mary. Won't she be disappointed on Christmas morning?"

He smiled. "Mary has four ex-husbands. All CEO's of major companies. You want to talk about power behind the throne? Let's just say each of them will ante up to keep Mary happy."

"How'd you meet Mary?"

"Through one of her ex-husbands. Even shiftless wanderers make friends once in a while."

She cast him a sharp glance. "You'll never forget what I said, will you?"

He smiled. "Not unless you give me a reason to."

She seemed lost in thought as they approached his house. He admired the blaze of light. His neighbors' puny efforts at tasteful holiday decorations paled in comparison.

"You know, I bet your house gives the airport fits."

He exhaled sharply. "Okay, I'll bite."

She slanted him a teasing grin. "How many planes have tried to land in your backyard because they thought they'd spotted the runway lights?"

He abandoned her hand and slid his arm around her waist, pulling her close. "What can I say? I'm a man of large appetites. I like bright lights, big houses, and warm women."

She molded herself closer to his side, and he tightened his grip. Funny how perspectives changed over the years. In high school, she'd been a pal. A little too serious most of the time. A little too disapproving of him.

Now? She'd never be just a pal to him again, not with the sizzle and spark that leaped between them. He was busy deciding how to explore all that sizzle and spark when he looked up to see Ridley waiting at the door. Not a good sign.

"Thought you were gone for the night, Ridley."

"Someone has to maintain your site, sir." He carefully pulled a white handkerchief from his pocket and wiped a smudge of dirt from his face.

Jenny looked puzzled. "I didn't know you helped Sloan with his website, Ridley."

"I was *not* speaking of a website, madam."

Dismissing Jenny, he turned back to Sloan. "I haven't the foggiest idea what you have in mind, sir, but making frequent trips to add water to it will, of course, count as overtime."

"Right. Overtime."

"You water Sloan's plants for him?"

"Hardly, madam." Ridley lifted his chin into the air and moved past Jenny.

Sloan watched Ridley climb into his car, then turned back to answer Jenny's obvious next question.

"What was he talking about, Sloan?"

Sloan rubbed the back of his neck to relieve the tension. "Who knows."

"You're lying. You always rubbed the back of your neck when you were lying."

Sloan dropped his hand. "Let's go in the garden room entrance."

"Why? What was Ridley talking about? What're you trying to hide? And why're we going in this entrance?"

Sloan turned his back to her barrage of questions as he unlocked the door, then turned around to face her.

"Why'd Ridley have dirt on his face? I don't—"

Wordlessly, he scooped her up in his arms, kicked open the door, stepped into the darkened room, kicked the door shut, then dropped her into his ornamental-pond-turned-mud-puddle.

Ignoring her shriek of outrage, he flipped on the dim lights hidden behind foliage. The many mirrors captured the scene of Jenny scrambling to her feet like some angry she-devil rising from a prehistoric swamp. At least he'd stopped her questions.

"You . . ." Words eluded Jenny. There weren't any that could describe her fury, her thirst for vengeance, her . . . *excitement*.

Sloan grinned at her, his smile a flash of wickedness in the almost-dark room. "Hey, I'm just granting your desire."

"I did *not* desire to be sitting in a mud puddle—"

"You typed it into my desire box."

"—with all my clothes on." She lowered her gaze to the area of his personal desire box.

"Then take them off, Flame. Take them all off."

His husky suggestion wrapped around her. *I want a bad man in the worst way*. Why not now?

Tonight, she'd get rid of her inhibitions along with her clothes.

Never breaking eye contact with the green glitter of his heated gaze, she stripped off her muddy coat and dropped it over the ornamental rocks beside the pond. "There's something more I forgot to type in the box."

"There's always room for more." His whisper promised that he was the king of more.

"A mud puddle's no fun alone." She couldn't

believe she was about to venture into the dangerous area of *fun*, which had an infinity of answers.

She turned her back to him and quickly unbuttoned her blouse. Okay, no stress here. She'd just modify his take-them-all-off statement. She'd get down to bra and panties, then they'd roll around and laugh just like the other time. *Then* she'd be ready. Her truth monitor's cluck clucks were *really* getting on her nerves.

She watched him in the mirror. His gaze never left her as he stripped off his Santa suit . . . and everything else. He'd always been an all-or-nothing guy.

The room's glow highlighted his body in shades of gold and shadow, stole away the boy she'd known in high school and replaced him with a hard, dangerous stranger.

He stepped into the mud, moving toward her with the measured tread of a predator, sure of his prey.

She took a deep, steadying breath. *Can the melodrama, there's nothing hard and dangerous about him.* She glanced in the mirror. Okay, nothing *dangerous*.

Closing her eyes, she anticipated the moment he'd touch her, wondered if she'd feel anything different this time.

"Don't move." His voice was soft beside her ear. His breath, warm against her neck.

His fingers slid across her shoulders, down

her arms, as he removed her blouse. When she felt his fingers move to the clasp of her bra, she could only shake her head.

"Whatever you want, Flame." His attention shifted. "It's your memory." Within seconds he'd removed her jeans.

Turning her to face him, he ran the tip of his finger down the front of her panties, paused between her legs. "Whenever you're ready." His whisper was hot need, and she clenched her legs against the urge to shout *yes*.

Too fast. Everything was moving too fast.

He was a dreamer. *I want him*. Okay, maybe he wasn't really a dreamer. After all, he had this place. *I want him*. He was totally right brained. Look at what he did for a living. Look at what he'd done to this house. *I want him*. Fine, so between his right brain and her left brain they'd have one whole brain between them. Good enough for one night of fun. After all, this was just a fling.

She wasn't sure. She didn't know. Biting her lower lip, she indulged in some mental hand-wringing.

"Shh." He slid his finger up over her stomach, between her breasts, and touched her lips.

"I didn't say anything." Should she close her lips around his finger, signaling that the fun could begin? Or should she bite him, thereby ending fun thoughts as he rushed to his local emergency room for rabies shots?

"Sure you did. I bet people blocks away could hear the battle between your brain and your baser instincts. Watch out. Baser instincts fight dirty."

While she was busy mulling that thought over, he slipped to his knees. All mulling came to a sudden halt as Sloan's hand glided up her bare leg.

"What do you remember most about the first time, Flame?" His hand continued up her thigh, and he fingered the lace at the edge of her panties.

Her legs wobbly, she sank to her knees in front of him. The mud felt cool against her heated flesh. "Mosquitos. Lots of mosquitos."

"Liar." Laughing, he pulled her down into the mud with him.

She squealed as he rolled her beneath him. Squealed? Clients would desert her in droves if they heard her. Squealing was not an accepted accountant noise.

She blinked up at Sloan. The truth? She didn't give a damn what her clients thought. She was having fun.

Suddenly, her laughter died. The mood shifted as he straddled her hips and studied her through eyes that gleamed beneath half-lowered lids. "I just remembered something."

"Uh-oh." She shifted her hips along with her attention to his most striking point of interest. *So close.* She could reach out and slide her fingers along his length, cup him in her palm—

"I remember writing a message on you."

She wanted to laugh, to restore the feeling of lighthearted fun. Nothing came out. "*On* me?"

"Yep." Slowly, he slid the mud over her stomach, and her stomach muscles clenched in anticipation. He allowed his splayed hand to rest there until his heat seeped into her, warming her. "Seemed like the right thing to do at the time."

"Sort of like when guys leave messages inside hearts on tree trunks? That kind of thing?" Her breathing quickened, her need to touch him, to clasp him in her hand, almost unbearable.

"I guess so." Dragging out the torture, he ran his fingers between her breasts, leaving a trail of mud and frustration.

Touch me everywhere. Now. "It must be a guy thing, like when bears leave claw marks on trees to mark their territory."

"Could be." Lingeringly, he molded each breast with his hand, then rubbed the pad of his thumb across each nipple.

Like a puppet whose strings were all attached to a master puppeteer, her hips arched at the bare-wire sizzle of his touch.

She had to share. Reaching out, she drew her fingernail the length of his erection.

He shuddered, then stilled. "Not a good idea, Flame. If you touch me like that, I could get serious real fast."

She smiled up at him, then purposely licked the dryness from her bottom lip. "How serious?"

He shook his head, and the slide of tangled hair across bare shoulders gleaming with mud strengthened the image of primitive male power. "Always the number person. On a scale of one to ten, I'm at about six."

"Hmm. Lots of room for serious growth then." Giving in to temptation, she clasped him. "But not here." She swallowed to clear the huskiness that had crept into her voice, the feeling that she couldn't get enough air.

"You'd be surprised." His response was muffled as he leaned forward and covered her mouth with his.

His lips were hot, hungry. He slid his tongue across her closed lips, and she opened to him. Deepening the kiss, he explored her, and she knew he could taste all her desires, the ones she'd dreamed and the ones she hadn't even thought of yet.

She was working hard on those unimagined dreams when he pushed away from her. As the clamor of her pounding heart and the harsh rasp of her breathing eased, she heard the voices of carolers in the street.

Sloan grinned. "Sorry. When it happens, I don't want to be lying in mud listening to 'Rudolph the Red Nosed Reindeer.' "

She nodded, the only movement she was capable of now.

"So don't you want to know what I wrote on you?"

She nodded again, fascinated by the rapid rise and fall of his gleaming chest. He'd been as much into the moment as she had.

Closing her eyes, she concentrated on the track of his fingertip between her breasts.

I. He'd traced the word "I." Made sense. What other word would fit in that narrow space? She kinda yearned for a longer word, though. One with maybe seven letters. He could start at one nipple, put the fourth letter right in the middle, then end up at her other nipple. Her nipples ached with the need for their very own letters.

He moved lower. Jenny frowned. Not a word, but a shape. She concentrated on the slide of his finger over her slick skin, tried to ignore the trail of goose bumps decorating his artwork.

A heart. He'd drawn a large heart. Okay, no reason to hyperventilate here. It didn't mean a thing. There were lots of messages out there with the same lead-in. I—heart drawing—cats, I—heart drawing—baseball. Millions of possibilities.

The only drawing space left was her lower abdomen. She wished she hadn't eaten that last Mario's hoagie. He had enough space down there to fill in the whole Phillies' roster, including the hot dog vendors.

She felt him edge her panties lower on her hips. Lordy, he couldn't need more room unless he intended filling in the amount of his last electricity bill.

He started on the last word. Strange, he was beginning in the middle of her stomach. Must be a short word.

She stopped breathing completely as he traced a long line down below her panty's edge, beneath the silky material still covering unexplored territory, then touched the spot that dragged a groan of pure sensation from her.

Jenny didn't care what word he was spelling, all she wanted was his finger to remain there, to rub that spot until tears trailed down her cheeks, until she screamed with raw pleasure.

Opening her eyes, she stared at his bent head with unfocused gaze, then reached out and grasped a handful of his tangled hair in a grip she hoped would anchor her to Earth.

Suddenly, his finger was gone. She mourned its loss with every disappointed cell in her body.

Slowly, she realized he was finishing the letter. *Y*. The "o" and "u" that followed were an anticlimax . . . until the meaning of the message hit her.

He lifted his head and gazed at her. She couldn't read anything in his expression, his eyes.

It had been a kid thing, something they would've laughed over ten years ago.

But now? She broke his gaze, glanced at the mirror behind him, noted dispassionately the image of his bare body crouched over hers—muscular, mature.

They weren't kids anymore, and somehow the message didn't seem like something to laugh at.

Chapter Seven

He'd managed to surprise himself, and that didn't happen often to Sloan. Why had he remembered that stupid heart after all these years? It hadn't meant anything.

Then why the basket thing? Why was it so important that she live with you in this house? Why're you so hot and hard you'd take her even if a dozen Rudolphs were singing outside your window? Figure that out, hotshot.

"It doesn't mean anything, you know." Jenny's voice echoed his thoughts.

And made him mad. "It *could* mean something. How do you know it doesn't mean anything?"

She lay in the mud, her body slick, her hair

sticking out in every direction, a smudge of dirt on her nose, and an uncertain smile on her lips. She was beautiful.

"I don't know." She shrugged, and her breasts lifted, hot-wiring his adrenaline. "But it could mean a lot of different things, like I admire you, or I get a kick out of you."

"I get a kick out of you?" He cast her his best you've-gotta-be-kidding look.

Her lips curved into a slow, deliberate smile. "What're we arguing about, Sloan?"

He drew in a deep breath. "Darned if I know. Want to share a cold shower?"

Her smile widened. "I don't think so, but wouldn't a roll in the snow be quicker?"

Sloan knew his gaze was heat and hunger. He didn't give a damn. "You watched me last night."

"Yes." She ran her tongue across her lower lip. "We could do it together. Now. I'm ready, and the carolers are gone."

The very thought of Jenny standing naked in the snow, her nipples hard from the cold, waiting for the warmth of his mouth . . .

"You're not ready."

"I can't believe you. Who're you to say I'm not ready? Are you waiting for Santa to leave a gift-wrapped announcement under your tree proclaiming that Jenny Saunders is ready?"

"I'll know when it's right." *When you come to me. With no questions, no reservations.* In what millennium would that happen? He didn't think he could wait that long. And why did it matter anyway?

She sighed. "Are we reversing roles here? Remember, I'm the careful one and you're the impulsive one."

"We're back to me being impulsive again, aren't—"

"Wait, wait." She met his gaze. "At first I thought impulsive was all bad, but look at me . . ."

He looked at her. At her lips swollen from his kiss, at her full breasts barely covered by her flimsy bra, at the curve of her stomach and hip. His eyes lingered on the small piece of silky cloth still guarding her femininity, and he wondered why the path of his gaze didn't burst into instant flame. "Okay. Looked at you."

"I said 'look,' Sloan, not burn and pillage."

"That wasn't burning and pillaging." He didn't smile. "You'll know when I'm burning and pillaging."

Her expression indicated a growing interest in the pillaging part. "Anyway, I've just done my best imitation of a mud wrestler. Can't get more impulsive than that. And you know something?" She reached up and touched each of his nipples with the tip of her finger. "I loved it."

"If you're looking for my power button, it's down on my surge protector." He couldn't control the huskiness of his voice anymore than the explosion mode of his surge protector. If he didn't disconnect fast, his whole system would crash.

He rose and moved away from Jenny. "So you're admitting that in some situations, impulsive actions can be good things."

"Yes." She slowly rose to her feet.

He should've helped her, but if he touched her again tonight, it'd be all over. And he had plans. Big plans that didn't include another roll in the mud. He was the king of desire fulfillment, and Jenny still had a few unfulfilled desires, even if she didn't realize it yet.

"Hey, it's a start. So where did you first get the idea that I was impulsive?"

He thought she wouldn't answer. She slogged out of the mud and sat on the bench beside the pond. He sat down beside her, making sure no part of him touched any part of her.

She sighed. "I don't know. A bunch of things. You always had these wild dreams in high school. You were going to contact aliens one day on your computer."

"Done that a few times."

She didn't smile.

"Lots of kids have wild dreams in high school. It's part of growing up." *Like drawing stupid hearts on women's stomachs.*

"Then you show up at my door sounding like you did ten years ago, telling my you'd been doing this-and-that. Didn't sound too stable to me.

And you have to admit, this internet business sounds a little bizarre."

She reached out and traced an aimless pattern on his bare thigh. He didn't move away, but he didn't react either.

"Great believer in giving a guy the benefit of the doubt, aren't you, Flame?" He didn't care if he sounded cold.

She withdrew her hand from his thigh. "I did give you the benefit of the doubt. I'm here, aren't I?"

"You're here for your fling. Character flaws don't matter much when you're only scheduling a one-nighter."

"Low, Mitello." She stood, still managing to look composed. "If you're finished with your mud slinging, figuratively speaking of course, then I'll go up to my room and take a shower."

There was nothing composed about the seductive sway of her bottom. Made him almost forget about being mad. Almost.

Jenny awoke to a discreet tap on her door and a surrealistic memory of the night before. She forced one eye open, then glanced at the clock. Yep, Ridley. Right on schedule with another bowl of yummy oatmeal.

Mumbling her hope that the IRS would audit him for the rest of his irritating life, she covered her head with her pillow.

Translating the mumble as permission to enter, he opened the door, strode to her bedside table, then plunked her breakfast where she could smell the tempting odor of congealing oatmeal.

Jenny yanked the pillow from her head and glared at Ridley. "I won't eat that oatmeal, and you can't make me." Lord, she sounded about six years old.

Ridley sniffed his disdain. "Madam left muddy footprints all the way through the house. I had to wipe up every one of them before I made madam's breakfast."

He was good. Very good. He'd sharpened guilt into a deadly weapon. Hating herself for doing it, she hiked the sheet up to her neck, sat up, then picked up her spoon and forced down a little of the cereal. "There. I ate some. Satisfied?"

Ridley cast her a contemptuous glance. "There were many, many footprints."

She sighed. "So I have to eat many, many spoonfuls."

He lowered his chin a fraction in acknowledgment. "Then of course, you'll want to enjoy your present."

"Present? What present?" She scanned the room, and there by the fireplace she saw *it*.

"Ohmigod, it's my *horse*. Sloan got me my horse!" All her childhood Christmas disappointments faded into the past as she gazed at the life-size carousel horse gleaming white and beautiful in the morning light. "If you don't want to see a naked woman, Ridley, you'd better run, because I'm naked and I'm getting out of this bed right now to look at my horse."

Ridley didn't hang around. "As you wish, madam." He hurried from the room with none of his usual dignity.

Jenny grinned. Her very own horse and a win over Ridley. Life was good. She wondered if Sloan would be surprised when he found out she'd thrown away her pj's. And he *would* find out.

Scrambling from her bed, she didn't even take time to fling on her robe as she rushed over to her horse. She slid her fingers along its smooth neck, touched the gold trim on its saddle and bridle, admired its upflung head and tail flowing in an imaginary breeze. "You're beautiful, sweetheart."

"I agree."

Sloan's low comment didn't even surprise her. She'd expected . . . no *wanted* him to show up. She didn't turn around.

"Thank you for the horse and . . . for sharing your dreams. Sometimes you don't realize there's anything missing from your life until your life changes." That was the closest she could come to telling Sloan how she felt. She hoped it was enough.

"Sounds like you did some thinking last night." He'd moved up behind her, and she could feel the scrape of his terry robe, the knot at his waist digging into her back.

"Heavy duty." She reached behind her and undid the knot, felt his robe fall open.

"Me too." She heard him shrug from his robe; then he molded his bare body to hers. "I realized all the shiny new things in the world can't wipe out old memories, good or bad. And some memories are worth saving, worth building on."

"Uh-huh." That's all the verbal response she could manage. What would he do? She shivered in anticipation.

"You know, this sorta reminds me of Godiva." He ran his nails lightly up the back of her thighs, then bent to kiss the sensitive skin behind her ear. "The lady, not the chocolate."

She grabbed the horse's saddle to steady herself. "Sure. Lady Godiva."

"She had a lot more hair though. Covered up a lot of great stuff."

He slid his fingers across her bottom and she swallowed a gasp.

"Like these. Nothing should cover these." He spread his palms over each cheek, then squeezed gently.

She clenched her thighs in response and took a firmer grip on that saddle.

"I just remembered something, Flame. Even ten years ago when I was pretending that we were just friends—"

She couldn't let that pass. "We *were* just friends."

"Maybe, maybe not. But even ten years ago I loved watching you leave a room. You'd wiggle that sweet behind—"

Outraged, she could feel her cheeks heating. Both sets. "I *never* wiggled my behind."

"Sure you did. Men notice that kind of thing. You were a champion wiggler."

"I . . ." What could you say to that kind of revelation?

"Shh." He turned her to face him, then lowered his head and kissed her.

Kissed her hard and long, his tongue tasting every part of her mouth, forcing her to meet his thrust, to meet his desire with her own.

Wrapping her arms around him, she slid her hands over the tense muscles of his shoulders, down the smooth expanse of his back, then grasped his buttocks, pulling him firmly against her. The heavy ache grew in direct proportion to his pressure as he slowly rotated his hips, teasing, tempting.

Suddenly, he picked her up. *Yes! Bed here we come*.

But she should've known. Bed was conventional, and this was the man who'd dumped her in the mud last night. Instead, he lowered his head and flicked her nipple with his tongue. Then before she could get attached to the idea of his mouth on her breasts, he lifted her onto her horse.

"You know, I think I'm supposed to have one leg on each side of the horse, Sloan." With her breaths coming in short pants, she was amazed she could string that many words together.

"Not for what I have in mind, Flame."

He rolled each of her nipples between his thumb and forefinger, then trailed kisses down over her stomach.

Grabbing the horse's mane and the back of the saddle, she tried to steady herself, and wondered why she just didn't slide off the other side like the glob of quivering Jell-O she was sure she'd become. Cherry Jell-O. She'd always liked cherries.

"Relax, Jenny, and enjoy the ride."

His low murmur did *not* relax her, and when he ran his tongue along the inside of her thigh she allowed a moan to escape.

To think that she'd had Sloan's mouth, Sloan's body at her fingertips ten years ago, and all she'd done was sit like a lump in front of the TV watching *The Man with the Golden Gun*.

She'd had her very own golden man and hadn't recognized him.

Suddenly, she realized that while she'd been busy with past regrets, her body was very much in the moment and taking care of its own needs.

She'd spread her legs to give him easier access to all of her. She wanted his mouth, his hands on every inch . . .

He pushed her legs further apart, then put his mouth on her.

His tongue touched her, stroked her, slid inside her, and she felt tears trailing down her face.

Abandoning her grasp on the horse, she clasped his shoulders, tried to pull him closer when closer wasn't possible.

"No, no, no!" *Yes, yes, yes*! Her chant picked up the rhythm of the spasms shaking her, and when the explosion came she celebrated it with a final scream of "No!"

She collapsed from the horse like the boneless rag doll she'd had when she was four years old. Sloan held her tightly until she stopped shaking, until *he* stopped shaking.

"Sloan, what about you? You didn't . . ."

"Shh." He kissed her eyelids. "My time will come. But not here, not now."

"Saving yourself for the right woman?" She'd meant the comment to be funny, but instead was shocked by a stab of pure jealousy. Jealous? Possessive? *Her*?

"Definitely." He grinned. "What's with the 'No' bit?"

Jealous. She frowned, considering this new unattractive facet of her personality. And beyond the jealousy, something even more sinister lurked. Violence. She wanted to blacken both eyes of Sloan Mitello's "right woman."

"Jenny?"

She blinked. "Sorry. Why'd I scream 'no'?" She cast Sloan a wicked-vixen smile. "Guess I'm just a contrary woman."

Sloan slipped into his robe, then headed for the door. "I like a contrary woman. Adds spice to a man's life." He threw her a lingering glance over his shoulder as he opened the door. "And I like my spices hot. Really hot." He shut the door behind him.

Jenny turned back to her intrepid white steed. "Who was that masked man?"

Chapter Eight

She'd been so wrong. About Sloan, about herself. *Christmas Eve*. Such a short time to make a lifetime of discoveries.

Over the past week, Sloan had slowly opened up about his ten years away from Haddonfield. She'd put together the pieces of his moves to various jobs, each gaining him experience in an area he'd need when he started his own company. She saw behind his words to the research he'd done on the burgeoning internet and its possibilities for someone who used it wisely.

When had Sloan gained so much depth? Maybe he'd always had it, but she had never looked beneath his surface charm, her own prejudices.

When had she started to let go of her past, stopped thinking in terms of absolutes like all dreamers are losers, and wish fullfilment is a cruel hoax? She didn't have to look past the moment Sloan Mitello walked back into her life.

The ultimate irony? Maybe her revelation had come too late. After the horse, he'd laughed and teased, but hadn't touched her again. And dammit, she wanted, no *needed* him to touch—

"Madam hasn't touched her oatmeal. It's difficult cooking breakfast along with the many other duties Mr. Mitello requires." Ridley managed to mold the sharp angles of his face into a expression of long-suffering, overworked servitude. "And when one's cooking isn't appreciated . . ." He shrugged, allowing her to guess at the depth of his disappointment.

"Uh-uh." Jenny shook her head and grinned at him. "Won't work this time." Up early after a restless night of dreaming about Sloan, she was dressed and ready for Ridley.

"Tomorrow's my last day here. Have any plans, Ridley?" *I sure don't*. Somehow this week had managed to become her life's entire time line. She couldn't conceive of a before or after.

"One manages." Ridley tried for pitiful and failed.

"You know, there's a lonely widow down the street who's looking for a strong man to organize her home. I bet she'd appreciate a man like you." *Forgive me, Mary*.

Ridley brightened. "Does she enjoy a hot bowl of oatmeal?"

"Yep. In fact, she said she really hated cold cereal." God would get her for that one.

Ridley looked happy, or as happy as he would ever get. "It sounds like the perfect situation."

Jenny handed him the address and phone number she'd written on a scrap of paper. "Here. I bet she'll be so impressed she'll want you to start immediately. It'll be hard coping without you for my final day, but your future is more important than a few piddling hours of discomfort on my part."

Ridley grinned. A sincere grin that surprised Jenny with its charm. "You'll make a bloody good liar someday, Madam. I assume you'll give me an excellent reference."

Jenny grinned back. "Right." Maybe she was actually doing Mary a favor. "How do you feel about playing Santa?"

Ridley frowned. "Santa?"

"Never mind." She pointed to the oatmeal. "Why don't you take that back to the kitchen? Give it to the kittens."

"They won't eat it." He turned and left the room carrying the dreaded oatmeal.

"Smart cats." Now to call Mary before Ridley did.

Jenny watched evening fall as snowflakes drifted past her window. Sighing, she returned her attention to her computer, but numbers seemed to have lost their charm for the moment.

Tomorrow. She'd pack her things, then go back to her off-white world. How could she walk away from Sloan?

Jenny stared at the numbers on her screen, then hit a few keys.

Better, but *scarier.* "Let us fulfill your desire. Sounds easy, doesn't it, horse?" She'd have to give her horse a name, but she'd do that when she got back to her apartment. She smiled at the thought of the fanciful animal in her blah apartment. It wouldn't be blah for long though. Changes were a-comin'.

Okay, she'd thought about her work, her horse, and her apartment. Anything else she could think of to put off the inevitable? Nope. She'd thought of everything.

She stared at the screen. What if he didn't respond? What if he wasn't interested? But he'd *promised* her a fling. Problem. She'd upped her expectations. A fling wouldn't be nearly enough now.

But what if he took back his promise? She'd never faced rejection before. *You never chanced anything before.*

Jenny took a deep breath. Somehow she knew this would be the most important chance she'd ever take. She typed.

375

I want a bad man in the worst way. A bad man with a golden bow.

She'd done it. She wouldn't worry about it anymore. He probably wouldn't even check his messages until after Christmas. She'd just go back to her work on the Chandler account.

Several hours later, she gave up. She'd probably be hearing from Chandler's lawyers if she didn't fix this mess. Later. She couldn't concentrate now.

He hadn't come.

Well, what're you going to do about it? Sit at your window and feel sorry for yourself like you did when you didn't get a horse? "No way. Wishes come true for those who make them come true. Right, horse?" Horse had no opinion on the matter.

Damned if she'd cower in her room, then spend the rest of her life wondering what might've been. Time to give destiny a kick in the behind. Turning off the computer, she stood and headed for the door before she could think of consequences, things like embarrassment and humiliation. *Heartbreak.*

As she was about to fling open the door, she spotted the piece of paper stuck beneath it. Probably nothing but a good-bye note from Ridley along with his recipe for making the perfect oatmeal. Still, her fingers trembled as she picked it up.

A bad man is waiting for you.

For absolutely no good reason, a tear slid down her cheek. Okay, she could change into something sexy or she could just go as she was. As-she-was won. She didn't want to waste one minute of her time with Sloan. Looking down at her bare feet, she shrugged. One less thing to take off.

Drawing in a deep breath of courage, she hurried down the hall. She paused outside Sloan's room to peer at the note taped to his door. *Bad man waits within. All desires fulfilled.*

Smiling, she remembered. He'd be wearing the gold bow. She pictured the exact placement of that bow and how much fun it'd be to take off. *Hey, have to cover up the gift part so it'll be a surprise.* She was still smiling as she opened the door.

Only a dim glow from the fireplace lit the room. The furniture was dark wood, dominated by a massive four-poster bed and the man stretched magnificently nude on it.

Sloan lay on his side, shadows thrown by the flickering flames playing over his long muscled back and strong buttocks as he gazed out the darkened window. "What do you want, Jenny?"

"I . . . I have a desire." She focused on the tangle of midnight hair that spread across one bare shoulder, and like a dark curtain, hid his expression, his emotions from her.

"Not a dream?"

"No." It was too deep, too strong. A hunger

she felt she'd never satisfy. "This is a desire."

"Tell me what you want."

What *she* wanted? Didn't he want a part of it? And why didn't he turn over to speak with her? "I want to touch you, all of you, the way you touched me." *No, I want more, much more.*

"And?"

"I want you deep inside me, filling me." *Completing me.*

"Come here, Flame."

As she walked toward him, she felt overwhelmed by the bed. Its rich wood gleaming in the firelight, it whispered of countless lovers who'd lain there, secrets it would never reveal. Ageless, it beckoned her.

The raw sexuality of the man lying atop the rumpled burgundy sheets made her catch her breath. Somehow, with the night, the bed, the man, everything had changed.

Sloan had reached out to her, drawn her into his life. Now he waited, silent, and she didn't know what to do. Okay, so she *did* know what to do, but the strangeness intimidated her.

"Touch me."

Well, that was pretty specific. "Turn over."

"Uh-uh." She could hear the laughter in his voice mixed with something darker. "It won't be a surprise if I turn over."

A surprise? She knew where the bow would be. "Too bad. I guess you won't be able to undress me. But I'll undress myself and tell you what's happening. You won't miss a thing."

"You'll pay, Flame."

She certainly hoped so. "Unbuttoning my blouse now. First button, second button—"

"Faster." He sounded as though his words were forced through gritted teeth.

"There, all done. Now I'm slipping the blouse off and dropping it on the floor." Even though the room was warm, she shivered at the touch of air on her bare skin.

"Describe your bra."

"My bra? It's black, and it has lace across the top. It's sort of cut low so it just covers . . ."

"Your nipples?"

"Yes." Her voice had turned hoarse. His words were almost like a touch—warm, intimate.

"Take the bra off."

"Like to give orders, don't you?" Did it matter? Reaching behind her, she unhooked the bra and let it fall. "It's gone."

"Touch your breasts, Jenny. Hold them in your palms, feel the warmth of flesh against flesh, then slide your thumbs across your nipples." His voice was low, urgent. "Imagine it's my hands cupping you. What do you feel, Flame?"

She didn't have to do this. He couldn't see what she was doing. But she *wanted* to. Closing her eyes, she lifted the weight of her breasts, imagined offering them to him. When she touched her nipples, imagined his lips closing hot and moist around each one, she moaned softly.

"God, you're killing me, Jenny."

She gloried in his torture. Another unattractive trait to add to her growing number. "Why don't you turn over, Sloan?"

"I can't." His voice was that of a man on the rack.

"Oh, well." Her voice might sound controlled, but she was glad he couldn't see her shaking fingers as she undid the snap of her jeans and slid them off. She should describe this, but she was having difficulty breathing, let alone talking.

"Talk to me, Jenny. I know you've taken off your jeans. I could hear you. What color are your panties?"

"Why're you so sure I'm wearing any?"

Once again, she sensed his amusement. "You're a follow-the-rules kinda woman. And the rules say you wear panties. So what color are they?"

"Black." She felt as mutinous as she sounded. He had her pegged as Ms. Predictable, but Sloan Mitello was about to get a surprise.

"Black. I like a woman in black." His voice was husky, approving. "Take them off."

She slid the panties off without comment. In a defiant gesture, she reached up and hung them on the top of the bedpost nearest her. She liked the effect. Sort of like raising the skull and crossbones flag on a pirate ship.

The excitement building in her was new, exhilarating, *freeing*. Jenny Saunders would take no prisoners tonight.

Chapter Nine

Kneeling on the bed, she gazed down at Sloan. What more could a woman want under her tree, under *her* on Christmas morning? *What more could a woman want for a lifetime?*

The thought touched her and felt right. But whether it was for a lifetime or just one magic night, she'd take what she could of Sloan Mitello. "Roll onto your stomach, Sloan."

"Someone else likes to give orders, but hey, it's your desire." He sounded intrigued. "This'll crush the bow."

"All in a good cause." She straddled his hips, almost groaning at the pleasure of having his body between her legs.

More. She needed him touching the ache that

had started the moment she'd seen him stretched out on the bed.

Scooting up until she was over his buttocks, she spread her thighs wide so that his flesh touched hers. Then closing her eyes, she slid back and forth, back and forth. The building heat had nothing to do with friction.

He moved beneath her, lifting his hips to increase the pressure. She could hear his heavy breathing matching her own.

Harder. She leaned forward to increase the contact, her nipples sliding over his sweat-dampened skin, and as her body begged to feel more of him, she raked her nails the length of his back, then followed the path of her nails with her tongue. She'd never thought of herself as a cat, but she was seeing some disturbing similarities. So who gave a meow anyway? Not her.

Her jungle-kitty act must've woken the sleeping tiger in Sloan, because with a hoarse growl, he turned over.

Scrambling into a kneeling position, she finally took a good long look at him. *All* of him. She swallowed hard, not sure if her voice would work. "The bow."

"Told you you'd crush it." His eyes gleamed in the firelight, giving away nothing.

"It's . . ."

"It's covering my gift to you."

"It'd take a mighty big bow to cover all your

gifts to me." She felt tears filling her eyes. Darn it, she wouldn't cry.

"Sure, but this bow is gift-specific." His voice lowered to a murmur. "It'll only cover the most important gift."

"It's over . . ." She reached out with trembling fingers and gently lifted the shiny gold bow from over his heart.

Jenny couldn't say a word. Tenderly, she kissed the spot where the bow had rested, then moved to his nipple. Sliding her tongue across the nipple, she gently nipped it.

His groan was all she could hope for. "Stop. Forgot something important."

"No." Not *now*. "Please don't stop me."

"Uh-uh. Can't go on without this." He picked something up from beside him, then handed it to her.

"Hershey's chocolate syrup?" A childhood quote came to mind. "Yes, Virginia, there is a Santa Claus." He was tall, muscular, and crying out to be served with chocolate.

She clasped the plastic container, but there was something strange . . . "This feels warm. How did you . . . ?"

"I heated it by the fireplace"—his gaze seared the length of her body—"and thought of you. Naked. I wouldn't need a fireplace to heat it now." He slid his fingers over his arousal.

She felt the heat from his body, steamy with

the scent of sex, and a want so powerful she imagined smoke rising from it.

"Use it, Flame."

He hadn't been too specific about how she should use it, but he'd soon find out she had a lot of ideas.

She concentrated on opening the top, ignoring Sloan's impatience. Good things were worth waiting for. He'd taught her that this week. "I've always had a passion for chocolate syrup. The smooth texture, the rich taste, the way it makes me feel good. That's why from now on I'll put it over everything I love."

She forced herself not to react to his sharp intake of breath. "I'll put it on my Cocoa Puffs every morning."

"You eat Cocoa Puffs?" His voice was nine parts sexual frustration and one part horror.

"All the time." She carefully dripped chocolate dots around his right nipple, then plopped one huge dot on top. She'd always thought she didn't have any creativity, but she kind of liked the pattern.

Too bad she was going to destroy it. Leaning over, she scooped up every dot with the tip of her tongue, except for the big one. She had plans for that.

Sloan sucked in his breath with every touch of her tongue, and she gloried in her power to give him pleasure.

He smoothed his hand over her hair with fingers that shook, and for once she wished her hair was long and flowing. Long enough to spread across his chest, glide over his flesh, and allow one more part of her to touch him.

Maybe she'd let it grow long. She'd think about it later. Closing her lips over his nipple, she swirled her tongue over it, then sucked the last taste of sweet chocolate from it.

He tightened his grip on her hair and forced her lips away from his nipple. "God, woman." That's all he seemed able to say.

"We were talking about chocolate syrup, right?" She skimmed her finger down over his stomach and enjoyed the ripple of his muscles. "I'll put it on my pizza, too."

His bark of laughter loosened sexual tension strung tighter than her monthly budget. Good. She wanted him to last a long time. But how long could *she* last?

"Bet you like anchovies on your pizza."

She widened her eyes. "Doesn't everyone?"

"That's disgusting, Jenny."

He didn't think it was disgusting a minute later when she poured a trail of chocolate over his stomach in the shape of a pepperoni pizza. *With* anchovies. She ate the whole pizza. Except for one anchovy that got stuck in his belly-button.

She was working hard with the tip of her tongue to scoop out that anchovy when Sloan reached out and stilled her.

"Leave it. I can't stand much more." His voice was hoarse with growing loss of control.

She smiled her wicked-cat smile. "If you want to go through life with an anchovy in your navel, who am I to stop you?"

"Where were we? Oh, yes. Chocolate syrup. I'll put it on spaghetti with Italian sausage and meatballs." She winced. That was too much even for her.

"Getting a little obvious, aren't you, Flame?"

Jenny glanced at her eventual destination. Obvious didn't begin to describe it. She slid her tongue across dry lips. She couldn't wait much longer. But she also couldn't let Sloan get away with thinking she had no imagination.

"Me? Obvious? I was just making conversation. I don't intend to do anything with it." Her nose would begin growing any second now.

"You'd better do something with it, and soon." His threat hung between them.

"Oh, I forgot. I'll put warm chocolate syrup on ice-cream cones." She scooted lower.

"Doesn't that make the ice cream melt?"

"Always." This would be her creative masterpiece.

She made twin swirls with a question mark in the middle of each swirl, then moved onto his main attraction. It was hard to make a dust devil design when your hand was shaking, but she managed it. At the very top of the dust devil she drew a big star, symbolic of her fulfilled desires. The star was a little lopsided, but an artist was allowed creative license.

"You're killing me." Sloan's voice was a tortured groan.

Me too. She slid her tongue across the swirls, leaving the question marks for last.

He bucked beneath her as she answered each question, and she could hear his harsh rasping breaths over her pounding heart.

The dust devil called for her tip-of-the-tongue technique. Around and around and around. She felt dizzy by the time she reached the star, and his hips were lifting rhythmically, brushing her nipples with each lift until they were so sensitized she felt she would scream.

The star. The heck with technique. She closed her lips over him, slid along his length, then worked her way up and down until she'd almost finished—

She didn't get to finish. There was still a little speck of chocolate left when Sloan heaved beneath her. Before she could gather her scattered thoughts, he'd pulled her beneath him.

He loomed over her. His long tangled hair trailed across her breasts, and she closed her eyes to savor the sensation of the dark strands sliding over her nipples. She was definitely going to let her hair grow.

"I wanted this to be long and slow, Flame. I wanted you to enjoy your entire desire, but God, I'm only human."

She opened her eyes and blinked at him.

"I'm going to fast-forward to the end." His face was dark shadows and tense angles. He smiled, a savage pirate smile. "We can rewind it later, then play it again. Slow and sweet."

Sounded good to her. She'd think of new ways to—

She did no more thinking as he lowered his head and captured her mouth in a kiss that took her breath away along with any still-functioning brain cells. He tasted of glowing firelight and dark nights. *Urgency*.

When he abandoned her mouth and kissed a trail over her throat to her breasts, she tangled her fingers in his hair, as though she could transfer her need through the dark strands.

It must have worked, because he slid his tongue around each breast, then drew a nipple into his mouth. She cried out at the touch of his tongue on what felt like bare nerves. And when she felt she'd shatter with what his tongue and teeth were doing, he transferred his attention to the other nipple.

She couldn't stand it one more second.

"*Now*. I want you now. And *yes* I'm ready."

"I don't want to rush this too much." She could hear the smile in his voice.

"*Now*, Mitello, or you . . . are . . . a . . . dead . . . man."

"You're homicidal. I like that in a woman."

Her breaths were coming in heaving gasps as

he pushed her legs apart. Only her senses spoke to her now: her wet readiness, an aching need to feel him inside her, the heat of his body, the scent of hot male desire.

He rose above her, and she closed her eyes so she could concentrate on *feeling*.

"I love you, Jenny Saunders." She almost didn't hear his whispered message as he pushed into her.

She felt his tension, his attempt to go slowly. No. She didn't want slow and careful. She wanted hard and fast.

Raising her hips, she wrapped her legs around him, clasped his buttocks with her hands, and pulled him to her hard. She knew her nails were digging into him, but she couldn't stop herself. She wanted him now. *Now*.

His body tensed and she felt the tightening of his buttocks just before he plunged so deeply into her that she knew *no one* would ever fill her this way again. Her brief pain was only a blip on the radar screen of her senses.

Again and again he thrust into her, a raw primitive rhythm that built until she felt, she felt . . .

When it happened, it wasn't pretty sparkling fireworks, it wasn't a heavenly choir singing. It was a massive explosion, and she didn't even have the power to scream as it shook her.

An explosion. There was no other way to describe it. Bits and pieces of her would be drifting to earth for days.

Her eyes landed first, so she opened them. Her voice was around somewhere if she could only find it. She probably wouldn't catch her breath for days. Heaven only knew where the rest of her was.

Sloan pulled her into his embrace until she'd stopped shaking. "I think we burned up during reentry, Flame."

She could only nod.

"I'd like to make love for the rest of the night." His eyes lit with anticipation.

Jenny gazed at him. "Six times. We have to do it six times."

"I have a confession to make." He stretched, feeling relaxed for the first time since he'd rung Jenny Saunders's doorbell.

"Confess away. No, let me guess. Those aliens you always wanted to contact switched bodies with you and you're really a native of the planet Zork. Kinky."

"Close. I know how attached you are to this house, but it isn't really mine."

She blinked at him. "What?"

"I built this house for Mom. I tried to tell you at the beginning, but you distracted me. This is Mom's desire. The biggest, fanciest house money can buy, filled with Christmas cheer to make up for all the bad years. We'll have to fly to California today to bring her home." He lowered his gaze in mock sadness. "Guess we'll have to make do with something smaller. Won't have all these great decorations either." He brightened. "But next year I'll buy all the lights you want. Can't have Christmas without lots of lights."

"I love you, Sloan Mitello."

Sloan slanted her a wicked grin. "Sure you're not saying that because we made love six times?"

She looked puzzled. "But won't we do that *every* night?"

"You'll kill me, woman. I'm glad I don't have to explain to anyone why I have fingernail marks on my butt." After last night, he didn't care where he had nail marks. "And I didn't know you were a—"

"Virgin?"

He nodded. "I knew you wanted a fling, but I didn't think it'd be your first time." His voice lowered. "You made me feel very special, Flame."

"You'll *always* be special to me, Sloan." She lay on her side, her fingers idly sliding across his still-damp chest. "I've figured out why no one I dated ever suited me. I guess, subconsciously, I was comparing them to you and they always came up short. Now I know I'm a never-settle-for-less kind of woman."

"We're like fine wine, Jenny. It was there in

high school, but we needed aging before we were ready to pop our corks."

"Makes sense to me." Her fingers slid to his stomach while her gaze turned thoughtful. "Desires are addictive. I feel another one coming on."

"Great. That's my job, let's hear it."

She leaned close and whispered in his ear. "I've decided to wear something special for our wedding."

"Okay, I'm open to suggestion." He looked puzzled. "Fancy white gown? Lots of glitzy stuff?"

"Something a lot more cost effective." She nibbled on his ear. "Something classic that never goes out of style."

"You'd better tell me right now, because you're not the only one working on a desire."

"A big shiny gold bow."

Five Gold Rings

Constance O'Banyon, Stobie Piel, Lynsay Sands, Flora Speer

In the Year of Our Lord, 1135, Menton Castle is the same as any other: It has nobles and minstrels, knights and servants. Yet from the great hall to the scullery there are signs that the house is in an uproar. This Yuletide season is to be one of passion and merriment. The master of the keep has returned. With him come several travelers, some weary with laughter, some tired of tears. But in all of their stories—whether lords a'leapin' or maids a'milkin'—there is one gift that their true loves give to them. And in the winter moonlight, each of the castle's inhabitants will soon see the magic of the season and the joy that can come from five gold rings.

___4612-1 $5.50 US/$6.50 CAN

Dorchester Publishing Co., Inc.
P.O. Box 6640
Wayne, PA 19087-8640

Please add $1.75 for shipping and handling for the first book and $.50 for each book thereafter. NY, NYC, and PA residents, please add appropriate sales tax. No cash, stamps, or C.O.D.s. All orders shipped within 6 weeks via postal service book rate. Canadian orders require $2.00 extra postage and must be paid in U.S. dollars through a U.S. banking facility.

Name_____

Address_____

City_____State_____Zip_____

I have enclosed $_____ in payment for the checked book(s).

Payment <u>must</u> accompany all orders. ❏ Please send a free catalog.

CHECK OUT OUR WEBSITE! www.dorchesterpub.com

Christmas Spirit

ELAINE FOX
LEIGH GREENWOOD
LINDA WINSTEAD

Three Heartwarming Tales of Romance and Holiday Cheer

Bah Humbug! by Leigh Greenwood. Nate wants to go somewhere hot, but when his neighbor offers holiday cheer, their passion makes the tropics look like the arctic.

Christmas Present by Elaine Fox. When Susannah returns home, a late-night savior teaches her the secret to happiness. But is this fate, or something more wonderful?

Blue Christmas by Linda Winstead. Jess doesn't date musicians, especially handsome, up-and-coming ones. But she has a ghost of a chance to realize that Jimmy Blue is a heavenly gift.

___4320-3 $5.50 US/$6.50 CAN

Dorchester Publishing Co., Inc.
P.O. Box 6640
Wayne, PA 19087-8640

Please add $1.75 for shipping and handling for the first book and $.50 for each book thereafter. NY, NYC, and PA residents, please add appropriate sales tax. No cash, stamps, or C.O.D.s. All orders shipped within 6 weeks via postal service book rate. Canadian orders require $2.00 extra postage and must be paid in U.S. dollars through a U.S. banking facility.

Name_____

Address_____

City_____State_____Zip_____

I have enclosed $_____ in payment for the checked book(s).

Payment <u>must</u> accompany all orders. ❏ Please send a free catalog.

BLUE CHRISTMAS

Sandra Hill, Linda Jones, Sharon Pisacreta, Amy Elizabeth Saunders

The ghost of Elvis returns in all of his rhinestone splendor to make sure that this Christmas is anything but blue for four Memphis couples. Put on your blue suede shoes for these holiday stories by four of romance's hottest writers.

___4447-1 $5.50 US/$6.50 CAN

Enchanted Christmas

Emma Craig

Noah Partridge has a cold, cold heart. Honey-haired Grace Richardson has heart to spare. Despite her husband's death, she and her young daughter have hung on to life in the Southwestern desert, as well as to a piece of land just outside the settlement of Rio Hondo. Although she does not live on it, Grace clings to that land like a memory, unwilling to give it up even to Noah Partridge, who is determined to buy it out from under her. But something like magic is at work in this desert land: a magic that makes Noah wonder if it is Grace's land he lusts after, or the sweetness of her body and soul. For he longs to believe that her touch holds the warmth that will melt his icy heart.

___52287-X $5.99 US/$6.99 CAN